IMMORTAL SORCERESS
BOOK 4

TIME OF THE SORCERESS

KRISTA WALSH

RAVEN'S QUILL PRESS

OTTAWA, ON

Raven's Quill Press

www.kristawalshauthor.com

Publisher's Note: This is a work of fiction. Names, characters, places, and incidents are a product of the author's imagination. Locales and public names are sometimes used for atmospheric purposes. Any resemblance to actual people, living or dead, or to businesses, companies, events, institutions, or locales is completely coincidental.

Cover Design: Deranged Doctor Design/2023

Time of the Sorceress / WALSH -- 1st ed.

Paperback ISBN: 978-1-998398-05-8

For Noelle - thank you for being Kat's loudest cheerleader

1

Katerina

I DON'T THINK this is working, Kat," Rhys complained as he squeezed his eyes shut so tightly his face turned red.

"You need to relax. If you keep on like this, you're more likely to give yourself an aneurysm than a vision."

He opened his green eyes on a huff and ran his freckled fingers through his red hair. "This is all I know. It's almost all I've been doing for the past four years."

I crossed my arms and leaned back against the couch with my legs stretched out in front of me. Rhys and I sat on the floor across from each other. Sunlight spilled through the south-facing windows to fill the basement rec room with the warmth of the July afternoon.

"That's probably the problem, isn't it?" I said. "You've never had luck forcing your visions. It's only when you've calmed your mind that you've been able to trigger them."

He dragged his fingers from his hair to rub his eyes. "I don't know what to tell you, Kat. It's like my second sight doesn't trust me anymore. Not since—"

His jaw flexed as he cut himself off, but I didn't need him to finish that thought. He was going to say not since he'd taken a vision-blocking potion to keep Alodie's searching fingers out of his mind. The sorceress had used him as a conduit not once but four times, and we'd all been afraid she would turn him on us—or on himself. To protect him, Poppy and Murisa, the witches who'd become such an integral part of my inner circle, had created a potion to effectively cut off his ability for a few days.

Almost three months had passed since then, and he hadn't fully recovered, but I didn't know how much of his regression was because of the potion and how much was his mind fighting against him.

I leaned forward and rested my hand on Rhys's ankle. "You'll get back to where you were, Rhys. I promise. Once you take the pressure off your shoulders. We'll keep working on it. We just need to move slowly."

He flinched and pulled his knees to his chest, escaping my touch. "That's great, but we don't have time to move slowly, do we? You need my help *now*. We have to find out who summoned Alodie's demon before they do anything else to get to you. I know what's at stake here."

I puffed out a breath and pushed myself to my feet. "Why don't we take a break? We've been at this for hours, and that can't be helping. Go take a walk, play a video game, get your mind off things, and maybe we'll have better luck when we try again."

Rhys bowed his head but stood up beside me. As he rose to his full height, I couldn't help but notice that the red-haired, green-eyed boy I'd known since infancy had sprung up another few inches, now towering over me by nearly a foot. He was eighteen—if he grew much more, he'd need to get his clothes tailor made.

He must have noticed my staring and misinterpreted the direction of my thoughts, because his cheeks flushed and he dropped his gaze. "I'm sorry, Kat. I know I'm disappointing you, I just—"

I held up my hand to cut him off. "Enough of that. You're not disappointing anyone. You are a gift, Rhys. Haven't I always told you that? Whatever help you offer, I appreciate, but I love you with or without your second sight. You're stronger than you give yourself credit for. We just need to break through these blocks."

The irony of me saying those words might have struck me as hilarious if it weren't for the pain in my friend's eyes. After all, hadn't my magic been stunted for a hundred years before I'd worked through similar mental blocks? The pressures of expectation and self-doubt had hidden my power from me until Emrick had helped me see my worth.

Rhys snorted at my attempted pep talk. "If I'm as powerful as all that, I would have been able to keep Alodie out of my head."

"If we'd realized how powerful you are, Adrian and I would have worked harder to find someone to train you years ago." I flinched at the mention of my vampire bestie. Three months he'd been gone, and I'd barely scratched the surface of my grief at losing him to Alodie's bloody games. "When the incredibly powerful fear demon possessing your body says he's good and comfy because of how strong you are, I think that's reason enough to believe it, don't you?"

Rhys raised an eyebrow. "Really? That's your best angle?"

I chuckled and wrapped my arms around his middle. "I know, it's weird, right? But in this, I think we can trust what Shogaur said. He's not drawn to weakness."

There was a lot to unpack around Rhys's possession back in March, but as yet he hadn't been up to talking about it. One of these days, I'd have to push the issue, but not yet. For the sake of fairness, I'd wait until I was ready to discuss the pain of losing one of my oldest friends. We all processed trauma in our own time.

"There's more to you than you realize, Rhys Byrne. We'll

find a way to ease you into it." I gave him one last squeeze, then gently shoved him away. "Now, go take your frustrations out on your… whatever the hell that monster thing is you've been trying to kill for the past three days."

A small smile spread across his lips, and I left him to his gaming console and his thoughts as I headed upstairs to my room.

While I meant every word, I couldn't deny Rhys was right that I needed help—and sooner rather than later. Every single day since Alodie's death, I'd been looking over my shoulder, ready for the next kick in the ass.

It had been five months since my life had taken a turn for the strange. I'd gone from burrowing under my blankets, doing my best to ignore the world and allow my immortality to pass me by without hassle, to being faced with regular reminders of my emotionally fraught past.

First there had been Mikhail, the blood witch with the immortality ritual I'd believed lost forever. Then there had been Shogaur, the fear demon who'd once burned me at the stake and who nearly stole Rhys from me. Both those monsters had been manipulated by Alodie—the traitor who'd massacred my family, and, unbeknownst to me until far too late, also survived the original immortality ritual. She'd orchestrated my downfall, and when that had failed, she'd tried to use me to regain the youth she'd lost due to a glitch in her spell.

I'd fought her and won, believing to the last that once she was dead I could finally move on with my life.

Except she wasn't the source of all my problems. She was yet another symptom. Someone had summoned the demon Alodie had been bound to with the intention of using the sorceress as a weapon against me. This someone was playing a very long game with the sole purpose of destroying me.

I had no idea who it was, or what they would try next, and until I had a better grasp on this looming threat, I couldn't afford to relax. Not when dropping my guard might mean losing someone else who mattered to me.

More fool me for becoming attached to mortals, I supposed.

I would have thought I'd learned that lesson centuries ago, but no, here I was with a family under my roof—a mix of mundanes and magicals, from the housekeeper who gave me crap every time I made a decision that hinted remotely at selfishness to the natural-born sorcerer, Alodie's grandson, who refused to accept what he was.

I wouldn't let anything happen to any of them, but that promise meant I had to be prepared for anything.

So far, I felt like I was floundering. Since Alodie's death, I hadn't stopped trying to figure out who might have summoned Fegor, Alodie's demon, but the answer eluded us as well as Alodie had for all those months following the Mikhail crisis. The summoning had to have happened decades ago, and even for an immortal, decades was a long time to collect enemies. Murisa and Poppy—or Muroppy, as I had named the pair—had worked tirelessly to narrow the playing field, but I could tell from their updates that they felt as defeated as I did.

As we all did. Rhys couldn't trigger his visions, and Maera—Rhys's mother and my housekeeper—struggled to keep the house going, visibly quailing under the weight of her duress and the thousand tonnes of baked goods she'd made over the past many weeks.

Gavin Yoon, the sorcerer who refused to accept he was a sorcerer, had opted to remain in Muskoka. He claimed he wasn't ready yet to return to his home or nursing career in Hamilton, not knowing how to adjust to his old life now that he carried fire magic in his veins. I might have worried about his decision to hide away in the middle of nowhere if it weren't for the fact that James Barrett was with him.

James Grumpy-Pants Barrett. Adrian's former human thrall, and the man Past-Me swore I'd cut out of my life at the first opportunity. Well, to my shock, I hadn't given up on him. On the contrary, I'd texted Barrett every single day since leaving Muskoka, checking in on him under the guise of asking how repairs to the house were going after the fire.

I suspected he knew the real reason, but whatever.

Somehow the son of a bitch had wormed his way into my family along with the rest of them, so he'd have to tolerate my involvement.

I hoped his eye twitched every time my ringtone sang at him—but even that hope had lost some of its old zing. The grief Barrett and I both suffered had bound us together. And although I didn't know how long it would last before we found our way back to hating each other, I'd realized I wasn't in a rush for it.

At the thought of my old friend, my heart clenched, and I rested my head against the door as I closed it behind me.

Eight hundred years with the vampire only a short trip away for advice or support, and now he was gone, leaving a giant hole behind. A wound that refused to heal.

It wouldn't happen again. Yes, the fight with Mikhail had been close—yes, Shogaur had almost won—and yes, Alodie had been within inches of wiping the floor with me, but despite the odds, I'd defeated them.

It was the only thought that kept me moving, kept me training. Whoever was coming after me, I hoped they were paying attention, because I didn't intend to lose now.

The next person to try to steal my family from me would go down in a wave of fire.

2

Katerina

ENCLOSED IN MY room, I shoved myself away from the door and headed towards my private balcony. With the time I had to myself, I meant to do some work on my own abilities.

Five months ago, I'd been a burned-out husk of my old self, worn down by depression, self-doubt, and exhaustion. The situation with Mikhail had hauled me out of my hibernation, but I was a long way from the height of my power. In whatever time I had before we tracked down Fegor's summoner, I intended to scrape off the last of the rust and come in strong. Blazing like a beacon of justice and balance the likes of which no mortal currently alive had ever seen.

Magicals of today might have heard rumours of me at my best, but most of them would believe the stories were exaggerated. Especially considering everything I'd shown them in their lifetime.

Those beliefs would benefit me when I proved every myth was nothing compared to the truth. Since we'd learned of Alodie's return, Emrick had been training with me, helping me regain my old strength. Slowly but surely, those muscles had woken up, and when the opportunity arose, I would put them to work.

I'd made it halfway across the room when the temperature dropped. A swirl of white mist swept over me, and a hand closed around my arm, drawing me to a broad, firm chest covered in an ocean-blue long-sleeved tee.

I slid my hands over the hard muscle of said chest and wrapped my arms around the unnaturally pale neck peeking over the collar. A pair of lips lowered to claim mine.

Emrick's tongue teased into my mouth, causing sparks to travel under my skin in tiny explosions.

I moaned against him and pressed myself closer. His right arm wrapped around my waist, pinning me against him, while his left hand crept into my hair. His fingers twisted the black strands, and he gave them a gentle tug to better angle my mouth against his.

"What's with this greeting?" I asked between kisses, a gasp escaping me as his lips trailed along my jaw and down my neck, his tongue dancing over my skin as he sampled me, promising endless pleasure to come.

"I've missed you," he murmured against my throat.

I dragged my nails across the back of his neck, and he wrapped both arms around my waist so he could pick me up and carry me to the king-size bed draped in its sage-green duvet.

"I've missed you, too." I let my head fall back, giving him better access as he kissed along my collarbone. "Ridiculous, really. It's only been a few days."

What were days to immortals? I'd gone seventy-five years without him, having sent him away in a futile attempt to save what was left of his soul, yet lately even an hour without his company left me empty.

"I don't care," he growled. "A minute away from you is an eternity."

His lips found mine again, his muscular frame pinning me to the bed, his arms caging me. The fingers of one hand stroked through my hair, while the other hand slid under the waistband of my leggings.

I clung to him, fisting his shirt to keep him pressed against me, needing to reassure myself that he was here—whole. It wasn't enough to feel his weight, not when the threat of him fading and leaving me behind remained a terror that haunted me both within dreams and without.

As a servant of Death, tasked with escorting magical souls into the afterlife, Emrick was forbidden to involve himself in the mortal world. Every infraction cost him part of his soul, and each lost fragment took him closer to becoming a shadow. A wraith. A shade with no memory of what we'd shared or how we felt for each other.

For centuries, he'd pushed those limits, refusing to stand by when I was in danger, bit by bit chipping away at himself until he'd faded to almost nothing. Today, his pale skin was nearly translucent, the blue veins running under the surface too visible. I tried to focus on the firmness of his muscles, the heat of his body—the proof that he was still here, still *mine*—but the fear of tomorrow made me desperate to have him, to keep him, to take him inside me and hold him there.

I spread my legs and let him settle between them, enjoying the comfort of his familiar weight, his warmth as it soaked through my shirt and travelled across my skin. My back arched as his hand snaked down between my thighs, seeking me out, drawing pleasure from the simple contact as my individual cells were jerked forward in time only to land back where they were.

His touch, fatal to mortals, served only to heighten every sensation in me. Our bond protected me, lay me open before him, and with every stroke, every kiss, I craved more. Centuries could pass with this man, and I would never tire of him.

Every roll of his hips had me responding. I reached for the button of his jeans, ready to release his hard length so I could satisfy the fire stoking between us, but before I could undo it, he froze. His body stiffened, and his lips stilled against my neck. Worse, his fingers, working their best magic, ceased their teasing caresses.

The moment passed, and with a groan of frustration, he bowed his forehead into the crook of my neck, withdrew his hand, and straightened my shirt.

I sank into the bed with a disappointed sigh and ran my fingers through the thick waves of his white-blond hair.

"Duty calls?" I asked.

"I hate this life," he grumbled. "I don't want to leave you again. Not so soon."

He lifted his head, his silver eyes sparking with regret, and I pulled him closer to catch his lips in a kiss that raised the temperature between us again. Not my intention, but I wasn't about to complain.

"When you get back, we'll pick up right where we left off," I said against his mouth.

"Promise?" He kissed me, and I rocked my hips against his.

"Try to stop me."

"*Mîn hiertan.*" My heart.

With one last kiss, his hands cradling my face as though I were the most precious thing in his world, Emrick rose off the bed and disappeared into the mist, leaving me alone, aching, unsatisfied. And, as always these days, worried he might not come back.

I smacked my pillow in an effort to expend some of my pent-up muddle of anxiety and desire, then rolled off the bed and continued to the balcony as though that delicious interruption hadn't happened.

Although reason urged me to refocus on the priority issue of getting my magic into shape, my thoughts refused to cooperate. Instead, they wrestled with the problem that had chased Emrick and me for centuries—the question of how we could be together without risking his future. *Our* future. Because if he became a wraith, the bond that tied me to this earth would still exist, but I would be alone.

Even more alone now that Adrian was gone.

The idea terrified me. The mortals I surrounded myself with today would be dead tomorrow, but I would remain. Trapped. Burdened with facing forever by myself, cut off from everything that kept me human.

A shudder ran through me, and I forced my thoughts in a different direction. As looming and severe a problem as my eternal loneliness was, we faced a more immediate concern. If the people trying to kill me succeeded, Emrick would be the one alone, stuck waiting until Death released him from his debt to join me in whatever came next.

The only solution I could see was the one I'd considered five months ago for very different reasons: retiring. Leaving the hunt behind me and disappearing into the world to live a quiet, peaceful existence. One that wouldn't cause Emrick to step in to save me when I got in over my head.

My stomach twisted in knots at the tangle we'd found ourselves in. I drew in a breath, emptied my head of thought altogether, and dropped into one of the Muskoka chairs that faced my private beach stretching into Lake Huron. As the season tipped towards mid-summer, the maples and spruces embracing the house were thick with foliage. Their shade spilled dappled light over my balcony, my legs, and the sand beyond leading to the water. The wind was sweet, touched with the scents of flowers and pine, of the silt that lined the bank, of the lake. I closed my eyes and drank it in, absorbing every last drop of life from the island I'd called home for the past decade.

Too long, probably.

After so many years, it was well past time for me to pack up and move on to some new safe haven.

The trouble with immortality was that you couldn't settle in one place for too long. People began asking questions, noticing that while they aged, their neighbour remained exactly the same. Having Maera and Rhys with me was both a help and a hindrance in that regard. While Maera ran most of my errands and was the more familiar face in our small community, aging normally—completely human—she also made my lack of change that much more pronounced.

The thought of leaving this place behind left me feeling hollow. In over eight hundred years, I'd never gone anywhere without discussing it with Adrian first, and he'd never landed too far from wherever I ended up. Since we'd met, we'd been inseparable. He was the only person I trusted most in the world aside from Emrick—and during the span where Emrick and I had stopped talking, the only person I trusted implicitly.

Without him, I felt adrift. Rhys's life was here, as was Maera's. I would be asking them to leave everything behind to come with me.

Or I would have to make the decision to leave them behind, and the idea of doing that bothered me more than it would have a few months ago. I'd lost so much in my life that I'd become possessive of everything I had left, including the mortals I'd worked so hard for so many years to distance myself from.

My life had changed dramatically since Alodie had targeted me.

Since someone had summoned Alodie's demon so she could destroy me.

I groaned and leaned my head back against my chair.

One more mission. I swore it to myself. One more mission to find out who wanted me dead, and then I would find the peaceful life. Then Emrick and I could have forever and not stress about forever being stolen from us.

I let that thought motivate me as I closed my eyes and sank into my meditation. My first step would be rediscovering the full breadth of my power and destroying my enemies. Then I could finally rest.

3

Katerina

BY THE TIME I finished my meditations, tapping into my magic and working to thin the barricades that kept its full strength locked inside my psyche, I was hungry, tired, and more than a little grumpy.

I trudged out of my room, through the living room, and into the kitchen, praying Maera had anticipated all my needs the way she usually did.

Sure enough, she stood at the stove, the white in her messy red bun catching the soft yellow glow of the evening sun, her green blouse and black pants fitting comfortably around her lean frame.

Without a word, she waved me to the table. I slid into my usual chair, facing the counter so I could watch her work as she poured water into the teapot and slid a few freshly made scones onto a plate. A small jar of clotted cream and another jar of strawberry jam rested on the tray beside the kettle. My stomach growled.

"I hope your day's going well," she said over her shoulder. "Rhys moped up here for a snack half an hour ago before moping back downstairs. I get the impression he's not making the progress he hoped to?"

"It's going slowly," I admitted, "but I'm trying to convince him he doesn't have to rush. I suppose it would come off more believable if I were able to relax a bit and let go of this sense of impending doom." I pulled my hair off the back of my neck. "All right, I confess I might be the problem."

Maera carried the tray to the table, her mouth curled in a soft smile instead of the disdainful grimace I might have expected. She was—understandably—not thrilled about her son's decision to step deeper into the magical world. She'd been worried enough when he'd wanted to join me in the fight against the blood witch Mikhail, and those worries had—again understandably—skyrocketed when he'd been possessed by the fear demon.

For the most part, she and I were on the same page when it came to her son. Whatever we could do to keep him safe, we would do it. Unfortunately, we were now faced with the challenge of his mental health being threatened by a crushing lack of confidence. I didn't envy Maera the position she was in, trying to be an encouraging mother while also wanting to clasp her forever-her-baby son to her chest to save him from the world's dangers.

She dropped into the seat across from me. "We all get where you're coming from, Kat. After years of quiet while you avoided the world, these last months have been… Well, no one was prepared for how much we'd have to deal with."

Maera Byrne, the queen of tact.

"He knows you have good reason for needing him to get back in the game," she continued. "He wants to help. We all do."

"And I want your help. I *need* your help. I've come to accept that I can't do this all on my own. But the more pressure he puts on himself, the less likely he is to improve." My shoulders drooped, and I shoved my fingers through my hair. "I can't help but take responsibility for his set-back. If I'd worked harder to protect him—realized what Alodie was doing so we could find a better way to guard his mind—he wouldn't be in this mess."

Before Alodie had twined her fingers through his visions, Rhys had made incredible strides with his second sight. In large part thanks to Adrian, who'd taught him a few breathing exercises to get him into the right headspace.

But my friend was gone, his wisdom was gone, and all Rhys had now was me, the sorceress who threw herself into a fight headfirst and often forgot the concept of patience.

I rested my cheek in the palm of my hand. "We need to find him someone better to train with. I don't want him feeling he has to prove anything to me. Maybe Muroppy know someone."

The witches knew everyone. Surely they had a Seer or two in their phone contacts. One of these days, I needed to start networking again myself, but while I could delegate to the mortals, I'd save myself the headache.

Maera poured two cups of tea and slid one over to me. It smelled of chocolate mint, lavender, and something else I couldn't place. My taste buds sang in anticipation. I needed a good, bracing remedy to anchor myself to the here and now. Stressing about the future was not going to help anything or anyone.

As she set a scone on a plate and nudged the cream and jam towards me, Maera said, "Rhys trusts you. There's no one else he'd want to walk him through this. You know my son. He'd be too self-conscious to work with anyone else, and the anxiety would get in his way and discourage him even more."

She was right, of course. Rhys reminded me so much of myself when I was a mortal sorceress in Palonia, working and failing to become what my community expected me to be. But if I was going to help him, I'd have to sort my own stuff out and find a way to work *with* him rather than pushing my own methods on him.

I'd never been a good teacher. Gavin was proof enough of that. Sure, he'd stopped setting things on fire, but he still refused to accept the magic that ran through his veins. And he still tended to walk out of the room whenever I walked in. I was demanding where I needed to be understanding, impatient when I needed to give space. It was the downside of being so isolated for much of the past nine hundred years. To suddenly find myself in the middle of a family again took a lot of getting used to.

I reached for my teacup as the steam settled and took a small sip. The lavender hugged my palate as the chocolate mint teased it, and a third flavour slid down the back of my throat with a strange bitterness.

I peered into my cup. "What's in this? It's interesting."

Maera shrugged and took a sip of hers. "Some new specialty brew. The herbs are grown locally, and they only sell it at pop-up markets. I'm told it's all the rage across the island."

"I understand why. It's good."

I took another sip, then set the cup aside to tuck into the scone. Before I could bring it to my lips, my phone rang, and I grumbled on seeing the photo of a grim-faced soldier pop up on my screen. I'd taken the photo myself when I'd caught Barrett at his most Barrett. I'd then updated his contact name in my phone from **Annoyance Demon** to **Tolerable**. Adrian would be so proud of me.

My hand wavered over the phone. Did I want to interrupt this lovely afternoon snack to deal with whatever dour mood my unfriend happened to be in today? The temptation not to answer was strong, but despite old habits, I couldn't ignore him. In an about-face of the ages, I needed to know he was all right.

Putting my once-enemy before my grumbling stomach, I accepted the call. "You can't possibly need me already. I know I promised to help with the house, but come on, Barrett. I thought you'd last longer than this."

Wanting to keep him in my life didn't mean not poking the bear at every opportunity. Some things weren't supposed to change.

Maera snorted a laugh, then stood up and started tidying. For the first time in a long time, she didn't immediately haul out ingredients to test another new recipe. Her nerves had relaxed enough to set the stress-baking aside. I hoped she wasn't being optimistic.

"I'm not calling for your help," Barrett said, drawing my attention back to the call. "In fact, I'm struggling to think of any possible way you could help me. Do you know contractors?"

"No."

"Do you know how to tile a roof?"

"No."

"Do you have any interest in helping me paint the new

foyer?"

"Not if my life depended on it."

"Then how—"

"Supervision, Barrett. Obviously." He grunted, and I allowed myself a smirk before reclaiming my expected role of Interrupted Harpy. "Then why are you calling? Did you lose Gavin? Dammit, Barrett, you have one job. Mind the sorcerer."

"He's right here, staring at me like I've lost my mind. Go do something useful. That trim needs to be finished." Barrett huffed, and I grinned down the line.

It had come as a surprise to all of us when Gavin had decided to stay in Muskoka with Barrett after Alodie's demise. He'd suffered the weight of a few nasty revelations in a short span of time, and I suspected he was still recovering from them. He had family and a nursing job in Hamilton—or at least he had family; I wasn't sure about the job anymore—but he'd opted for the middle of nowhere with a magic-hating ex-vampire thrall. Every day I expected to get a call saying he'd either gone home or spontaneously combusted, but instead, he and Barrett had seemed to develop a friendship.

I didn't know what was more shocking: that Gavin was choosing to stay in contact with the magical world or that Barrett was capable of having a friend.

Now that Barrett and I had gotten the essentials out of the way and I was sure both he and Gavin were all right, I relaxed in my seat. "The renos are going well, then?"

"Well enough. The reconstruction is complete, and the interior is nearly finished. I assume you'll be more interested in lending us a hand once the manual labour is done? I can't imagine you not wanting a say in the decorating."

A lump formed in my throat, and I took another sip of tea to help me clear it. "I'd like everything the way it was. If you're okay with that."

There was a pause on the line before he said, "I agree. I'll see if we have any pictures lying around to replicate everything."

"No need. It's all in my mind. Let me know when you're ready, and I'll micromanage the placement of every piece of furniture to the last detail."

I prepared for him to push back on my suggestion, but he grunted his approval, and the lump in my throat grew more painful.

I would have thought that after so many centuries, change would have become second nature to me, but maybe that was why Adrian's death had hit me so hard. *He* had never changed. Everything about him—his life, our life together—had been a steady force in the chaos. A flagpole in the storm. A rock in the rapids.

If I was playing with the notion of packing up and finding somewhere new to plant my roots, Adrian would have been considering the same, yet I couldn't bring myself to change even the hue of his foyer.

My stomach twisted, and I curled my hand into a fist on the table, digging my nails into my palm to offset the discomfort.

"So what can I help you with today?" I asked, eager to change the subject. "You have the sorcerer under control, the house in hand. What's up?"

My stomach churned again, and I closed my eyes against the sudden nausea. He better not be calling with bad news. I couldn't handle it. Not after everything that had happened over the past few months.

To settle my nerves, I pulled my plate closer and took a small bite of my cream-and-jam-slathered scone. The sugars tickled my tongue, but the bread caught in my throat on its way down, making me cough. Crumbs flew from my mouth, and I sucked in a breath, taking another sip of tea to clear my airway. As I made to set the cup back down, my fingers slipped, and the tea spilled across the table.

"Shit."

"Never mind, I've got it." Maera grabbed a rag and pounced on the spill before it ran off the side.

I frowned at my clumsiness and turned my attention back to my phone. "Sorry, you were saying?"

"I wasn't," Barrett replied. "I'm calling to see if you've learned anything about the people Alodie said were coming for you. I—" He cleared his throat. "I wanted to offer my help in tracking them down. Now that the house has been settled."

I didn't bother to hide my smile as my head swam with relief. Not bad news, then. Not for me, anyway. I was sure Barrett felt a little morose at realizing he wanted to stay in my life as much as I wanted to stay in his.

Not wanting to spoil the mood, I didn't call him out on his sentimentality. I'd wait to do that in person. "Nothing yet. Rhys and Muroppy are doing some research for me, but I—"

Pain sliced through my stomach, and I bent double in my chair with a cry.

"Kat?" Barrett called over the phone at the same time Maera dropped the rag and set her hand on my shoulder.

Sweat broke out over my forehead and down my back as another spasm clenched my middle. The room spun, and I fell out of my chair onto the floor, smacking my elbow on the edge of the seat as I went. When I hit the smooth tile, I curled my knees into my chest. The comforting position did nothing to stop my insides from twisting, a sharp agony that stole my breath.

"Kat, are you all right?" Maera asked, and I heard Barrett's firm voice through the phone demanding to know what had happened.

"She collapsed," Maera told him. "I don't know what's going on. Katerina? Can you tell me what's wrong?"

Another scream was the best I could manage. It felt like

knives were slicing through my guts, paring my organs, filleting my blood cells. I couldn't make out Maera's face, and her voice had moved farther away, even though her hands were still on my arms. Holding me steady?

"Mom, what's—holy shit."

I wanted to groan. Rhys didn't need to see me like this. Whatever this was. But I couldn't warn him away. Couldn't tell Maera where the pain was—which was all over.

Whiteness encroached on my vision as my limbs grew more distant, and then all that was left was nothing.

4

Emrick

I STARED AT the empty frame of the aged witch where she lay in her bed, then shifted my attention to the spirit hovering beside her body. Instead of the waifish creature tucked between the sheets, her spirit stood as a pillar of golden light, with only a hint of facial features deep within the glow.

"I thought it would be more dramatic than this." Her voice came out tinny and distant, crossing the divide from the afterlife to the world of the living.

"It is for some people. You're one of the lucky ones."

She shrugged. "I would have liked a better story. I don't suppose you could throw some blood around? Knock over some furniture? Give something for the neighbours to talk about?"

I chuckled and offered a grimace of regret. "I wish I could."

She cast a longing glance at her corpse. "Ah well. Probably for the best. My nephew wouldn't know what to do with a murder investigation. Very well. What's next?"

I raised my hand and summoned the mists that served as the doorway to the afterlife.

She sniffed, unimpressed with the performance, and I gestured for her to lead the way. With one last look over her shoulder, she left the mortal world behind and stepped into the afterlife, the liminal space where souls came to rest before moving on to whatever came next.

I stepped past her so I could guide her to the river, but the light of her soul reached out to me, drawing me to a halt. She hesitated to voice her reason for stopping, and while I waited, I stared across the barren wasteland of home. The murky whites and pasty greys of sky and cracked, empty field. The dried blades of grass. The empty trees with their leafless branches stretching into the black, starless sky. Beautiful in its reflection of the life it represented.

"What's it like on the other side?" The question came so quietly—her uncertainty such a contrast to the brash, vibrant woman I'd met minutes ago—that it took me a moment to shake off my surprise and form my answer.

"I don't know, I've never been. I only take people as far as the river. After that, it's as much a mystery to me as to those I escort."

"Hmm. Not terribly reassuring, you know."

I chuckled. "You should mention something to management. Maybe they'll give me a tour."

I'd spent almost fifteen hundred years guiding magicals across the border between life and death, unable to make the passage myself. For centuries, I hadn't cared, accepting the consequences of my deal with Death to save the woman I'd loved. The woman who'd left me as soon as she'd recovered from her illness.

Once I'd put Gabrielle behind me, I'd wondered if I'd ever have the opportunity to make the crossing. These days, my only solace was the woman who waited for me in the mortal world, the sorceress who held me bound by a ritual gone wrong and a love so fierce it kept my lingering humanity alive.

Though that solace was offset by the ever-growing fear that I would soon be the one leaving her. I'd traded too many fragments of my soul helping Kat across her nine hundred years of immortality, and my losses were showing with increasing severity. My memories of my time with Kat had begun to either fade or disappear altogether. The pigments of my hair were leaching out of me. I was becoming a shadow of the man I'd been—the man I wanted to be—and no solutions had presented themselves. None beyond abandoning Kat and salvaging what was left of myself. A trade I wasn't willing to make.

A shudder ran through me, and I closed my eyes to centre

myself. I hadn't faded yet. We had time to figure things out. All I needed to do in the meantime was stick to the afterlife as much as possible and keep my hands off Kat's fate. No matter what happened or who was after her.

It was a demand on myself I wasn't sure I could keep.

The spirit started to say something else, but a searing pain cut through my chest that left me doubled over. I set my hand against my sternum, putting pressure on the fiery, stabbing agony of an impossible wound.

"Are you all right?" the woman asked. "Is that normal? I thought you were supposed to be my escort. Is this some sort of test? Am I supposed to help you get to the good place?"

I couldn't answer. I felt as though the air had been sucked from the world, leaving me in a vacuum that was trying to drag me through a narrow tube. The scene in front of me wavered black to white before returning to normal.

The sensation of something being ripped out of my centre was gone, but something was seriously wrong.

"Is—is everything okay?" the spirit asked.

"It's fine. I'm fine."

I wasn't. Not even close. It was like someone had grabbed hold of my bond with Kat and was tugging with all their might, snapping the fragile threads that connected us. The sensation was more painful than anything I'd felt before. The world around me spun, and I forced myself to stay steady.

Anxiety tore through me, urging me to leave this place and run to Kat's side. Death had already warned me what would happen if I turned my back on the terms of my deal—if I continued to put my sorceress first.

But I couldn't ignore this feeling—like something was being torn out of me piece by piece. Shredded, then cauterized. I couldn't stand not knowing what was happening. I had to check on Kat. I'd leave and be back once I was sure she was okay. There was quite a distance to the river, but Death would have to forgive me.

I turned to the spirit. "I need to go. I'm sorry. I'll be back as soon as I can."

"Wait—but—"

I summoned the mists and prepared to step through to Kat's bedroom but was shoved back by an unseen force. I stumbled, caught my balance, and tried again, but again I was blocked. Panic gripped me, and I threw myself at the barrier between this world and the mortal one, desperate to break through. If Death was keeping me away, what did that mean for Kat? What the hell was going on?

"I don't understand." The spirit sounded so terrified, so confused, that it sliced through my panic and left me numb.

With my heart thrashing against my ribs, I forced myself to suck in one deep breath after another. My place was here. My obligations were here. I wasn't allowed to leave until I'd seen them through.

The thoughts dropped into my mind as though someone beyond me had spoken them, and I bowed my head. Death didn't allow for broken deals.

Swallowing the anguish of leaving my other half to suffer unknown torments, I turned to the woman's spirit. "Everything is all right. Forgive me. Please, follow me."

The pillar of light hesitated only a moment, and I sensed her fear, her uncertainty. A pang of guilt cut through me. I'd failed her. My purpose was to guide, not to scare.

I did my best to shake off my terror and set the agony in my heart aside. I had responsibilities—a debt to repay. I would escort this woman to the river, and then I would hurry to Kat's side.

If Death allowed it.

I prayed to Kat's gods that my delay wouldn't cost me everything.

5

Katerina

I ROLLED ONTO my side but didn't make it any further before my joints locked, complaining at every subtle movement. The hip pressing into the mattress ached with a cold, burning throb, and my knees and ankles grated as though they'd been filled with sand. Even my toes whined.

My upper half was no better. Elbows, shoulders, wrists, knuckles. The skin on my arms, the soft tissue between my ribs.

Nausea welled in my belly as I processed the multiple layers of discomfort, and when I tried to push through it and sit up, a sharp pain lanced up the back of my skull and pierced my eyeballs.

With a groan, I collapsed onto my pillows, but even that small motion jarred my strained body and caused every muscle to spasm.

A sob escaped me despite my efforts to hold it back.

My spine wracked with a shiver as the temperature in the room dropped ten degrees—not in the familiar way of Emrick stepping in from the afterlife, but an icier, unpleasant chill. I pulled my blankets up under my chin.

What the hell was wrong with me?

I hadn't been sick in… well, ever. Not like this. Why wasn't my body healing itself? How long had I been in bed? Maybe it wasn't long enough. Soon, I'd be back on my feet, laughing off whatever human ailment I'd picked up.

Yet even as I tried to give myself the pep talk that my suffering was temporary, more pain swept through me, followed by a muted, hollow sensation in my middle that scared me more than everything else. I rubbed my sternum, hoping the contact would ease the ache, but the emptiness lay deeper than some surface wound. It felt more like something had been plunged under water, leaving it frigid and distant. The sensation was worse than my grief after Adrian's final death.

I curled onto my side again, swallowed the whimper that eked out the back of my throat, and squeezed my eyes shut. More sleep, that was what I needed. A few more hours of rest, and everything would be back to normal.

It took a while for sleep to come, and when it did, it was accompanied by nightmares the likes of which I hadn't experienced in centuries. Dreams of my magic inflicting the full force of my power on me. Nerves burning, freezing, enduring electrical charges that sent my whole body into convulsions. The pain was so real, it chased me into wakefulness, but when my eyes opened, the agony continued, leaving me flailing against the bed with nothing to hold me down except the heavy comforter that was at once too stifling and not enough to battle the tremors that swept through me.

Where was Emrick? He should have been back by now. I needed him here to explain what was happening. But instead, I was alone. Alone and terrified and confused. I tried to scream, but the sound caught in my throat. My breath stopped along with my voice until my lungs burned.

Pain crashed over me in wave after wave until I didn't think I could bear it any longer, but when it finally ebbed, I wished it would come back, because the numbness that followed was more terrifying than the discomfort.

For a long while I lay with my eyes closed, braced for the torment to return. Ready for some new nightmare to grab me. When the minutes passed without any indication of a fresh onslaught, I gave my fingers and toes a tentative wiggle. More to reassure myself they were still there than anything else. Just lying here, I couldn't be sure.

Everything felt so far away. Out of touch. Unreal. I didn't know if I'd fallen back to sleep, or if I was drifting along the line of wakefulness. Either way, it was a relief after everything that had come before. I wanted to stay here in this nice, safe bubble.

"Kitty Kat?"

The soft voice enveloped me, familiar but filled with a worry sharp enough to pop my comfortable bubble and send me tumbling back into full awareness.

Except the awareness remained distant. As though I were trapped in my body. I murmured some kind of response with an uncooperative tongue, and that small effort left me drained.

"It's all right, Kat," the voice said. Poppy. It had taken me too long to place it considering I'd spent the better part of four months in her company. "We're going to figure this out, all right? You're not alone."

Like hell I wasn't.

Her words dragged me closer to consciousness, and with my increasing lucidity, anger-infused fear came with it.

She wasn't in my body enduring this endless cycle of pain and emptiness. She wasn't dealing with the feeling that someone had punched a fist through her chest, grabbed her heart, and stuffed it into the depths of the ocean, leaving her choking, suffocating.

But I couldn't say any of that. Not only because I didn't have the energy to utter a syllable, but because I was grateful to hear someone's voice other than mine. Especially the voice of someone who sounded so confident they could help me.

All I'd wanted was a cup of tea and a snack before returning to the task of finding out who wanted to kill me. Apparently that decision had pushed me into the fires of hell, where I was now burning for the sake of a scone.

Life was cruel.

As I imagined flames sweeping over my skin, my thoughts were dragged to the pyre where I'd been bound eight hundred years ago. It wasn't possible. Shogaur had been cast back to the infernal realms, and people didn't tie witches to the stake anymore. Not in Canada, anyway.

There was no fire. This heat was all in my twisted, broken mind.

I tried to reverse my fire magic to summon a layer of frost, anything to cool myself down and soothe the aches, but no matter how far I reached, I couldn't find a single spark of my power.

I tried again, keeping it simple. I would have been happy to summon a tiny flame into my palm and risk setting the bedsheets on fire.

Nothing.

My stomach twisted again, this time from sheer panic, and I tried harder, scouring my blood for the smallest trace of magic.

"Kat? What is it?"

Poppy's voice came closer, and the mattress shifted beneath me as she settled on the bed. She rested her hand on my shoulder and brushed my hair out of my face. The contact was both a comfort and a torture, reassuring me and making it all the clearer that this was no nightmare I would wake up from. Something inside me was wrong. Missing.

"Can I get you anything?" she asked.

It took too long for me to make my lips work, but finally I breathed out the word, "Emrick."

I needed him here. He would hold my hand and help me find my strength to figure this out. His presence had always been enough to chase away the worst of my fears—or at least to help me face them.

More than any of that, I needed him to tell me everything would be okay. Anyone else could say the words, but he was the only person I'd believe.

"Of course you'd task me with the impossible," Poppy grumbled. "Not like the guy has a phone in the afterlife. I'll do what I can, all right?" She stroked her fingers through my hair again. "Get some rest, kitty Kat."

The bed lurched as she stood up, and the room fell quiet.

I was alone, and I didn't want to be alone. Not with my thoughts, not with this numbness, not with my absent magic.

I rolled onto my back, groaning with every tiny movement, and sank into myself. Three deep breaths, just as I used to do during my earliest training with Emrick, when he used to tease me for wasting time anchoring myself when the enemy might close in and lop off my head. When all I'd longed for was to be able to hurl a fireball at my problems, and instead, I'd wound up possessing more power than I ever imagined possible in my tiny frame.

But no matter how many breaths I took, no matter how many exercises I practiced to focus my magic when it was being stubborn, I came up with nothing.

Not even the slightest stirring in my blood.

Tears sprang into my eyes and streaked down my cheeks. I didn't know how it was possible, but deep in my cold, terror-ridden bones, I understood.

Somehow, I'd lost my magic.

6

Katerina

THE NEXT TIME I opened my eyes, the sun was rising.

Most of my pain had eased, with only a lingering ache in my joints and soft tissue. I could only compare it to a post-workout discomfort—or so I assumed. I hadn't experienced that particular pain in so many centuries I could only base what I felt off other people's complaints. My body should have healed itself while I slept. I should have been bounding out of bed ready to torment Poppy with questions about what had happened to me.

Unless Poppy had been a dream?

Curious, I looked around my room, but there was no sign of the glittery necromancer or her girlfriend and fellow witch, Murisa. The two of them were inseparable these days. If one was here, the other one wasn't far.

Yet just as I decided Poppy must have been a figment of my imagination, my eye fell on a grey lump at the end of my bed. A grey lump with yellow eyes. A stinky grey lump with yellow eyes.

Cuddles, Poppy's resurrected cat.

"*Mrowr*," he intoned, a monotonous, undead sound that made me think of dusty crypts and decaying corpses. He'd been brushed recently, which hid the patches where clumps of his long fur had fallen out during his time buried on the edge of a Toronto cemetery. He flicked his kinked tail and curled it next to his body.

If he was here, the witches definitely were, and I was ready for answers.

A tickle in the back of my mind urged me to draw on my magic and wrap myself in its comfort, but anxiety gripped me at the thought.

Not wanting to think too closely about where my fear came from, I reached for my phone on my bedside table to text Poppy, but it wasn't there. Its absence left me with another twinge of unease. I always put my phone on the table in case of emergencies, insomnia, and the need to check the news first thing in the morning to ensure the world wasn't facing some new magical crisis.

Not having it also meant I had no way of reaching out to

anyone in the house. Except by yelling.

"Maera?" I shouted as loud as I could. When my house-keeper didn't immediately barge through the door, I tried again. "Rhys? Poppy?"

Still no one ran in to see what I wanted, which left only one option.

Summoning my strength, I slid my feet out of bed and persuaded the rest of my body to follow.

I wore the same clothes as when I'd collapsed—the blue-and-teal leggings, a blue T-shirt, and my elbow-length leather gloves I'd thrown on for magical practice. In my present murky mood, the vibrant colours mocked me.

Cuddles stared at me in condescending disapproval, but I ignored him. His judgement was not what I needed right now.

A moment later, I was standing, if that's what it could be called when the wall was doing most of the work.

I took a few steps towards the door before my legs gave out, and I crumpled to the floor in a heap.

The door opened, and an exasperated huff sounded over me.

"Really, Katerina, I heard you calling. You couldn't have waited a moment?" Maera asked. "Come on, let's get you into bed."

She tucked her arm behind my back and eased me to my feet.

"I don't want to be in bed," I grumbled. "I want to be up

and dressed and finding out who wants to kill me. And what the hell is wrong with me."

"You need to rest. If Poppy and Murisa are right, whoever wants you dead almost succeeded." She helped me the few steps towards my bed, and I sank onto the edge of the mattress with no more complaints. Those six steps had taken the wind out of me. My eyelids sagged, and I forced them open.

"What are you saying?" I did my best to wade through the haze of exhaustion. "You think whatever just happened, it was the result of an assassination attempt?"

"It didn't *just* happen, Kat. It's been over a day."

My heart clenched. A day? Where the hell was Emrick?

I mentally prodded the muted, stifled feeling in my chest, and another wave of panic gripped me. Was he all right? If something had happened to him, I—

I cut off that line of thinking. I would know if something had happened. The tether between us was still there. It felt strange—different—but it was there. He was fine, and he'd be here soon to explain where he'd been. Everything would be all right.

"Poppy took some of your blood while you were asleep," Maera continued. "Those two have been running all kinds of tests. All they've found so far is that you must have consumed something that's wreaking havoc with your system."

"What?"

She frowned. "They're not sure yet, but they're testing a few ideas."

I thought of the bitter flavour mixed in with the lavender and chocolate mint, the one I hadn't been able to identify. "That tea."

Maera averted her gaze, and a flush crept up her neck to fill her cheeks. "It's possible."

She knew something. She had to know something more than she'd told me; otherwise, she'd look me in the eye.

"Maera?"

She fluffed my pillows and helped me sit back. Only when she finished ensuring my comfort did she settle beside me and raise her gaze to meet mine, perhaps nervous about what she would find there. Or what I would find in hers.

Guilt. That was why she was avoiding me. Of course she'd be worried that if the tea had done something, I'd hold her responsible for it.

But I wasn't angry. I was terrified.

"My magic is gone."

The words came out barely above a whisper, but it was enough to shake the foundations of everything Maera believed in. Or so it seemed by the change in her expression.

She gripped my hand, her fingers so tight around mine my knuckles screamed. "Are you sure?"

Tears stung my eyes, and I wiped them away with the heel

of my palm. "I've been trying to call on it since the first time I woke up. There's nothing. Not the smallest flicker."

Her throat bobbed. "I should go get Poppy. Maybe this will help her narrow down what it was."

She stood up, but before she left, she squeezed my hand tighter. "We'll sort this out, Kat. What you need to do is go back to sleep. Don't let this worry you. All will be well."

I forced myself to nod, needing to show strength when all I wanted to do was curl up and cry. I was the head of this household. If I broke down, where would we be?

Maera offered one last pat on the back of my hand and left the room. In the silence, my thoughts ambushed me. My magic was gone. What did that mean for me? I had people trying to kill me, and my best defence against them had been stripped away.

My *identity* had been stripped away. For almost nine hundred years, I'd been the immortal sorceress, guardian of the balance between magical and mundane. What would immortality mean if I'd lost my power—and why wasn't my strength coming back?

I imagined an eternity of aches and pains, of slow recovery after every magic-less battle.

My breathing turned rapid, jagged, and it was a relief when Maera returned shortly after, rushing behind a frenetic Poppy, who burst into my room as though it were hers.

"What do you mean your magic is gone?" she demanded. "Like you can't summon it or like you can't access it? Does it feel out of reach or gone-gone?"

Cuddles must have objected to the sudden energy in his quiet space because he leapt off the bed, waving his bent tail behind him as he slipped out the door.

Poppy's tight curls bounced as she hurried towards me, hypnotic in their movement as I tried hard not to think of anything else.

Everything about Poppy was distracting. If someone were to describe what they thought a powerful necromancer might look like, Proserpine Lister was probably the opposite in every respect. The tips of her dark brown hair were always dyed some bright colour—at the moment a vibrant blue, which matched the talons of her gel-tipped fingernails. She lacked her usual berry-hued lipstick, and her face looked more wan than I'd ever seen it, but she hadn't skimped on her outfit, wearing a bright purple hoodie over a white T-shirt and tight jeans covered in butterfly-shaped patches.

The pants looked familiar. I was pretty sure they were Murisa's.

"Kitty Kat? Did you hear me?" She snapped her fingers in my face, and I wanted to respond by flicking an ember in hers... except I couldn't.

"Gone-gone," I mumbled. "That's how it feels, anyway. I've

tried meditating on it, I've tried ignoring it, I've tried forcing it. There's nothing there."

I understood my magic being stubborn, and I understood it being weak. I'd struggled with both before I'd reached the heights I had. Not having my magic at the top of its game was almost second nature to me.

This was different.

This was like having my arm sawed off and someone asking if I was one hundred per cent certain I didn't have fingers.

Poppy leaned over me, and I pulled my head back to create more distance. She ignored my signals and leaned even closer, peering into my eyes. She reached for my face, and I dodged her touch. I wasn't prepared to be poked and prodded now that I was awake.

"What are you doing?"

"Looking to see if there are any physical explanations for what happened."

"I'm sorry, I didn't realize raising corpses made you an expert in magical anomalies."

She huffed. "I'm not an expert, but Murisa is pretty damned close. She told me a few things to look for. She's in our room going over your blood again or she would have come in to see you herself."

"Thanks for getting consent for the blood, by the way."

"You're welcome for trying to save you. What the fuck, Kat?

We were supposed to be done with getting thrown into the deep end. That Alodie bitch is dead. We know someone else is after you, but we were supposed to have the upper hand here. What is this shit?"

Her uptick in cursing and the way her brown eyes glittered with unshed tears told me anger wasn't her driving emotion. Not towards me, anyway.

"I think it might have been the tea." I glanced over Poppy's shoulder to where my housekeeper stood in the doorway. She'd stayed back, letting Poppy do her thing, but now that I'd acknowledged her, she stepped closer.

"I'm so sorry, Kat. If it was the tea, I just—"

"You said you got it at the market?" Poppy asked.

She nodded. "There was a lineup for it, and they were giving out sample boxes."

"Have you tested it yet?" I asked Poppy.

Poppy looked between us. "Murisa's run a few basic scans with what she has at hand, yeah, but until we know more about what it's done to you, there's not much we can do in a hurry. These things take time."

"Maybe that's what these people want?" Maera suggested. "Throw Kat out of the game so they can carry out… whatever they plan to do?"

I crossed my arms, winced at the stretch in my shoulders, and let them fall at my sides again. "I thought what they wanted to do was kill me. If so, they failed. I guess I should be happy about that."

I didn't feel terribly happy, though. I felt angry, and sore, and afraid of what else in my body might have changed that I wasn't aware of yet. The fact that *anything* in my body had changed was enough to make the world fall out from under me. Almost a thousand years of waking up to the exact same *me* every morning, and here I was faced with having been stripped of a defining element of my being.

My chest tightened, and I struggled to draw in a full breath. Instead, I sucked in air with quick, shallow gasps, and within seconds my vision grew black along the edges.

"It's all right, Kat. Don't pass out on us now. Try to take a deep breath, all right?"

Maera's hand was on my back, but I couldn't heed her advice. I needed answers. I needed Emrick. My world was falling apart, and I was falling with it. The farther I tumbled, the more I appreciated just how deep this void was—and I had no idea if I would survive the landing.

7

Emrick

THE MOMENT I delivered the woman's spirit to the shores of the river, I once again drew on the mists to step into the mortal world. The strange sensation in my chest hadn't faded, and the unfamiliar pull demanded my attention. Without knowing the cause of it, I was left imagining the worst. If I didn't get to Kat soon, I would lose my mind.

Now that my obligations had been met, the mists came when summoned, and I soon found myself in Kat's bedroom.

My heart lurched on finding Poppy and Maera hovering over Kat's bed, but my worry eased when I saw Kat sitting up, awake—alive.

A moment later, fear crept back in. Something about her was different. She looked… small. Frail. Breakable. None of which fit with the indomitable sorceress I'd come to love so fiercely I was willing to defy Death itself to stay by her side.

"What's wrong?" I asked. "Are you all right?"

I rubbed at my chest, disappointed the discomfort hadn't faded. I'd hoped that being near her, confirming she wasn't in trouble, would ease the pain.

Kat's gaze dropped to my chest, and she rubbed her fingers against her sternum in the same place I was. Did she feel it, too?

A sob caught in her throat, and I strode towards her, needing to touch her, to wrap her in my arms and protect her from whatever had caused her distress. Her eyes were red, her cheeks stained with tears. Whatever had happened had been bad enough for her to break down in front of other people, something so rare that any relief I felt on seeing her sitting up was washed away under another wave of dread.

As I approached, Maera's eyes widened. She scurried out of my way and pressed herself against the door. It wasn't like her to be afraid of me, but I didn't spare her a glance. My only thought was getting to Kat.

I reached for her, but before I could make contact, Poppy lurched between us, swinging the lamp from Kat's bedside table. "Don't touch her!"

The lamp burst against my arm. Ceramic shards flew in all directions, mixed with glass from the shattered light bulb.

"What the *fuck*, Poppy?" Kat yelled, pressing herself against the headboard to avoid the spray of sharp fragments.

I stumbled backwards, as confused as I was furious. Who did this witch think she was trying to keep me away from Kat?

Poppy remained between us, one hand raised towards me, the other towards Kat. She pinned her gaze on me. "You have to stay away from her."

The temptation was there to brush her aside and ignore her, but something in her expression made me freeze. Uncertainty—terror. What the fuck had I missed?

She looked at Kat over her shoulder. "Kat, you've lost your *magic*."

Her words landed like a blow to my gut, and my breath left me in a whoosh. "You've what?"

I looked from her to Kat, who was staring at Poppy as though she were trying to unravel a knotted ball of yarn. Only now did I catch the slight glaze to her eyes, her struggle to focus.

A deeper horror grabbed me, and I dropped my arms to my sides.

At my shock, Kat's face scrunched up, and more tears streamed down her cheeks even as she fought to hold them back.

"It's gone," she croaked. "I can't summon it. I'm sore, I feel like I've been dragged behind a car, and my magic is gone."

The floor beneath me rocked, and I reached for the wall to steady myself—realizing as I did that in my haste to get here,

I'd forgotten to put my gloves back on. No wonder Maera had fled from me. One brush of my skin, and I would have reduced her to dust.

And if Poppy was afraid for Kat…

None of this made sense. Kat's magic was gone?

I pulled my gloves on and looked to Maera. Of everyone here, she was the one who always had the answers. She had to know what was happening.

But instead of the usual reassurance and confidence the woman exuded, she crumpled in on herself. "We think someone poisoned her. We don't know anything for sure yet."

Everything in me turned cold. Black curled around the edges of my vision, and everything else disappeared except Kat. "Details, please."

Her *magic* was gone?

Poppy exhaled sharply. "We took some of Kat's blood, and Murisa is checking it for any obvious poisons, but all she has on hand are magical tests. It's not like we have a full technical lab in our bedroom. It's going to take time."

"What about my lamp?" Kat demanded, sounding so much like her normal self for this one, brief flash that I hoped everyone was mistaken. Something had shaken my sorceress, but she was fine.

But when I took her in—her pale skin, her sunken eyes, the tremor in her hands where they rested in her lap, I knew she wasn't. Worse, I suspected the issue ran so much deeper than her magic. I rubbed my chest again—that bizarre, uncomfortable burn.

The necromancer rolled her eyes, bent down to pick up a piece of broken ceramic, and grabbed Kat's arm. Kat tried to pull away, but Poppy tightened her grip. Before I could object, before Kat could cry out, Poppy sliced the jagged edge across the outside of her bicep, between the sleeve of her T-shirt and the top of her leather glove.

Kat yelped, and I bared my teeth, holding myself back from shoving the witch away from her, but Poppy held her ground as firmly as she did Kat's arm. And as I watched the blood well up from the wound, drip over the side of Kat's arm, and keep bleeding, I got it.

I didn't understand how it was possible, but I appreciated Poppy's speed with the table lamp more than I would ever be able to say.

Kat stared at her arm without blinking, without swallowing, without moving a muscle. With every second that passed, we waited for the wound to seal. It didn't.

"Kat…" Her name slipped through my lips on a breath.

How was it possible? I felt the bond between us. It was still there. She was still a part of me.

But the connection didn't feel right. Somehow the poison had struck so deep it had altered the tether that bound us. Left it fragile, ready to snap.

Kat didn't look at me, but her face grew even paler as the full weight of her situation crashed over her—and I couldn't even comfort her. The one thing I had left that wouldn't break Death's rule—the one role I'd held since I'd led her away from the bloodstained hills of Palonia—had been torn from me by some poison.

It didn't make sense.

"If he'd touched you, you'd be dead," Poppy said softly, as though she realized Kat needed a push into accepting the truth. "I wasn't sure, but with your magic gone, I wondered." She turned to me. "I couldn't take the chance."

"Thank you, Poppy." My voice sounded like it came from a million miles away. "You saved her life. I'd take a thousand lamps to the chest if it kept her alive."

Kat's tears mixed with the blood streaming down her arm, and she squeezed her eyes shut. A low keening slipped from between her lips as she hugged her arms around her middle. Blood smeared across her clothes, making her appear even more vulnerable than she now was.

My heart shattered, and I sagged against the wall. Someone out there had done what Death had failed to do for nine hundred years. They'd stolen her immortality.

8

Katerina

Everyone seemed to accept my condition more quickly than I could.

They probably would have denied it, but what other explanation was there for the speed with which Maera and Poppy rushed to console me? Within moments, Maera left the room to inform the rest of my team what had happened. Poppy followed not long after to return to her research.

They were able to breathe. Think. Move.

I was trapped in my body, unable to do anything but sit and stare and suffer the pain of my sliced-open arm.

Since the twelfth century, time had carried on without affecting me. Now that Poppy had pointed out what should have been obvious the moment that suffocating hollowness had squeezed my middle, I felt the seconds running through me, tugging on my skin, my hair, my blood. Time burrowed into my joints and muscles and made itself at home among my pores.

I *felt* myself aging.

By the tick, tick, tick of the clock on the wall, I was getting older.

For most people, that wouldn't matter. But for most people, it was a given. As soon as they were old enough to accept their mortality, they forgot about it unless confronted with a direct reminder.

For me, whose cellular makeup had remained unchanged for over three hundred and twenty thousand days, it was like my system had been thrown into hyperdrive.

How long would it be before I got my first wrinkle? My first chronic ache?

How long before Emrick escorted me into the afterlife, unable to follow?

Panic jabbed its fingers through my lungs and applied pressure to my diaphragm, making every breath, every heartbeat a struggle.

My magic was gone, which meant Emrick no longer had a claim on my soul. When I died, it would be some stranger assigned to the mundanes who led me out of the mortal world. Unless Death came for me directly again. Would it bother now that I'd been shoved into the proper timeline? Put back in my place?

Those fingers of panic pressed harder until black spots danced in my eyes. Would I follow in my family's footsteps to whatever had awaited them after they died, or would I be sent somewhere else now that I wasn't magical?

I thought of my time in the fog after Alodie's spell circle had killed me. How alone I'd felt, lost in the nothingness with no one to greet me. Was that my future now that everything had been torn away from me?

What if there was nothing after death at all, and in the space of a few heartbeats, everything I'd come to love about this world would be gone and there would be nothing left of me and—

"Breathe, Kat," Emrick said as he sat at the end of my bed.

I didn't want him that far away. I wanted him beside me. I wanted his warmth wrapped around me to chase away the chills that had taken over my weak, aging body.

"It's going to be okay." He rested a gloved hand on my leg. Over the covers, of course. Because we needed layers between us now to avoid speeding up my visit to the emptiness of the next life.

Although I wanted to hide, to live in denial of what had happened, I forced myself to look at him. In his face, I found all the confirmation that this nightmare was real. He looked stricken—haunted. Caught between shock and horror. His silver eyes burned with desperation, and he rubbed his sternum as though the pull of our bond were a physical pain.

Maybe it was. The muted compression in my chest was an agony, and I suspected it wasn't only with emotion.

"You feel it, too?" I whispered, rubbing the same spot.

He nodded. "It's like that poison lit a match and taped it to our bond. We're still connected. I still feel you here. But it's not… solid." His brow furrowed in frustration that he couldn't find the right word, and he curled his hand into a fist.

Tears dripped onto my fingers where they clutched my comforter. I tried to follow his instructions and take a breath, but every inhale came through an increasingly narrow tube, and I didn't know if it would ever inflate. How could it? In the space of a single cup of tea, my life had grown immeasurably smaller.

Emrick rallied first. He drew his shoulders back and lifted his chin, every inch a man determined to win. "It doesn't end here, Kat. Muroppy haven't failed us yet with everything you've thrown at them, and if there's anything I can do, you know I will. If you think the poison or whatever the hell did this to you came from the tea, then I won't hesitate to raze the entire fucking country to the ground to find out who made it. Do you understand me? Whoever did this to you will pay—with more pain than they can possibly conceive. None of us will rest until our bond is as strong as it was before."

Rage snowballed in his voice, and by the end of his impassioned speech, I half-expected my bedding to catch fire. I appreciated his battle cry, but we both knew our limitations. He might want to destroy the world to save me, but doing so would ensure I lost him forever. Our best bet rested with the witches. And while Emrick was right that they were the most brilliant and persistent women I'd ever met, there were only so many miracles they could perform.

I opened my mouth, wanting to reassure him that no matter what happened, it wouldn't change how I felt about him. That I wouldn't blame him if we never found our way back to each other. That I needed him to be safe more than I needed to be immortal.

But the words dried up at the intensity I found staring back at me. Emrick's entire body was tense, coiled and ready to strike. If he told me he was about to lead a Crusade through the mists to wipe out every last person between me and whoever had come between us, I would have believed him.

And that I did believe him was a terror all on its own. He'd told me before that if I died, he would prefer being a wraith to being without me. I prayed he didn't rush down that path too quickly—my time on this earth would be short enough if we couldn't reverse what had been done. If my time with him ended with my final heartbeat, I didn't want to lose a moment.

"I love you, Katerina. I fell in love with you the first time I saw you, and that love has only grown by the day. Whoever thought stealing you from me was a good idea has made the worst decision of their pathetic life. They're going to suffer for every lost second."

"I love you, too." It sounded frail compared to his proclamation of devotion, but I didn't have the words for how deeply my soul yearned to be safely bound to his again. My love, my fear, my anger, my confusion—they tumbled inside me with the force of an unbalanced load of laundry, teetering so far off-kilter my body felt stretched to the point of breaking.

Emrick reached for me, then pulled back. Then he growled and shoved himself off the bed and tore his hands through his hair. "I can't stay here. To be here but not able to touch you—it's torture."

I understood what he meant, but it fractured my soul to hear him say it. There was no winning. Either he stayed and kept his distance, or he left me alone with the maelstrom in my head. Both options were a personally designed hell.

"If I'm limited to the afterlife, that's where I'll start," he said. "I'll scour every inch of that plane for answers." His throat bobbed, and he met my eye, his expression pleading. "Don't lose hope, Kat. Soon enough, I'll have the ashes of the bastard who did this clutched in my hand."

He squeezed his fist as a promise, and then the temperature in the room dropped, the mists came, and he disappeared.

9

Emrick

I STORMED THROUGH the afterlife, my thoughts buffeting around my skull as though caught in a hurricane.

No. *I* was the hurricane. Someone had come after the only person who kept me human, who kept me *alive*, and they would suffer the consequences. I wouldn't rest until I knew who was behind this.

Kat was *mortal*.

The concept hadn't settled, still whirling about in the gale.

Someone had taken a formidable guardian and brought her to her knees. Not only had they stolen her magic, but her purpose in this life. How could she protect the balance between magical and mundane now that she was vulnerable? *Mundane.* A mundane couldn't stand before a basilisk and drive stakes into its eyes so someone could dart in and cut off its head. A mundane couldn't face ogres or a nest of vampires.

I stumbled to a stop and followed that line of thought. Someone wanted Kat out of the picture. They might have failed to kill her, but they'd effectively knocked her out of the hunt. Kat had gained many enemies over the centuries, so the list of suspects was long. Too long to pare down. She'd dealt with most of them, but how many more lurked in the shadows? Forget the people who'd poisoned her—how many more would rise to take advantage of the void she'd left?

How long would it be before word spread throughout the magical world that she'd fallen?

A shudder ran through me at the thought of the chaos magicals might create if they were allowed to exist unchecked. The witch hunters, vampire hunters, and Hunter's Guild—the three international organizations who strove to achieve a fraction of what Kat and Adrian had accomplished over the years— would be forced to step in to do what they could, but they'd proved often enough how ineffective they could be. Their goal was to crush magicals when they stepped out of line, not ensure the balance.

Without Kat's guiding hand, it was more than likely the world would tip into outright war, with magicals doing whatever was necessary to protect themselves while the mundanes in the know fought to destroy them.

I was prepared to push my limits as far as they'd go to help Kat regain herself, but our success or failure to protect the world would extend well beyond one no-longer-immortal sorceress. Kat and her team needed to figure this out soon, or the afterlife was about to get incredibly busy.

If I followed the trail of Kat's enemies, however, maybe I wasn't at a dead end. I was a master in this afterlife. If anyone she'd taken down lingered here—if anyone knew who this new threat was, I would find them. And I would tear their souls to pieces to get our answers.

10

Katerina

I**F I WAS** worried I'd be left alone with my thoughts after Emrick left, I shouldn't have been. Within minutes of him stepping into the afterlife, Rhys knocked on my door.

"Are you all right?" he asked as he dropped onto the bed beside me. He sat so much closer than Emrick had, and I hated my pang of resentment that it should be my friend and not my lover offering the comfort of his presence.

My shoulders drooped, and I sank into my pillows. "Not at the moment. But I will be."

Rhys took my hand, and I squeezed his fingers, grateful for the contact. Somehow reassuring him soothed some of my own aches—and did he ever look like he needed reassurance. His face was whiter than pale, his green eyes wide. He reminded me of a child's doll, his features exaggerated in every sense, but instead of being comical, it broke my heart.

"I triggered a vision." He delivered the news with a seriousness that matched my mood, but I caught the flicker around his mouth, the tightness in his jaw as he tried and failed to hide his relief that his second sight had cooperated.

I wanted to celebrate with him that he'd gotten over his block but kept quiet, readying myself for whatever he might have Seen.

"It wasn't much," he warned. "Only a flicker. But there was blood. A knife in the shadows. A broken fence?" His lips twisted in thought as he worked to remember, and his shoulders slumped. "I'm going to keep trying, Kat, I promise. You're not in this by yourself. Murisa hasn't left her room since she got here, and Poppy's been in and out getting ingredients for whatever they're working on. Mum is trying to remember everything she can about the person who sold her the tea, and with every detail she gives me, I'll use it to direct my visions, okay?"

I tugged him to me, and he wrapped his arms around my neck. I sagged against him and squeezed my eyes shut to press back the tears threatening to choke me. "Thank you, Rhys. I appreciate everything you're doing."

He pulled back but kept hold of my hands, dropping his gaze to our fingers. "I know what it's like to be stuck in your body. Knowing what you should be able to do and not being able to do it."

I held my breath. In the four months since Shogaur had possessed him, he'd rarely brought up the subject himself, and never had he spoken about what he'd suffered. Maera and I hadn't wanted to push him, figuring he would share when he was ready. Even now, I held my tongue, not wanting to say anything to make him shut down.

"It's terrifying, isn't it?" he said softly. "To feel so out of control? After you got Shogaur out of me, it took me a while to feel comfortable in my own skin again. He had hold of me for a single day, but nothing felt familiar."

I'm sure it hadn't helped that he'd been recovering from a knife wound to the gut at the same time. Delivered by me. The guilt of which I was still working through.

He squeezed my hands. "You'll get there faster than I will, I think. You're strong. So much stronger than these assholes think you are. They don't know you like I do—they don't know how bad they've screwed themselves."

His words of confidence gave mine a bit of a flutter. It was a half-hearted wiggle, but more than I'd felt since waking up.

His voice dropped again. "Does it hurt?" He cleared his throat. "I mean—well, no, I guess that is what I mean. To not have your magic. To not be immortal anymore. Are you in pain?"

"Nothing extraordinary," I answered as honestly as I could.

"Waking up was unpleasant, but my body seems to have settled into its new state of… whatever this is. I have aches and pains, but nothing I can't push through." I frowned at my arm. "Poppy gave me the worst of it."

I supposed I should look at cleaning and bandaging the nasty gouge in my flesh. I'd never had to worry about that before, and no one else had thought of it, either.

Rhys puffed out a breath of relief. "Good. Like, I know it's not. It sucks. But I'm glad you're not, like, sore because of it."

I forced a smile but didn't have to exert myself for long before he added, "Mum called Barrett. He and Gavin are on their way."

He couldn't have delivered worse news.

I imagined Mr. I-Hate-Magic standing over me, gloating, while Mr. I-Hate-Myself-For-Having-Magic stared on with envy, wondering if there was any leftover tea for an easy solution to his self-loathing.

I didn't need either of them in my face.

"Do me a favour, Rhys?"

"Anything."

"Keep them out of my room."

After Rhys left, I dragged myself out of bed, steadier on my feet this time. Halfway through getting changed into a clean pair of black leggings and a heavier navy-blue sweater—despite the summer temperatures, I was freezing—Maera swooped into my room with anti-bacterial ointment, gauze, and a tray of tea and cookies. She patched up my arm, got me settled on the balcony in my Muskoka chair, and left me to eat my feelings.

Within five minutes, I went back inside to grab a blanket from the closet. Never mind that it was over twenty-five degrees Celsius with a cloudless sky and barely a breeze to rustle the branches past the house, I couldn't warm up. I suspected my body had forgotten how to regulate its temperature without the perks of my magic to help it along.

A failure on my part, perhaps, to have relied on my power too much, but what else was a sorceress expected to do when she was able to channel fire or create a layer of frost over her skin?

I devoured the cookies, but the cup of tea sat on the table beside my chair, cold and filmy. I hadn't touched it. As sad as it made me that I couldn't enjoy my go-to comfort, the memory of pain was too recent. While I doubted Maera would have served anything beyond boxed, brand-name leaf after last time, I was off hot beverages for the time being. Any beverage, really, unless it came from my own tap.

It was possible the precautions were unnecessary. If the

poisoner's goal had been to strip away my immortality, they'd succeeded, which meant they could now sit back and laugh at having finally bested me. They'd essentially killed me, even if my death was a few decades out.

If their goal had been my more immediate end, they would undoubtedly try again. Next time, though, they wouldn't catch me off guard.

As I sat in my chair, staring out over the glittering waters of Lake Huron, I considered my options. Murisa and Poppy were in their room casting whatever spells they could think of on my blood. Barrett and Gavin were on their way to do… something. Emrick was in the afterlife hoping to pry answers from the dead. Where did that leave me?

I stared down at the palms of my leather gloves, and with a rattle of combined grief and fury in my heart, I yanked them off, baring my arms to the late-afternoon sun. What did I need them for?

I ran my fingers over the supple leather. These gloves had been with me since I'd come into my power at fourteen years old. What little power I'd had back then, anyway. They were a gift from my grandmother, Palonia's Seer, who'd foreseen greatness in my future. She was the only member of my family who ever had, and she hadn't survived long enough to watch her vision come true.

These gloves had been out of my possession only once, when

the Crusaders had confiscated them in the thirteenth century, days before they'd tried to burn me at the stake. Emrick had rescued them years later.

All those years, all that magic, and, with only an occasional clean and polish, the leather looked as new as when I'd first received them. That was the magic of the runes. Protection and containment. Immunity to time, magic, and general wear and tear.

A bitter laugh escaped me. They were in better shape than I'd ever be now.

I traced one of the runes, tilting the leather to catch the faint silver shimmer deep in the etching, the lingering traces of the magical compound that made the gloves what they were.

Then I set them next to my untouched teacup and tried to forget about them. They wouldn't serve me anymore—not nearly as much as a baseball bat once I had a target. Because I had no doubt someone would be able to send me in the right direction soon, for revenge if not for a cure.

Once they did, I would need to reassess quite a few things about my purpose on this earth.

The sun shifted through the trees as the hours passed, each minute ticking by with a swiftness that astounded me. But not even the adrenaline rush at the concept of my impending death kept my weary body from falling prey to the warmth on my skin as the sun pierced the trees to my right. My eyes closed, my muscles relaxed, and I fell into dreams of fire and ash. Alodie pointing and laughing at me, telling me I'd finally gotten what was coming to me. My parents standing behind her looking so disappointed that I hadn't anticipated this kind of covert attack. I sought out my son among them, both dreading and hoping a memory of him might grace my thoughts.

Before I found him, an awareness of someone moving beside me pulled me out of the darkness of sleep and back to the sunny balcony.

Which was a little less sunny now that the day had begun to close. It was early enough on this July evening that the heat lingered in the cedar wood of my chair but late enough that shadows encompassed most of my surroundings, including the wide, surly man sitting in the matching chair beside me.

James Barrett.

I barely glanced at him. It was enough to know he was here—against my wishes. But I didn't need to look directly at him to take in the stretch of his wide biceps in his green T-shirt, the way the cotton stretched across his well-defined pecs, or the thick thighs caught in black denim. The man was a wall, each muscle an individual stone set in place by the grout of tendons and ligaments.

He held a bottle of beer between his large hands, rolling it between his palms.

"Rhys is fired," I grumbled to the trees.

"Kid did his best," he replied gruffly. "Only so much he could do. I outweigh him by at least seventy-five pounds."

I arched an eyebrow. "Did you manhandle my protégé?"

"Of course not. I told him his mother was calling for him, then came in when he went to find her."

Rhys and I would have to have words about what playing interference meant. Rule number one: do not be fooled by false calls from your mother.

Whatever. The damage had been done. I would do my best to ignore the talking tree and let his smugness flow over me. His opinion meant nothing. His sense of superiority could not affect me.

"How are you holding up?" he asked.

I waited for the follow-up question. The laugh. The biting comment to put me in my place about how all my beliefs about my magic had been disproved and how it was about time life knocked me down.

Nothing came. The silence stretched out between us, and while I wouldn't say it was easy, it carried no weight of words unsaid.

I adjusted my blanket to cover my toes. "All right, I guess."

Another drawn-out pause. "It's a big change."

When I still heard nothing except basic thoughtfulness, I shifted in my seat to face him.

Barrett's wide jaw was covered in stubble, and his hair had

grown out just long enough to brush the tops of his ears, something I'd never seen before on the ex-soldier. Dark circles lined his brown eyes, setting off the angles of his once-broken nose. The shadows caught the myriad scars on his face—one that cut across his chin, two tiny ones on his right cheek, and another that crossed the middle of his forehead.

Some of them he'd received while in service with the special forces; others had come during his decade-long tenure as Adrian's human thrall.

Some he'd received while working with me.

We'd been through so much together over the past few months. Usually against our will, usually at odds, but we always had each other's back when things turned tough. A realization that surprised me as much as it warmed me.

"It is," I said. "I don't think I've processed it yet."

He dipped his chin in a slight nod and rested his ankle over his opposite knee as he relaxed in the deep chair.

I blinked. I had never seen Barrett relax in my presence. I hadn't realized the steel rod could bend.

"That's understandable. Magic is a big part of who you are."

I snorted. "For the worse, right?"

"No."

The man could have pushed me over with a feather. "Excuse me very much? You are James Barrett, are you not? You're not some shapeshifter wearing his face?"

The corner of his mouth kicked up in the faintest of smiles—which for him was a great, beaming grin. "I have my opinion of magic. I have my opinion of magic users. And then I have my opinion of you. Call me a hypocrite if you want, but over the past few months, those opinions have"—he tapped his fingernails against the bottle—"shifted."

I cleared my throat and picked at a thread on my blanket. "I call you a lot of things, Barrett, but never a hypocrite. An asshole, sure, but the most level-headed asshole I've ever met."

"And you are the most realistic magic user I've ever met," he countered.

I frowned. "Realistic? That's the best you've got?"

He shrugged. "Look at Mikhail. That guy wanted to massacre hundreds of witches so he could bond his soul with a demon's and live forever. Same with Alodie. In my experience, people who run with magic seek unlimited power. They might only get it bit by bit, but give it enough time and there's nothing they won't do to reach the top." He took a swig of his beer, then went back to rolling it between his palms. "You've been alive for almost a thousand years. You've held incredible power in your hands, and you've only ever used it to help. You're the kind of magic user the world needs more of, Kat. It's what Adrian saw in you. It's why he kept pushing you even when you felt so low that all you wanted was to hang up your cape and leave it to the moths. So no, I'm not happy about your situation. I'm not about to stand over you and cheer or whatever you thought I might do—whatever reason you told Rhys to keep me away. Someone came after you. As a member of my family, that means someone came after me, and I don't let that shit stand."

Well, crap.

The bastard had gone and made me cry.

Shithead.

"From here, I see two ways forward for you," he continued, staring at the bottle and peeling the label off from the corner. "You can sit around and wallow, waiting for someone to find out who did this so they can kick some ass and discover the why and the how."

"Or?" I breathed, watching his deft fingers remove the label with such careful precision that there was no tear, no fragment left behind.

Once the label was off, he put down the bottle, set the label beside it, and turned the entire heavy chair so he could face me. His deep brown eyes met mine, and in his stare was such strength and drive my broken soul awoke.

"Or you can train with me, learn the limits of your mortal body so you can push past them, and go out there and rip this fucker apart yourself."

11

Katerina

BARRETT'S WORDS LIT a fire inside me—a fire that flickered precariously when he led me to the back patio carrying two yoga mats.

I expected him to tell me we were about to practice some kind of cool fighting technique, but nope. They were for yoga.

"There are a lot of things about being human you haven't had to deal with," he said as he guided me through a basic sun salutation that had my quads shaking. "You've always been able to jump right into a fight without suffering any of the repercussions. The rest of us base mortals benefit by stretching before we go into battle. Yoga is not only good for keeping the muscles and joints limber and flexible." He slid into a Warrior One position, his right thigh impressively parallel with the ground while his back leg stretched firmly out behind him. "It's also good for centering the mind. A moving meditation."

He shifted from Warrior One to Warrior Two, deepening the lunge in his front leg.

If Emrick had been in front of me, I would have been too distracted by his mouth-watering body to replicate the pose, but Barrett's muscles didn't entice me—they terrified me. He was more than capable of Warrior-Two-ing me into an early grave.

Earlier grave.

So instead of complaining or gawking, I did my best to follow his movements, wincing with each lunge, squat, and back-bend.

By the time we finished, my arms trembled, my core screamed, and I felt amazing. For the first time in almost nine hundred years, I was using my body in new ways, stretching the life back into it. But more than that, I was doing something, which felt a hell of a lot better than hiding in a Muskoka chair.

"Now that we've warmed up," he said, pulling a knife from somewhere on his person. "We can dust off your other skills."

He drew a second blade and handed it to me, hilt out. I accepted with a grin and allowed myself to sink back in time. Despite what Barrett thought about me, I was no stranger to the art of knife-fighting. Adrian and Emrick had taught me well, believing I should always have a backup defence if ever I couldn't access my magic.

They'd meant if I ever found myself stuck in a public space filled with mundanes, or if my reserves ran dry. None of us ever imagined I might lose my power altogether.

But whatever skill I had was nothing compared to what Barrett possessed. He'd honed his mastery professionally and privately every day for almost twenty years, and the result was a graceful flow of dexterity mixed with brute force.

I suspected all the training in the world didn't explain the speed with which he moved—and had my guesses about what lay behind it—but had no time to ask about it as I struggled to keep up.

He flew towards me, blade glinting in the evening light. I didn't have time to fight him off, so I settled for ducking under his arm and backing away from him. The hilt of my knife felt uncomfortable and unfamiliar in my hand, and although I attempted a few strikes in response to his assault, I didn't come close with any of them.

On the contrary, my own hand was bleeding before we passed the hour mark, sweat having loosened my grip on the hilt so the blade slipped and sliced my palm.

I regretted taking my gloves off. Their original purpose might no longer serve me, but they would have protected me against myself.

My heart pounded against my ribs, and my muscles screamed at the exertion, but I refused to bow out. My pride rebelled at the mere idea. My fear at being helpless and trapped in this mortal body pushed me to try harder, to reclaim the knowledge that had grown lax over my years of apathy.

Tears of exertion streamed down my face and mixed with beads of sweat. My vision blurred, and Barrett landed the edge of his knife against my throat.

He held it there for a moment, both of us breathing hard, his muscled chest inches from my face.

"We're done." He stepped away and turned to roll up his mat.

I used my shoulder to wipe my eyes clear as I stomped after him. "No, we're not. We have to keep going. I'm not good enough yet. I won't stop until I am."

Barrett sheathed his blade and grabbed hold of my wrist, twisting enough that I gasped and dropped the knife into his hand. Without releasing his hold on me, he slipped the weapon into the sheath at his waist, tugged me closer, and looked me in the eye.

"You are good enough, Katerina. If I had any doubt about that, I wouldn't waste my time with you. But pushing yourself right off the bat will burn you out and leave you as useless as you're afraid you are. So we're going to take this slow. You're going to deal with your hand, you're going to shower, eat something, get some sleep, and at the ass-crack of dawn tomorrow, we'll meet back here for another round. Rinse and repeat until you can beat me without breaking a sweat. I believe you can do it, and I believe you'll do it quickly, but if you doubt yourself, you're going to fail. That's life, Kat. The hard truth of it."

He loosened his grip but didn't let go as he pulled me towards the house. Without saying a word, he nudged me towards my room, and I obeyed. It was strange taking orders from him, but stripped as I'd been of all forms of power, I couldn't do anything else. Until I found my footing, Barrett was the better leader, and it would only serve me to accept it.

His words echoed in my head as I stripped out of my damp clothing and stepped into a hot shower.

The son of a bitch was right.

I couldn't afford to doubt myself, and I couldn't afford to make mistakes. And pushing myself to exhaustion would certainly be a mistake.

I had to prepare. Properly. Carefully. Whoever had poisoned me would expect me to be weak and afraid, so it was on me not to play into their expectations. When I finally tracked them down, I might not have magic, but I wouldn't be powerless— and my enemy would feel it.

Washed, dried, and dressed, all of which was made difficult by my still-bleeding hand, I returned to the kitchen, where Barrett waited for me at the table with the first-aid kit lying open in front of him.

"Shouldn't Nurse Gavin be the one patching me up?" I

asked, staring warily at the kit as I sank into the seat beside him.

His jaw flexed. "He said he'll check it out if I think it's bad enough."

In other words, the sorcerer didn't intend to follow in Barrett's footsteps of gracing me with a pep talk.

While Barrett prepared the disinfectant and bandages, I dropped my gaze to my hand, waiting for the slice across my palm to heal itself. For the tissue to draw itself together and the skin to itch.

Instead, it kept bleeding.

He scooched his chair closer and held out a cotton ball. "You ready? This is going to hurt like a son of a bitch."

I curled my other hand around the seat of my chair. "Try not to enjoy it too much."

A hiss cut through my teeth as disinfectant met wound, and I squeezed my eyes shut against the pain. I was no stranger to injuries. I'd taken knife wounds, gunshot wounds, blasts of magic. I'd been burned, pushed down stairs, hit by cars. Bitten, clawed, gored. In this moment, none of those past wounds hurt as much as this stupid cotton ball.

"So," I said, hoping to distract myself from the pain, "vampire blood?"

Barrett stiffened but didn't look up from his dabbing. "Excuse me?"

"You're good with a knife, Barrett, but you shouldn't be

that good."

As Adrian's human thrall, Barrett would have taken a drop of blood now and then to make him a stronger defender of Adrian's sleeping form—and as a gift from one lover to another. Heightened senses, quicker healing, improved speed and mobility. Not enough to push him into magical levels, but enough to keep him safer in a fight.

I'd wondered what Barrett would do now that Adrian was gone, but it seemed my old friend had thought ahead.

Barrett's brow furrowed as he nodded. "He left me enough for a while. A long while."

His shoulders were stiff, as if he were braced for me to mock him for indulging in the magic he hated so much. A tiny voice in the back of my head was tempted, but I found it easy to send that voice away.

I squeezed his hand with my cleaned-up one. "Good. We don't know what we're moving against here, and Adrian would have wanted you to be protected." A ball formed in my throat. "Besides, it kind of keeps him here with us. I'm grateful for that."

His throat bobbed with a hard swallow, but he said nothing else as he moved on from the cleaning to the much less painful bandaging.

"That should be good for now," he said after he taped it. "It doesn't look too deep, and it was a clean cut. Keep an eye on it, change the bandages at least once a day, and let me know if it starts to look nasty. If it gets infected, you'll have the joy of experiencing the Canadian health care system."

A shudder ran through me, and I swallowed hard to stop myself from crying. It was fine. I didn't have a fear of hospitals, I'd just never had the need of one beyond visiting other people. Or of doctors. Or of medicine.

There was a lot about this modern world I hadn't experienced firsthand, and I didn't relish the idea of that changing.

"How's the patient?" Maera asked as she came into the kitchen with Rhys close behind her.

"Not vomiting." I cleared my throat. "Yet."

"Good, then maybe you can check in on Muroppy. I think they've learned something."

I couldn't have stood up faster if she'd mentioned cinnamon pancakes. Learning was good. Learning meant progress, which meant finding an answer—and maybe a solution—to what ailed me. Namely, life.

Rhys and Barrett followed close behind me as I headed downstairs to the rec room, but I barely spared them a glance as I first knocked then threw open the door to Poppy and Murisa's room.

Poppy jerked up from the round table where she'd been leaning and pressed her hand to her chest. "Jeez Louise, kitty Kat, give a girl a moment. What if we'd been in a compromising position?"

"Then I'd have backed away, closed the door, and pretended not to have seen anything. Maera said you've learned something?"

Murisa nodded and moved herself to the next chair over, giving me space to approach the microscope set up at her seat. "It's not much. *Please* don't get your hopes up."

Hugging my hopes to my chest despite her pleading, I bent over and set my eye to the eyepiece. At first glance, all I saw was a smear of red and some floating cells.

"What exactly am I looking at?" I asked, realizing I probably should have asked first, looked later.

"It's subtle," Murisa said. "You can notice it more along the outside of the sample. In the sort of yellow-ish clear bit."

I squinted. When that didn't help, I relaxed my face and tried to look at what she'd described.

Finally, after what felt like ages, I spotted a faint sparkle in the blood. "Is that a light reflection I'm seeing?"

"It is *not*," Murisa said, and by the note of excitement in her voice, I knew I'd flagged the correct detail. "*That* is *magic*."

My eyebrows brushed against my hairline, and I leaned over to take another look. If I'd hoped that having a name for it would make everything clear and the sparkles in the blood pop out like rainbow confetti, I was disappointed. It didn't look any different from my first glance, and even with Murisa telling me what it was, I didn't understand.

"Kat's magic?" Rhys asked.

Murisa grimaced. "Unfortunately not. It's…" She huffed and shifted in her chair. "Let's see if I can explain this. There's innate magic and created magic, and the two show up differently. A person's magic is genetic, so we can only see evidence of it in cellular data. A potion, however, shows up the way a radiation dye might, only much more subtly. That we found it here tells us a lot."

My shoulders slumped. "I'll have to take your word for it."

Her smile softened, and she rested her hand on my arm. "It means we're one step closer to an answer, Kat."

Poppy set her hand on my shoulder, leaving me squeezed between the two witches. It was a strangely comforting position to be in.

"It means whatever dosed you was magic, kitty Kat."

I tried to dig up the same excitement shining in their eyes and failed miserably. "So? We already suspected that."

"But now we *know*." Poppy put her other hand on my left shoulder and turned me towards her. "I know you've never thought much about what we witches can do, but there's one thing about our magic that all your sorcery lacks."

I barely had the heart to ask. "Oh?"

"Every spell has a counterspell. If there is any way to reverse this magic, Murisa and I will find it."

12

Emrick

I STALKED THE shores of the afterlife hunting for witches.

Normally I didn't care who drifted along these empty roads while they waited for their escort across the river. My role in their lives was over.

Today was my exception.

Time and again, Kat had made me promise not to help her when she was in trouble. Every time I interfered with the mortal world, Death absorbed a fragment of my soul, bringing me closer and closer to wraithhood. Memories gone, all colour drained from my life. I would become a permanent resident of the afterlife, a spectre, a classic pop-culture reaper. And Kat would be alone for eternity without even my presence to keep her company.

Something that was especially out of the question now that Adrian had met his final death.

But the situation had changed. Kat was mortal. She had maybe six or seven decades left on this planet before Death claimed her overdue soul.

If we didn't find a way to reverse whatever had weakened our bond, becoming a wraith would be a kindness to me. But I wasn't about to let either event happen without a fight.

So here I was, walking that razor edge between interfering and sticking to my lane. In this place I was free to ask questions and to exert my power. To a point. And I was willing to inch as close to that point as possible if it meant saving Kat.

Someone in this afterlife had to know something. Kat had ruined a lot of lives, many recently, and the odds of their souls having already crossed to the next plane were slim. Some of them might have glided right onto the first ferry across, but others would have lingered. Not everyone knew where they wanted to go when they reached this place. Some wanted to wait for their loved ones, some fought against their new reality. Some were simply too broken to have a clear idea of what the next stage looked like. Until they made up their minds, they were stuck here.

So I searched, keeping my senses open for any familiar souls among the crowds.

The busiest region of the afterlife was along the river, so

that's where I directed my feet. Balls of light floated past me, while in other places glowing pillars remained in place. A few souls were little more than wisps—souls so lost they would never find their way across.

I drew on my power as a servant of Death to bring the pillars into sharper focus. Out of the light came human forms, their facial features blurred but distinct. Most I didn't recognize. I swept past them, and they ignored me, which made my journey quick. Every time I met a soul I'd escorted in the past few months, I stopped to ask questions, but most didn't remember anything of their mortal lives. They'd accepted their fate and left the living world behind them, holding on to their most precious memories and letting the rest go.

A few stood out. Most of them were witches who'd died in Mikhail's bid for power. They resented being here. Their anger seeped into the light around them like shadows, twisting their features into monstrous dimensions.

With them, I pressed harder, asking them about Kat, about any known plot against her. All I received in response were insults and vitriol.

"I wouldn't tell you a goddamned thing," one man said. "That bitch deserves whatever she gets. As far as I'm concerned, you've just given me the closure I was missing."

The shadows around him thickened and deepened, and I watched with disgust. If he kept on this way, he'd tear himself apart and join the other aimless wisps. I wouldn't mourn his loss.

"Mikhail knew someone was up to something," another soul said. Their shadows weren't as deep, ebbing and flowing with their lighter half. "He joked about it. Believed they'd fail. Promised to take care of it for them. We know how that worked out."

A frisson ran through me. "Who's they?"

The soul wavered. "I don't know. I can't see their faces. I can't remember. Why can't I remember? Where am I?"

The shadows darkened as the soul struggled, and I left them. Without the reminder of what came before, the spirit would settle and continue waiting.

But now I had a target.

My blood rushed in my ears, my hands clenched and unclenched at my sides.

Although I knew I was inching too close to the edge of my limits, I pumped more power into my veins, drawing on the essence of the afterlife to clear the clouds around these souls further. Or maybe bring myself further into the essence of the afterlife. I didn't think about it too hard, not wanting to consider the consequences when I was so close to getting the answers I needed.

When I finally found Mikhail, he was standing on the edge of the river, staring out over the water with a deep furrow between his eyebrows.

Although I'd escorted him here after Kat killed him, I'd never encountered Mikhail in life. Kat had sent me away long before her first run-in with him, and he had every reason to be relieved I hadn't. Promise to Kat or not, I would have been tempted to turn him to dust the first time he'd targeted her. Even now that he was dead, I squeezed my fists to suppress my desire to throw his soul into the river to disintegrate.

Eyes like onyx blazed out from under his thick, dark hair, and his brown skin with its copper undertones had, I'm sure, been a large part of his draw when he was alive. He'd been in his late-sixties when he died, with model-pretty features and the confident bearing of a dictator. Which, by all I knew of him, was apt.

His clothes were all white, from the loose shirt to the flowing trousers, and he was barefoot.

It took a special kind of person to hold on to their pretentiousness in this place, and I swallowed my contempt as I approached. That kind of thinking wouldn't be useful when I needed him to cooperate.

I swore to myself I'd be on my best behaviour as I stepped onto the shore beside him. "Searching for something?"

His dark gaze flicked my way, scathing, irritated at being interrupted. Bad luck for him I had no intention of taking the hint.

"A way out."

"All you need to do is pick a direction and someone will be

along to take you there."

"I don't want to cross the river. I'm not looking for a way forward. I'm looking for a way back."

"This is a one-way road. Going back isn't an option."

Mikhail scowled. "So I'm beginning to appreciate. Which is bullshit, of course. I'm not supposed to be here. It shouldn't have been possible for me to be here."

He was almost right. A few more minutes, and he would have summoned a demon, bound his soul, and become as immortal as Alodie had been. I bit back my laugh.

"It wouldn't have been how you imagined it, you know."

Now I had his attention. His eyebrow arched high as he turned to face me. "What would you know about it?"

I shrugged and shoved my hands in my pockets. "Abigail, as you knew her."

"That bitch," he spat. "She didn't tell me the sorceress could shoot *lightning* from her fingers. She wanted me to fail. Probably laughed the whole time. I should have killed her and her demon when I had the chance."

"That probably would have been smart," I agreed. "Too late now, though. She's dead."

Mikhail sniffed. "Good."

"She was old."

"She said she was looking into a solution for that particular problem."

"She wouldn't have found it. Her solution was you, then Katerina. Even if Kat had wanted to help, she wouldn't have been able to."

"Oh?"

I could practically see the wheels in Mikhail's head spinning. He was hoping I was about to supply him with the answers he sought, and in a way, I was. He just wouldn't be happy about it.

"Demons age. Not quickly and not in the same way humans do, but they get old. They get more powerful as they get old, and they don't die. This was what Alodie experienced. What you would have experienced. Power and a failing body."

He didn't need to know that Alodie's ritual had gone wrong. It was possible if he'd performed it properly, he wouldn't have suffered that particular side effect.

"What about the sorceress? The bitch who killed me?"

I shrugged again. "She's bound to me." Less so now, but I didn't want to dwell on that.

Mikhail scoffed. "And you don't age, is that it?" His eyes widened. "Wait. You were there. You were the one who brought me here." He frowned and crossed his arms. "Well, that's hardly fair, is it? She ends up bound to Death and gets everything she wants?"

Hardly, but he didn't need to know that, either.

I canted my head. "You wanted her dead."

"Of course I did. She's an interfering pain in the ass who

should have been put in the ground centuries ago. I never should have gotten in their way."

I didn't think—didn't even realize I'd moved until I found myself staring down at Mikhail, my hand wrapped around his throat where I pinned him to the ground. Without planning, I'd drawn on more power, sunk deeper into this plane until Mikhail was as corporeal as I was. He thrashed against my hold, but I held him down without effort. In this place, he would never overpower me.

"Whose way?" I growled. "Who else wants her dead?"

"Everyone wants her dead. You might be the exception." Mikhail squirmed again before he gave up. His eyes were wide, but the uncertainty was greater than his fear. He was already dead, so he knew I couldn't kill him again—unfortunately— but he didn't know what I *could* do.

Neither did I, but I was willing to find out.

"Tell me who."

A sly gleam crept into his dark eyes. "Ah, I see. Some- one else has made an attempt on dear Katerina's life, haven't they? And you already said Abigail is dead, so it's not her." He threw his head back against the ground and let out a laugh that made me wish I could tear out his throat. "Oh, this is so sweet. You expect me to give away all my secrets so you can go and save your precious sorceress. Well, I won't help you. If there's even the smallest chance they'll succeed, I want to give them a running start."

I curled my fingers into his neck and hauled him to his feet. When I let him go, he rubbed the spot where my nails had torn into his flesh. There was no blood, no wound, but I hoped he felt my touch for the rest of his long, long wait on this shoreline.

My pulse throbbed in my temples, my throat, my chest. I felt the pull of the afterlife tugging on my energy, draining me bit by bit, and knew I had crossed a line, but I wasn't finished here. Not yet.

Baring my teeth in a wolfish grin, I closed the distance between us. I had a few inches on Mikhail, and I used them to full advantage, towering over him and holding his gaze until I caught the faint tremor in his lip.

"I hope you enjoy the view here, Mikhail. I can make it so no one ever comes to get you. You're in my world now, and I can guarantee you stay here. Death has what it needs. Everything beyond this river is a gift. One you don't deserve."

The first flicker of pure terror danced in the darkened embers of his eyes, and I latched on to it. "You wanted to know what an eternity feels like?"

I stepped away from him, giving him time to sit with the idea of forever in this muted, silent space.

"Wait!" he called, and I bit down on my smile before turning back. "I can't give you names. I don't know them. But it's a group. They're the ones who summoned Abigail's demon almost sixty years ago. They told her about Kat. She didn't tell me all of it when she found me—trained me—but she told me enough. Whoever they are, they're big and they've been around a long time."

A group that big would have made a name for itself somewhere in the mortal world. With that information, Kat's team might have luck figuring out what that name was. Assuming I could figure out how to pass the information along to get them started.

I nodded my thanks and continued down the path, releasing my hold on my magic until Mikhail's features faded back into a pillar more shadow than light. The tug on my soul staggered me for a moment, but I drew myself together. I was still here, still me. I still had Kat. I wasn't sure if my efforts had cost me anything, but I wasn't in a rush to try it again to find out.

"Wait!" Mikhail's voice drifted towards me again. "You'll get me across now, right? You won't leave me here. Tell me how to get out of here!"

"That's on you, Mikhail," I called over my shoulder. "It's always been on you. You need to figure out what's waiting for you on the other side."

The sound of his weeping followed me out of the afterlife and back into Katerina's bedroom.

13

Katerina

I‌T WAS WELL past midnight, but although I lay in bed, I hadn't yet fallen asleep.

Not that I'd tried very hard to get there.

Every time I closed my eyes, I became all too aware of the figurative ticking clock, every passing second singing my name, dragging my body closer to the grave. Every time I opened my eyes, my brain surged with thoughts about who might have done this to me, why, and whether I would have the opportunity to repay the favour.

My sleeplessness meant I was all too aware when the temperature in the room dropped. Goosebumps rose on my bare arms as shivers scurried down my spine. Habit made me reach for my fire for warmth, but when no heat surfaced, I went lax, pummelled with defeat.

Emrick stepped through the mist, and my throat tightened when he kept his distance. In my periphery, I watched him lean against the wall with his hands tucked behind him—the posture he used when there were untouchables nearby. Anything to reduce the risk that he would make contact and turn them to dust.

He'd never taken that posture with me. I'd always been the exception. *His* exception. That I was now one of the masses hurt almost as much as my lack of magic.

"Any luck?" I asked, keeping my attention on the wall next to the door. To look at him would be to want him, and my inability to have him would be one more push towards the breakdown that hovered just out of sight. If I tumbled over that edge, it would take me forever to claw my way back. And I no longer had forever.

"Some." His voice was soft, but I heard the effort behind his veneer of calm. His grasp on control had to be as fragile as mine was, but if he slipped, he could do so much more damage than I could right now. "I happened on an old friend of yours in the afterlife. He offered some insight."

He couldn't have said anything more compelling. My impending breakdown slipped beneath a treacherous flicker of hope, and I rolled onto my back. "Who?"

Emrick didn't move, but when his silver eyes met mine, his

presence swept over me with its familiar weight. "Mikhail."

That made me sit up. Of all the names I'd expected to drop from his lips, that wasn't one of them. "I hope you passed along my giant fuck-you."

"I may have offered something along those lines."

The silence that followed was uncomfortable, like a favourite sweater that had shrunk in the wash. Even during those seventy-five years when I'd ordered him to stay away from me, our banter had possessed more bite than this. We were like two people who knew they were about to break up but neither of them wanted to be the one to end it.

My chest tightened, and I forced myself to take a breath and calm down. Our relationship wasn't the priority right now. It couldn't be, because, as things stood, it couldn't exist. Him being in my room, him talking to me, researching my situation—all of it went against Death's rules. How much further could he push his luck before Death believed he'd gone too far and stole whatever was left of the man I loved?

I opened my mouth to ask him to leave. Whatever he got up to in the afterlife, it would keep him safer than spending time with me. But the words stuck in my throat, and, despite myself, the question that came out was, "Can you tell me what he said?"

He couldn't—not directly. I knew that. But he wouldn't be here if he didn't have something to share.

Emrick scratched his jaw, then tucked his hand behind him again. "He claims not to know what group sent Alodie after you. Maybe that will set off some memories for you. Maybe some underground society you pissed off in the last half-century or so?"

His shoulders tensed as he braced himself—worried he was about to lose another part of himself? A moment later, he relaxed, and I prayed that meant whatever information he'd shared had snuck under Death's radar.

Now it was my turn to parse through what he'd said and figure out where the clue lay. It took me a few replays, my thoughts still foggy with stress, but I landed on the word *group*. Not a one-off magical with a vendetta who'd summoned Fegor but *many*. Lucky me.

I snorted and tucked my hair behind my ear. "I've pissed off so many people, I couldn't begin to narrow down the list. Covens, vampire nests, shifter packs, dragon thunders, geese gaggles—you name it, I've crossed it. I don't know why any of them would want to work with Alodie, though. A coven *maybe*, if they felt they got something out of it, but I don't know if my death would be a big enough motivator. Even if they killed me, the witch hunters would replace me quickly enough. They've wanted to do it for few centuries, so they have everything in place."

Emrick raised an eyebrow. "Not a bad place to start, then.

They might have an idea about who this other group could be."

I hated to admit it, but the hunters had kept their ears closer to the ground than I had over the past few decades. Not enough to pin a giant red flag on Abigail, but maybe they were sitting on information they didn't realize was important.

"I'll talk to Barrett tomorrow and see if he's willing to give his contacts a call." I groaned. "There's also the Death Raisers. Every step of the way, that coven has nagged at me as a potential threat, but I've gone against my instincts and ignored it. Poppy told me it isn't them, but since when do I take other people's word as fact?"

If my failure to check in with them had led to my current condition, I'd never forgive myself.

"What about the tea angle?" Emrick asked.

I shrugged. "Maera and Rhys are asking around about it. The pop-up table closed, but for everyone that bought some, no one else has fallen ill, so whatever poisoned me, it's not harmful to non-magicals. Thank the gods for that, at least."

Silence settled around us once more, the awkwardness gone but the tension so much greater. Emrick's expression grew pained, haunted. He pushed himself away from the wall and stepped towards the bed, stopping a metre away from the end. "This is killing me, Kat."

A dark laugh escaped me. "You're telling me. I'm the one dying."

His jaw flexed, and his throat bobbed. "Don't make jokes."

"Sadly, it's absolute fact. What do you think?" I tilted my face to show him my profile. "See any wrinkles yet?"

"Kat."

My name dropped from his tongue as though it weighed a hundred pounds, and I gave up trying to sound strong in the face of his brokenness.

My shoulders drooped, and I sagged against my pillows, wishing I could take his hand and pull him onto the bed with me. Wishing I could turn back time and not drink that tea. Wishing I could have stopped Alodie from setting off that last spell circle until after I'd dragged the information about who'd summoned her from her stubborn lips.

But what was the point of wishing for the impossible?

Maybe it would be better to be grateful for everything I'd had until now. I'd had a good run. The bulk of it with an amazing man by my side. It was more than most people got.

"Is it our fault, do you think?" I asked.

Emrick frowned. "How could this possibly be our fault?"

"Maybe we rubbed our happiness in fate's face too often. You, me, Adrian. Saving the world, having each other. Do you think this is the gods' way of getting back at us? Ha ha, now you have no future."

The corner of Emrick's lips curled upwards as his silver eyes gleamed. "It does seem like something that would happen to us, doesn't it?" Tentatively, he reached out his gloved hand and swept a single finger over my comforter, well away from where my toes lurked under the blankets. "I love you."

His voice was husky with emotion, and the sound caused my heart to clench. "I love you, too."

He nodded and held my gaze for another heartbeat, then he bowed his head and disappeared into the mist.

Fair. There was nothing more to be said.

14

Emrick

I COULDN'T STAND returning to the afterlife after leaving Kat the way I had.

There was so much more I'd wanted to say. I wanted to reassure her that we would reverse whatever this was. I wanted to swear that I wouldn't stop until we'd exhausted every possibility, and I didn't care if it took three years or thirty years, I would love every wrinkle that added to her beauty.

She wasn't dying. Whatever jokes she wanted to make to hide her terror, I refused to allow the possibility. She would survive, and we would be together. Gods, fate, enemies be damned. She and I would find a way because that's what love did.

Wasn't that what Adrian had said to me once? *Bond or no*

bond, immortality or no immortality—you find a way.

The thought of my old friend pulled me through the mist to the empty library in Muskoka.

With Barrett and Gavin in Spring Bay, the house was dark and quiet, but I didn't need anyone to play host. I stood in the middle of the room that still smelled of Adrian—old books and blood and a hint of cologne—and closed my eyes against the bittersweet pain that gripped my heart.

If he'd been here, he would have known exactly what to say. He would have been there for Kat. For me. He would have helped us navigate this foundational shift that had wiped our feet out from under us.

"So?" I asked the darkness. "What words of wisdom do you have for me, my friend? How do I help Kat when I can't even stand beside her?"

I squeezed my hands at my sides and breathed through the tightness in my chest as my heart raced. "I'm helpless here, Adrian. She's still living, still breathing, but she's as far from me as if she were dead, and there's nothing I can do. And she's terrified. She's trying to hide it, but it's obvious. She's acting like someone clawing at the side of a mountain, struggling to find a good grip but knowing one shift of the rock is all it'll take to send her flying."

I rested my hands on the mantel over the hearth and bowed my head. This would have been the point where Adrian would chuckle or sigh or rise from his armchair.

In all my years, I've seen every pain immortality has to offer, I imagined him saying. *We see so much, but so much happens beyond us that when it happens to us, we don't know how to react. It's our greatest curse, is it not? To spend so much of our lives unchanging that when the world pivots beneath us, we feel it so much more deeply than the mortals for whom change is constant.*

I huffed a laugh and leaned more weight on my hands. I pictured Adrian standing beside me, his hands in his pockets, staring thoughtfully into the fireplace.

Katerina is strong enough to adapt. Once she has a target, she'll pour all her fear and rage into destroying it. That drive will ensure her life remains on her terms, regardless of anyone else's aims. As for you, my friend—you are helpless in this.

I shoved myself off the mantel and paced the room, taking in the spines of Adrian's books, the stack of them sitting on the table. In this room, Barrett had kept everything the way Adrian preferred it, making his presence all the more real.

Maybe that was why I heard a whisper on the nonexistent draft that raised the hair on the back of my neck.

But you're not useless. Love, Emrick. Your love for our sorceress will see her through the pain. It will guide her through the darkness. Don't give up on her, don't give up on your bond. You will find a way.

I spun around, certain I would catch Adrian's spirit drifting through the room. Although the library remained empty, the whispers burrowed into my head.

My bond with Katerina was frayed and she'd lost her immortality, but my love for her only burned hotter for the forced separation. If that's what it would take to reach the dawn through this moonless night, then that's what I would offer.

We would find our way.

15

Katerina

AFTER EMRICK LEFT, I finally stole a few hours' sleep. The next morning, fueled by the possibility that Barrett's contacts might lead us in the right direction, I rushed through my shower and got dressed in a pair of burgundy leggings and a long charcoal-grey T-shirt. One tiny silver lining of not being able to summon fire into my hands was that I was less likely to ruin my clothes, which meant I could pull out all my favourite outfits.

At this point, I was desperate to grab hold of every benefit I could find.

Once dressed, I went in search of Barrett. I thought I'd find him in the kitchen or the rec room in the basement, but it wasn't until I went outside that I found him and Gavin on the edge of the shore.

They sat side by side on the rocks that curved along the side of the beach, cross-legged, hands clasped in their laps. They weren't talking, weren't moving—the only way I knew they were all right was the rise and fall of their shoulders as they worked through some kind of breathing exercise.

Meditation, then.

Not wanting to interrupt them but also not wanting to put off my conversation with Barrett, I made my way towards them. Although neither man reacted to my approach, I didn't doubt for a moment that Barrett heard me. With the touch of Adrian's blood in his veins and his own training, the man's hyperawareness was just shy of magical.

I stepped carefully across the water-slick rocks until I found a comfortable seat beside Barrett, rolled up my leggings, and dipped my bare feet into the water. The summer sun had warmed the lake enough that my toes only suffered the faintest pinch of cold before my skin acclimated to the temperature. I sank into the soothing tickle as the water ebbed and flowed in gentle laps and lowered myself onto my back so I could stare up through the thick leaves, enjoying the softness of the dappled light on my skin.

The minutes passed—too quickly—and before long the temperature of the air rose. Significantly.

I opened my eyes and yelped on finding Gavin's arms

covered in fire. The flames licked over his forearms and caught the edges of his shirt. He cursed, and Barrett shoved him into the lake. Steam rose from the surface of the water, and a moment later, Gavin pushed himself out, his black T-shirt clinging to his thick pectorals and defined abs.

He wobbled to regain his footing and accepted Barrett's hand to climb back onto the rocks.

I sat up and braced for them to exchange a few nasty comments. These two had fallen in with each other from the moment they'd met, and although I'd been impressed more than once by the way they trained together, using their unique positions to help the other develop their skills, I was certain they spent an equal amount of time solidifying the other's opinions. Barrett's hatred of magicals would only reinforce Gavin's self-loathing, while Gavin's self-loathing would confirm Barrett's hatred.

With my expectations firmly in place, I nearly fell over when Barrett clapped Gavin on the shoulder and said, "That was better this time. You had more control."

Gavin scowled and slicked his dark hair out of his face. "Not enough."

"You'll get there." Barrett gave his shoulder an extra squeeze, then let his hand drop.

Gavin's gaze followed it until it reached his side, then he gave himself a shake as a faint pink touched the tips of his ears.

"Hopefully I won't need to. I'm going to go dry off." He started towards the house, casting me a quick glance as he passed but not offering any sort of hello. He and I were still working out our footing when it came to each other.

"He must be so jealous of me."

Barrett's gaze followed the sorcerer as Gavin slipped through the patio door into the rec room, then his attention shifted to me. "He is. He's disappointed Muroppy didn't leave any of that tea untouched. He hopes we track down the people who dosed you so he can get some for himself."

It didn't surprise me, but it pained me nonetheless. The man had worked such wonders with his power and had the potential to do so much more, but instead of leaning into it, he longed to escape it. I wondered if that would have been the case if his introduction to the magical world hadn't been so traumatic. I also wondered if he would ever come around to appreciating the gift he possessed.

As though he'd read my thoughts, Barrett smiled. At least that's how I chose to interpret the slight upturn of his mouth. With him, it was difficult to tell.

"He thinks he knows what he wants. I have my doubts."

"Time will tell, I suppose." I forced my thoughts away from the sorcerer's magic and back to my missing power. "I don't suppose you've chatted with your witch hunter buddy lately?"

Barrett's eyebrows rose in surprise. "Tony? Not since—" He

cut himself off, cleared his throat, and tried again. "Not in a few months. The way they dropped the ball with the Alodie situation hasn't encouraged me to reach out."

I understood that well enough. The witch hunters claimed not to have known who Mikhail's patron was despite all the power she'd accumulated over the years. Considering the trouble I'd had finding anything about Alodie, I believed she'd done a great job hiding her tracks, but I also believed the hunters had allowed hubris to blind them to the threat she posed. No one had stopped her in time, and the result had been Adrian's final death.

I claimed a decent amount of guilt for my own role in what had happened, but I was with Barrett—the witch hunters deserved to shoulder part of the blame.

"It might be time to put them to work again. See if they can uphold their sworn mandate for a change."

"Oh?"

"Emrick swung by last night." I aimed for casual as I said it, not wanting to give in to the feelings of despair that accompanied my thoughts of him. From the flicker of sympathy in Barrett's eyes, I failed. "Seems Mikhail's chosen to make himself comfortable in the afterlife, and he let slip a few details about who's behind the attack. A big group, been around for a while."

Barrett frowned. "Doesn't narrow things down much, does it? I can't think of any group that hasn't been hunted down and broken up by either you or the hunters."

"That was my thought, too, but according to Mikhail, that's who we're looking for. I thought maybe Tony and his band of merry men might have some ideas. With all their tech and spy networks and snazzy futuristic gimmicks, maybe they have their finger on something we've missed with our traditional paying-attention skills."

"I'll give him a call," Barrett said. "It can't hurt to check in with them, anyway. They owe me some updates."

Curiosity tickled me. "Are you sure you're not one of them?"

Barrett chuckled—a low, rumbly sound I'd never heard before and found myself wanting to hear again to ensure I hadn't imagined it. Bit by bit, the stony facade he'd worn around me for ten years was crumbling, revealing the man who'd won the heart of a vampire.

"I'm not," he said, "but I understand why you'd think so. I'm practically a poster child for the organization."

"I'm surprised they never tried to recruit you."

"They did. If I'd known of them before I met Adrian, maybe I'd have accepted. By the time they approached me, I was already bound to Adrian, and they had issues with my vampire *master*." He said the word with distaste. While there had always been a vampire-thrall dynamic between he and Adrian, their relationship had never been one of master and servant. Adrian had held far too much respect for the ex-soldier to see him as anything less than an equal.

It was what had made Adrian so special, the son of a bitch.

Unable to compartmentalize my grief with everything else going on, I shoved all thought of my friend aside and focused on this smidge of back story I was finally getting from the man who'd always claimed to hate me.

"If they didn't approve of your relationship with Adrian, how did you get to know Tony?"

Barrett nodded his chin towards the house, and I pulled my feet out of the water and accepted his offered hand. Together, we started up the path to the back door. "We kept our bond a secret at first. Adrian thought it would be a good idea for me to find out what the hunters were up to. I learned what they did, helped them with a few missions, made my way through their recruitment process. They did some digging and found out about Adrian, and that was the end of it. Easily nine years ago now. Even if they didn't want me in their ranks, I'd impressed a few of them with my skills—"

"And your loathing of magic."

He nodded. "And that. I respect what they do. What all the hunters do. You may be good at maintaining the balance, Kat, but you're one person. These groups move internationally. Their reach far surpasses yours."

I suddenly felt old and tired. "I know. It's why I thought it might be possible for me to stand down and let them take over.

I was so sure of my place for so long, but even if this unknown group hadn't come after me, I don't know if there's room for me here anymore. Maybe it's a good thing I've lost my power. Maybe it's a sign that I've done all I can."

Barrett drew to a stop and moved into my path, forcing me to stop as well. "Bullshit. The witch hunter organization may be large, and they may be determined, but as a whole they lack perspective. They're like me. They believe all magic is unnatural. Doesn't matter if the witch in question uses her knowledge for good or ill, they see it as a threat, and one that should be wiped out as thoroughly as possible. You see the nuance, and it's important."

I crossed my arms and struggled to keep my jaw from dropping to the ground. "This coming from you? You've surprised me often enough over the past couple of days, Barrett, but this takes the cake."

"I know what you think of me, and I know what I've always said, but Adrian—" He rolled his lips between his teeth. "It took a long time, but I guess all of Adrian's lectures and explanations and appeals had more of an effect on me than I realized. Since his death, I've had time to think about it. Often. In depth."

"I would have thought his death would solidify your opinions considering how he died."

"You'd think so, but somehow it brought home everything

he tried to teach me. There has to be balance. Without magic, he and I never would have met. I never would have had those years with him. I may hate most of what comes out of your world, but I can't wish it doesn't exist. And since it does exist, we need people like you to keep it in check."

I could have hugged him. I didn't, because that would suggest some part of him was soft, and I worried he would murder me for the assumption.

He smirked as though he knew what I was thinking. "Come on. Let's go call Tony and see if we can ruin his day."

16

Katerina

WHEN BARRETT PULLED up in front of Tony's house in Etobicoke, I felt as though we'd stepped into the past—a weird, twisted past where everything was contrary to how it used to be.

The first time we'd come here, Barrett and I were barely on speaking terms, my magic had been rusty but present, my mindset rough and reluctant. If it hadn't been for Adrian's encouragement, I wouldn't have been here at all.

Now I was here with Barrett as my new BFF, my magic was non-existent, and Adrian was gone. But never had I been more determined.

The drive here had been long but strangely comfortable. I hadn't tried to piss Barrett off by blasting music I knew he'd hate, and it turned out we both had similar tastes in classic rock.

More than anything, I'd been relieved to get out of the house and away from all the people fussing over me. Muroppy hadn't made any further progress on my blood samples, and the waiting was agony. Maera and her guilt were popping into my room every fifteen minutes to see if I needed anything, and Rhys was there just as often to ask how I was doing.

As for Gavin's avoidance, it was almost as loud as everyone else's concern.

The only person I wanted to see was Emrick, and he'd disappeared again.

When Barrett had called Tony and wrangled an invitation for us to visit him, I'd jumped at the chance to take a road trip. Now that I was here, I worried about how the encounter might go. On our last visit, Tony had made his opinion about my magic and my role in this world pretty clear. While no one else had crowed over my fall—shockingly—I was ready for him to be the first. If not with smugness, then perhaps relief. Congratulations, maybe.

My stomach twisted, and Barrett nudged my shoulder with his as we made our way up the steps to the front door of the comfortable suburban bungalow.

Not long after he rang the bell, the door opened and there stood Tony, looking exactly as he had the last time, right down to the cheese powder all over his graphic tee.

"Barrett, nice to see you." He pulled Barrett into an elaborate handshake. When he caught sight of me over Barrett's shoulder, he narrowed his eyes, surprise mixing with a hint of disdain. "Sorceress."

Had Barrett not mentioned I was coming with him? Naughty boy.

"Tony," I replied, matching his tone.

"Come to get more information out of me about some magical you're trying to put down?"

I shrugged. "In a way. More specifically, I'm trying to root out who put me down."

Confusion twisted his face and pushed his eyebrows high on his wide forehead. "Oh?"

"Someone drugged her," Barrett explained. "We think they tried to kill her, but they failed."

"They did strip away my magic, though." If we were here for help, it made sense to share what we knew, even if I wanted to vomit around the confession.

The lines around Barrett's mouth hardened. "We need to figure out who might have that kind of power."

Tony's eyebrows climbed higher, and he gave me a more thorough once-over. I couldn't have felt more exposed if I'd been wearing a slinky nightie. It didn't matter that his attention was more analytical than lecherous, I still felt gross.

"Come on in." He stepped aside to give us space, but his

gaze remained firmly on me, as though he were trying to pick my insides apart. "Is it true? Your magic is gone? That's amazing. I'd love to get a blood sample. If you're okay with that."

"No." Barrett got to it before I could, and both Tony and I looked his way.

"No?" Tony asked. "But, Barrett, man, come on. Some kind of magical drug that wipes out magic? This is exactly what the witch hunters have been trying to make for generations. If someone actually succeeded, this could change the course of the world."

"Which is exactly why it shouldn't fall into anyone else's hands," Barrett said.

I could have high-fived him, but I was too busy gawking. Despite what he'd said to me before we left, I struggled to merge this man, with his reasonable outlook, with the man who'd given me nothing but nasty stares for the past ten years because of what I was.

Tony turned to block our entry into the dining room. "I don't know why you're here, then. I'm kinda busy right now and don't have time to waste trying to figure out who's doing my job for me."

"Me," I said blandly. "I was doing your job for you. Long before you started and better than you did it if the last few failures are anything to go by."

His cheeks flushed pink, but I held his stare. If he wanted

to turn his back on me because of some twisted belief that I was less than he was, he could go fuck himself.

"We're not asking you to break a sweat or even interrupt your gaming session for longer than a few minutes," I continued. "All we're looking for is information you might have about any group that might have summoned a demon a few decades ago."

He barked out a laugh. "Oh, is that all? As if you people aren't summoning the bastards by the hour."

There was some truth to the stereotype, but I liked to believe most people kept their summonings to low-level demons they could banish with a word.

"This particular group summoned a demon bound to a sorceress. Abigail, actually. You know, the witch your organization failed to notice for sixty years? The one who taught a nasty ritual to a blood witch? The one who summoned Shogaur? The way I see it, it would be worth your while to put this group down before they summon anything else."

I left it at that, happy to watch the series of expressions flitting across his features. He had no idea what to think, which way to lean, or where to land, and I relished his lack of balance. Misery loved company and all that.

"Fine," he grumbled. "Let's go see if we can dig anything out of the hunters' records."

I bowed deeply at the waist. "I thank you."

Barrett winked at me, and I followed both men through the dining room and downstairs into the basement.

The Bat Cave.

The epicentre of Tony's life.

It reeked of sadness.

The desk was covered in pop cans and snack bags, and the garbage can on the floor was full of more of the same. An assortment of high-tech gadgets littered most available surfaces, surrounding the computer that took up the majority of the desk's real estate.

"You can sit over there." He nodded to the couch, the shade of which I could only generously call puce. A rough crocheted afghan hung over the back, and I wasn't sure whether I was more terrified to touch the blanket or the couch cushions.

At almost any other point in my life, I would have preferred to stand, but my shift to mortality had left my muscles weak and aching, and all that standing around waiting for Tony to get his head out of his ass had drained most of my energy.

So, trying not to think too much about it and making a note to burn these clothes when I got home—goodbye pipe-dream of not ruining today's outfit—I settled on the very edge of the couch and leaned forward so I could see as much as possible of the computer screen.

Barrett, the in-shape bastard, chose to remain on his feet, reading over Tony's shoulder as the witch hunter scanned his computer files.

The warriors of the modern age.

"Most of this stuff is confidential," Tony said, shooting Barrett a look, "but considering who you are and the fact that most of these cases were closed by the sorceress, I'm not going to stress too much about that."

And I would try not to let those words go to my head. But damn right they were.

"What else do you know about this group?" Tony asked.

Barrett shifted to include me in the conversation, and I tried to remember everything Emrick had passed along. It was a twisted, multi-dimensional game of telephone, and I could only hope some of the details were correct.

"It would be a few decades old. Alodie's demon was summoned in the late-fifties or sixties. I don't know if their goal from the start was to use her against me, but eventually she wound up being the voice in Mikhail's ear."

Tony's jaw clenched. "I really wish the hunters had been the ones to take that blood witch down. It would have been a satisfying victory after the chase he led us on."

Barrett shot me a look, and I bit my tongue. He didn't have to warn me to keep my mouth shut. We'd come here for information; information we weren't likely to get if I pointed out all the ways the witch hunters had failed—horribly—in their attempts to stop Mikhail.

"This group also supplied Alodie with some strong enchantments and spells when she came after us," Barrett added. "So whoever we're looking for, they're dealing in power."

Tony scrolled his database. "There are dozens of covens and demon-worshipping groups in Toronto. Any of them might have had a hand in bringing that woman and her demon to this world and supplying her with everything she needed. You'll have to give me something more specific."

I wanted to bash my head against a wall. We didn't have time for this. If he needed me to micromanage every moment of his life, it would be better to drag him out of that chair and have Barrett take over. "Can you read some of them out to me? Maybe a name will ring a bell. If they want me dead, I have to have crossed paths with them at some point, right? I know I'm a bitter pill to swallow, but I don't see a complete stranger wanting to kill me."

"I don't know about that," Tony mumbled, but I ignored him. He was just grumpy because I'd cut into his game time. My future was more important than his boss fight, thanks.

Even so, he read out two dozen names as he ran through the list, pulling the most likely candidates and throwing them my way. None of them did anything for me. Some were too new, some not powerful enough, some were obviously rookies trying to sound tough by giving themselves names like The Yonge Wizards. It was endearing but not useful. After half an hour, all I had was a sense that I'd wasted my time.

"Wait a minute." Tony leaned closer to his computer screen. "Just a second here."

I found myself leaning so far forward, I lost my balance on the edge of the couch. To cover my clumsiness, I rose to my feet and stood next to Barrett.

"There is a group. A coven of necromancers. The Death Raisers." A low groan escaped me, which Tony didn't miss. "You know them?"

"We've crossed paths a time or six."

It obviously should have been seven or eight.

I didn't offer any other information. Tony didn't need to know one of the higher ups the last time I'd shut that coven down was Poppy's mother, Hera Lister. According to Poppy, Hera wasn't likely to have summoned Alodie's demon or be involved in any other shit the sorceress had gotten up to in her final weeks, but so far her old coven was the only name that stood out.

"Thanks, Tony," I said, not even tasting the bitterness of expressing my gratitude. "We'll start there."

He raised an eyebrow. "Just like that? You're not going to press me for the full list?"

The smart move would probably be to let him keep reading, but with this lead in front of me, I was champing at the bit to get moving.

Barrett clapped him on the back. "If you find anything else that might help, get in touch."

"Sure."

I left them to their handshake and headed upstairs, thoughts swirling through my head. At their height, the Death Raisers had been a force. I'd faced an entire army of undead when I'd torn them down almost forty years ago. It had taken me weeks to get the stench of rotting flesh out of my nose.

When I'd asked Poppy about them, she'd told me Hera was more invested in her new coven these days, focusing on beauty regimes and fundraising galas.

Like the masquerade where I'd met with Mikhail.

That fundraiser had been on behalf of the League of Magical Freedom, a group that advocated for reduced oversight in the lives of witches and their covens. I'd always assumed their target was the witch hunters, or all the hunter organizations, but now I had to wonder if they'd included me in their push for autonomy.

I stepped outside and took a deep breath of non-cheese-powder-filled air.

I didn't want to do it, and Poppy wouldn't be thrilled, but it was time to face down her mother.

17

Emrick

I RETURNED FROM Adrian's library impatient and determined to find some way to safely pitch in. Kat wasn't home, and I was almost grateful she was gone. The need to see her was a constant ache, but I could only say the same things so many times. I needed something firmer to stand on, and the only people I could think of to give me that footing were the witches.

I paced the length of the rec room, giving the table where Muroppy had set up their workspace enough distance that I didn't crowd them. They'd pulled the round table out of their room and set it close to the back doors to catch the evening light streaming through the floor-to-ceiling windows. The floor at Poppy's feet was covered in papers she'd discarded, and the space around Murisa was filled with petri dishes, hot plates,

Bunsen burners, and more I couldn't identify.

Murisa was bent over her microscope, writing notes without looking away from the eyepiece. Poppy stood over her mortar and pestle, grinding what had to be her fortieth combination of herbs and potions to attempt another reversal spell.

So far they'd had no success, and I could tell they were both getting frustrated. So discouraged they were reaching for increasingly wild ideas.

My presence wasn't helpful at all, but I had no intention of leaving. I wanted to be in the house when Kat and Barrett returned from their trip to Toronto. I wanted to be here if Muroppy had any breakthroughs.

More than that, I couldn't wander the afterlife waiting. Suffering the agonies of *not knowing*.

Poppy shot me a dark look. "Can't you go hang out with Maera? She's upstairs baking again."

I scowled. "Maera can't help Kat the way you can. I'm staying."

She shook her head and took her irritation out on the herbs in the bowl. "If you think standing there is going to make us work faster—"

She didn't bother to finish her sentence. We all knew they were working as hard as they could. I wasn't here to rush them—no matter how badly I wished I could.

"What about Rhys?" Murisa asked. "Has anyone checked

on him?"

He'd been in his room for the past hour. We hadn't heard anything, and I'd assumed he'd fallen asleep. But what if he'd had a vision?

Giving the witches a reprieve, I walked across the basement and knocked on Rhys's door. A mumbled voice replied, and I stepped into the darkness within. The window was open, filling the space with the soft scents of tree and lake, but his east-facing room didn't allow for much sunlight at this time of day and the lights were off.

Rhys sat on the floor, legs crossed, eyes closed, hands in his lap. His chest and stomach expanded with every deep breath, and I dropped onto the edge of his bed to watch him. How long had he been trying to trigger a vision? I knew if he'd had any success, he would have said something, but the silence of his second sight only made me worry more. With the Alodie situation, Kat had blocked his visions to keep him safe, but the potion Muroppy had brewed to redirect his second sight had long worn off. So why couldn't he See?

I scrubbed my face, forcing myself to stay quiet. Badgering wouldn't help Rhys any more than it would help the witches. He knew what he was doing better than anyone else in this house did. I had to have faith he would succeed.

My strained patience was rewarded when his eyes flew open, the bright green irises washed out under a film of milky white. "We face betrayal from those we trust. A blade from the shadows. Magic hidden in kindness." His voice was low, empty. I'd heard him in the throes of horror before, and this wasn't it. If anything, he sounded pained, as though each word wounded him. "Spiders approach, building their webs, ready to trap their target and drain it of everything it is. Fire extinguished, lightning fizzled out, ice melted. A future of emptiness and destruction."

None of it meant anything to me except that Kat's future held no guarantees. Someone close to her was involved, and if we didn't figure it out, she would stay as she was for as long as her shortened life lasted. None of that sat well with me, but it didn't offer any way for me to help, either.

Rhys sucked in a gasp and pressed his hand to his chest as his eyes cleared. I stayed where I was on the edge of the bed, waiting for him to come around.

"What else did you See?" I asked gently, just as Kat would have done. She always hated not giving him a chance to shake off the effects of his visions, and I understood why, but I didn't have it in me to wait.

Rhys jumped at the sound of my voice, and a horrified awareness seeped into his expression. "I don't even know. Spells flying and doing nothing. This sense of—of something huge. Bigger than anything we've faced, and all coming from someone we'd never expect." He shuddered. "I wish I could See something more specific, but it's not coming. It's like it's there, but it's hiding behind all these unknowns."

Frustrated, I rose to my feet and strode towards the door.

"What do I do?" Rhys called after me.

I turned and met his eye. He knew I couldn't answer him. But I didn't need to—one look at my face and his expression hardened with resolution. "Right. I'll call Kat."

I replied with a small smile. It was exactly what I would have recommended.

A faint glint of pride swelled in Rhys's eyes, and he pulled his shoulders back. "That was the first time in a while I've Seen so much and remembered it. Maybe this means I'm back?"

"I have no doubt," I said. "Kat will benefit by you being here."

His pride grew with warmth, and he nodded as I returned to the witches.

"Anything?" Murisa asked.

"He'll fill you in," I said as I found a space against the wall to lean against. I had more reason than ever to keep my eye on them. If we were looking at a betrayal, I needed to stay aware of everyone's movements. No one would get another chance at Kat's life.

Poppy released a drop of Kat's blood into her readied mixture, and her face fell when nothing happened.

"I don't get it. Whatever this spell was, it was strong enough to erase someone's magic, but it's not reacting to anything else I mix it with. Not a nullifying spell or a warding spell. It's like they created something brand new for our sorceress. I know she's a pain in the ass, but this is dedication."

I must have made a noise because she gave me a wide-eyed look and cleared her throat.

"A pain in the ass for magicals who break the rules," she amended. "You can't deny there are going to be a lot of happy campers across the world when word gets out about what happened."

A tingle crept across the back of my neck, and I instinctively reached for my bond with Kat—the presence that had been my comfort for so many centuries. A fresh burn welled up along the tether, sending pain shooting through my chest. I latched on to it, taking hold of the small reassurance that as long as that burn remained, we stood a chance of repairing what was broken.

But Poppy made a good point. I'd been so wrapped up with Kat's mortality, I hadn't considered the more immediate threats she might face. She had enemies on every continent, and not a small number of them would cross any distance to catch her at her weakest to taste revenge.

If they needed to cross a distance.

Would strangers with grudges take advantage of the opportunity Kat's magicless state presented them, or would the threat come from closer to home as Rhys predicted?

I watched as Poppy dumped the failed mixture and gathered ingredients for another attempt.

How hard was she trying to find an answer? I'd been a sorcerer in my mortal life but knew little about modern witchcraft. She and Murisa seemed to be working hard for a solution, but their skills meant they were just as capable of creating the original spell.

Murisa was new to Kat's circle, but Kat and Poppy went way back. Kat had threatened to kill her, forced her away from her magical path, ruined her reputation, and was the reason her shop was rubble.

Was it so unbelievable that Poppy craved revenge as much as any of Kat's known enemies?

For now, I had nothing but suspicions against the people in this house, but if any of them had betrayed Kat, the last thing they'd feel was my hand on their neck.

18

Katerina

ARE YOU SURE we shouldn't let Poppy know where we're going?" Barrett asked as we returned to his SUV.

"Let's leave it for now. From what little she's told me, she and her mother aren't in a good place these days. Why add to her stress?"

"You don't want Poppy giving her mom a head's up we're coming," he interpreted.

"Here I was, trying to be diplomatic…"

I climbed into the passenger seat and shut the door, leaving Barrett no choice but to get in if he wanted to continue the conversation.

Control over my life was slipping in every direction, and I intended to cling to it anywhere I could—like in continuing to make his life difficult.

My state of mind wasn't helped by the phone call I'd received from Rhys as Barrett left Tony's house. While I was thrilled my young friend had successfully triggered a vision, the contents of said vision hadn't left me feeling warm and fuzzy. Someone close to me had torn me down. Someone I considered an ally was planning something very big and very bad.

I didn't want to believe the worst of anyone I trusted—not when my trust wasn't so easily earned—but that didn't mean I wouldn't be on my guard. Starting with keeping my plans close to my vest.

"I don't suppose Tony had an address for us? I didn't think to ask."

I shifted in my seat, then fiddled with the air conditioning to hide the reason for my fidgeting. In truth, I was nervous. Going to speak with a powerful witch would have been nothing a few days ago, but now it made my bones rattle. Hera Lister made Poppy look like a novice, and from what I'd heard of her husband, he was no slouch, either. Even Barrett, with all his skills and strength and practice, was stronger than I was. For the first time in a very long time, I would be the weakest person in the room.

In no way could I let Hera know that. In front of her, I would have to pretend to be everything my reputation had built me to be and pray she didn't sniff out the deception.

"The address on file is in Burlington. Do we want to take the trip today or wait until tomorrow when we're better rested?"

After I'd had a chance to gather myself, he meant. I appreciated *his* attempt at diplomacy, strange and unusual as it was, but all it did was steel my nerves. Or at the very least make me appreciate how much I didn't want to go back to Adrian's Kensington Market house to spend a sleepless night staring at the ceiling there instead of my own.

"Let's get this over with. If she did have something to do with what happened to me, I'd rather know now and deal with the consequences."

Without offering his opinion, Barrett put the car in drive and pulled out of the driveway. As I looked back at the house, I found Tony staring at us from the dining room window. The curtain fluttered shut, and a chill scurried down my spine.

The drive to Burlington felt twice as long as normal as I scrambled to put all my questions in a row.

What could Hera be involved in these days that she'd benefit by removing me from the picture? Had she resurrected the Death Raisers while I wasn't looking, or was this some new venture?

One argument against the Death Raisers being behind my

fall was the timeline. I'd dismantled them in the eighties. If they'd already summoned Alodie and her demon, why not send her after me then? Why let me decimate their numbers?

Unless Hera had been working without the Death Raisers knowing? She'd been one of the few to survive, but what if that had been by plan and not by coincidence?

Unease ran through me as the next question rose unbidden: was Poppy working with her?

I'd met Poppy around five years ago when her coven had attempted to start a war with a rival group. Poppy hadn't been in a good place, having started down a dark road with her necromancy, but I'd seen enough of her personality to understand her true passions lay in knowledge, not in destruction. It was why I'd spared her. Except I hadn't just let her go, had I? I'd made a deal. If she followed the rules, she got to live.

It was a deal I'd held over her head as recently as a few months ago.

Was it so far of a stretch to believe she resented me for it? Enough to want revenge?

My stomach tightened, and I bowed my head in my hand. I couldn't afford to think about this. Not yet. Not if I wanted to present Hera with a strong, confident front. If Poppy was working with her mother against me, I'd find out. Until I knew for sure, I would act as though I were walking into a low-stress information-seeking session.

Regardless of what happened, by the time I left, I'd know more. Win.

When Barrett pulled the car up in front of the address Tony had given us, my jaw dropped, my brain needing a minute to hold what I was seeing beside what I knew about Poppy.

Poppy with her comfortable apartment above her cozy occult shop.

Poppy with her plush carpet and sunken chairs.

I struggled to put that woman together with the mini-mansion in front of me.

Three storeys of epic proportions. Ostentation blended with cold elegance.

A curving driveway connected a four-car garage to the right of the white house. A patch of grass out front was filled with flowers that probably cost a thousand dollars before upkeep. Concrete steps led to the double front doors, with more flowers in urns tall enough to reach my shoulder. Large windows with black shutters glowered down at me, and I found myself adjusting my shirt to ensure I met with their approval.

My mouth was dry, my palms were clammy, and I braided my hair over my shoulder to give my fingers something to do while Barrett got out of the car and came around the side to open my door.

Not that I needed or expected him to open my door, but for some reason I couldn't find the courage to do it myself.

"She's just a woman," he said in a low voice as he offered me his hand.

I wiped my palm on my pants before accepting his help, not wanting to repay his kindness with sweat.

Which in itself was a strange feeling. Old Kat wouldn't have hesitated to smear Old Barrett with sweat. Then again, Old Kat wouldn't have worked up a sweat at the prospect of meeting a witch.

How times had changed.

Barrett led the way up the stairs and rang the bell. My throat closed when the familiar notes of "Eine Kleine Nacht-musik" sounded from inside, and I caught Barrett squeezing his eyes shut.

It had been Adrian's favourite musical piece. How many nights had I woken to the sound of violins?

I didn't have time to express any words of empathy before the door opened and I found myself staring at the most imposing woman I'd ever seen. Not in stature, of course. She was slight and slim—my five-foot-four gave me nearly an inch on her—but in presence she towered over me, and I suspected that would have been true even with my full power and the security of my immortality.

From what little Poppy had told me about her, Hera was in her mid- to late-sixties. The afro in the photo from the Death Raisers' file had been shaved, and she sported a head of greying hair that added to her air of authority. Few wrinkles lined her face, with a notable lack around her eyes. This was not a woman who indulged in the simple pleasures of life. Like smiling.

Where Hera of the eighties had dressed in bright colours, much like her daughter did today, the present Hera wore a grey three-quarter-sleeve, cowl-necked top and white slacks. I suspected this level of business casual was her relaxed wear.

Her dark eyes scanned Barrett first, dismissed him, and landed on me. In a blink, her expression changed, darkened, shuttered, and she pulled her shoulders back into a posture so flawless the headmistresses of Victorian England finishing schools wept.

"Ms. Palon." Her voice was deep and rich. "You can turn around and leave my property at once. I have nothing to say to you."

I'd only just arrived, I hadn't even said a word, and the door slammed in my face.

19

Katerina

SOME PEOPLE MIGHT have turned around and given up.

I had no real reason for believing Hera wanted me dead, beyond some forty-year-old connections to a defunct coven, and no other suspects from within the Death Raisers, so why should I waste my time?

But the speed with which she'd ignored Barrett and the vehemence with which she wanted me gone broke through my recently developed sense of inadequacy and tapped into the ego that had kept me going for eight hundred and seventy-seven years.

Barrett crossed his arms and stepped back, allowing me to take the lead as I brought the side of my fist down on the door.

Minutes stretched without an answer, but that didn't deter

me from knocking again, and again, and again. I wasn't about to walk away until I knew where Hera stood with me. Even if she had nothing to do with the attempt on my life—even if the Death Raisers were as buried as I'd left them—I wanted to speak with her. The group that had summoned Alodie's demon was out there, and Hera's finger on the pulse of the witch community put her in a perfect position to give me information I needed.

"Can I help you?" a man's voice floated our way from the garage, and I walked down the steps in search of him.

We found him at the end of the third car bay. He was a handsome man in his mid-sixties with dark hair, tanned skin, and a warm smile. At first glance, he wasn't familiar at all, but after a few seconds taking in the familiar shape of his eyes and the line of his jaw, I recognized Poppy in his features. Her father, then. Perhaps it was to her advantage that Poppy had taken after him more than her mother. Hera was the more striking of the two, but she was also a bitch.

I walked towards him. "Hi. Are you Arnold Lister? Proserpine's dad?"

His brown eyes sparkled with pride. "I am. You know my Pom?"

"I do. We go way back. I was in the area and thought I'd swing by and say hello. She's been so busy these days working on a million different projects or else she would have come with me."

He snorted and opened the garage door, revealing the glossy black Corvette inside. "I doubt that. My daughter hasn't come by to see me in over five years. An old man can dream, though. But any friend of Pom's is welcome here if it means I can have word of her. She's well?"

"She is."

Homeless, jobless, currently overworked trying to solve a magical mystery. But she had Murisa, so I suspected she was happy enough.

Unless she's a traitor, a small voice spoke up in the back of my mind. For now, I shushed it. I needed to stay focused on the potential enemy in front of me, not the possible enemies back home.

"Good. Would you care to come in? Have a coffee? You can tell me all the news and then explain why you're really here, Ms. Palon." My poker face must have slipped because he smirked. There was no joy in the expression. "Oh yes, my dear, I know who you are. But please, come in. My wife may not be curious, but I confess I'm not as indifferent."

He walked into the house and didn't look back to see if we followed him.

Barrett and I exchanged a glance. He shrugged. I shrugged. We fell into step behind Poppy's father and entered the house through the garage.

Slate-grey granite tile stretched out across a sea of foyer. A wall of mirrors lined the entrance closets, causing the already large space to double into the square footage of my entire house.

Indoor versions of the giant urns on the front step sat in every corner, the plants within more ferny than blossomy. I was afraid to get too close in case the greenery snapped me up in invisible jaws.

Was this the house Poppy had grown up in? If so, no wonder her adult self had embraced chaos and comfort. Anything to break away from this gilded cage. The more I saw, the more I struggled to picture mother and daughter working together on anything. Where would they meet? Either Poppy's home or Hera's would cause the other's brain to leak out their ears.

Arnold led us through the foyer into a sitting room, where Hera sat at a card table. Instead of a game of Solitaire set out in front of her, there was a tarot spread, and I longed to know what her future foretold. I hoped it read that I would be a huge pain in her ass and she would be better off cooperating with me to save herself time.

"What is that person doing here?" She flipped another card, not sparing us a glance.

"She's come to ask us some questions, my dear. I couldn't send her away without learning what those questions are."

Arnold walked behind his wife and bent to kiss her cheek. The show of affection speared me with jealousy, and I forced myself to keep my smile in place. These people didn't know how lucky they were that they could enjoy such easy, simple contact with the person they cared about.

I supposed I should be relieved to see Hera was capable of caring for anyone. It meant she wasn't a complete harpy devoid of human emotion. For Poppy's sake, I rejoiced.

Arnold left Hera's side and poured himself a cup of coffee, though perhaps cup was a generous definition. Thimbleful would be more precise. He offered to pour for Barrett and me, but we both passed. What would be the point? One sip and it would be gone, leaving me awkwardly holding my cup for the rest of our chat.

"Please, sit." Arnold gestured to the couch, and although I braced for the cushions to be as comfortable as the concrete steps outside, I did as he said. Barrett sat beside me, appearing far more relaxed, as if he weren't fazed at all by the display of wealth and pomposity.

"All right, Ms. Palon," Arnold said. "Ask your questions."

"Quickly," Hera added without looking up. She flipped another card. "We have a dinner to prepare for."

I flashed her a smile. "Sounds fun. I'll jump straight to the point. Did either of you hire someone to kill me? Recently, I should add. I'm not here to resurrect the past."

Necromancer puns were always in vogue.

I'd hoped to shock Hera into some kind of reaction, but

her concentration on the tarot deck never wavered. Not even Arnold appeared surprised.

He leaned back in his chair, crossed his ankle over his knee, and sipped his coffee. "I can't say we have. What exactly was this attempt on your life?"

I watched his body language closely. I might feel small and inferior, but I was coming to this conversation with hundreds of years of practice in reading people. His tilted head suggested interest, but the lines around his mouth were loose, as was his hold on the coffee cup. His fluffy eyebrows had risen ever so slightly, but nothing else about him had tensed. If he was guilty, he wasn't showing any signs of it.

"A poisoning. Someone sold my housekeeper some tea in an attempt to get rid of me."

Hera hooted a laugh, but no smile touched her features. "What fool would try something like that? Rumours tell us you're a step below the gods. Untouchable. To me, that sounds like a waste of good poison. Better to use it on your pets if someone wanted to get you out of the way."

"One reason among many I don't keep any pets," I replied. "Don't you?"

Her dark gaze flicked ever so briefly to Barrett. His jaw flexed, but it was the only hint that he was irritated by the comment.

I sucked a breath in through my nose to steady my temper.

"Yes, well, hopefully they don't consider that approach next time. You don't know anything about it?"

"Ms. Palon, I could not care less if you lived or died. My daughter seems to have taken a shine to your inane mission of—what is it?—*maintaining the balance* of the magical world, but I don't have time to entertain your idealistic dictatorship. I have a coven to run, spells to work, and fundraisers to organize to keep our freedom out of the hands of the witch hunters. You don't even register on my radar."

"You're too kind." I didn't dwell on her blatant attempts to insult me. She wouldn't chase me away that easily. "What about your old coven? The Death Raisers."

Arnold chuckled. "The foibles of youth, eh, my dear?" He smiled indulgently at his wife, but the smile faded as he returned his attention to me. "You did us a favour when you dismantled the Death Raisers, Ms. Palon. Pauline was a menace. Our original purpose was to bring the greatest minds back from the afterlife to learn what we could and relay the secrets of their genius to the world. When we realized that what past generations considered genius was merely luck, logic, or practice, our high priestess thought to syphon power from the dead instead. Hera and I weren't thrilled with the change, but we weren't in a position at the time to leave. You solved that dilemma for us, and we veered in a different direction."

Hera didn't bother to add anything, and Arnold uncrossed

and recrossed his legs. "Either way, it's been a good forty years. We've formed another coven—the Hydrangea Circle. We focus on life these days, not death. Healing. Beauty. Longevity."

Inwardly, I cringed. Mikhail had probably offered the same spiel in his recruitment material. In his case, the longevity was only for him, and it came at the expense of all his followers.

Barrett frowned. "You still practice necromancy?"

Arnold shrugged. "Once in a while as part of our regular practice, but it's not a priority. Simply a useful skill. An occasional means to an end."

"If everything you do is aboveboard, you wouldn't have an issue with me speaking to some of your coven members, then, about what sort of thing you get up to at your meetings?" I asked.

Hera finally sat back in her chair, ankles crossed, hands clasped in her lap. Although our seats were on a level with each other, she appeared to be staring down at me, and I forced myself not to drop my gaze.

"Katerina Palon. A sorceress turned immortal in the twelfth century, bound to a servant of Death, sworn to uphold the balance of the magical world in an effort to redeem herself for the death of her family."

I wanted to punch the woman in the face, but I didn't flinch.

"Your story is no secret to me, my dear. The details of your turning, the battles you've faced. Oh, I'm sure there's much I don't know, but everything you've done over the past sixty years has been on written record in each of my covens. A reminder to my followers not to stray into your path, but also an example of the arrogance of too much power. You believe you have a say over what we do? You are nothing. I don't care if you can summon enough magic that this very house crumbles over my head—all that would prove is you can make things happen. But so can we all."

I didn't bat an eyelash, though it took all my restraint not to react. For the first time since I'd woken up magicless, I was glad my power was gone. It removed the temptation of lighting Hera's perfectly creased slacks on fire. Instead, I was able to come off as calm and collected, dredging up centuries of practice in keeping my expression blank.

If she was intimidated by my lack of response, she didn't show it.

"You came here because someone made an attempt on your life. Whoever it is, it wasn't the Hydrangea Circle, but someone put you on to us. Who was it, I wonder? Someone looking to cause trouble for my coven, I have no doubt. You scurry back to them and let them know their intelligence was faulty. Our circle doesn't dabble with removing people who don't concern us, and you would do well to remain out of our way."

Her gaze flicked to the card table, and the first hint of a

smile touched her lips. It added no warmth to her face.

"Change is a condition of life, isn't it, Ms. Palon? Something we all must face, whether it be a blessing or a curse." She picked up a card between her index and middle finger and flicked it at me. My reflexes felt slower than usual, but even so, I caught the card before it hit me in the face.

Death.

I returned my gaze to Hera.

"Tell my daughter I say hello."

20

Emrick

I MOVED BACK and forth between the rec room and the after-life, unable to stay in one spot for too long.

Rhys had gone upstairs to sit with Maera after Murisa had suggested they work on the tea-seller angle, and although I'd spent a bit of time pacing the kitchen, Maera had quickly ordered me away. I'd listened, but only because Kat's house-keeper was low on my list of suspects for people who might betray her. Yes, she'd been the one to serve the tea, but the woman had been with her for over fifty years. Although they had their issues, that was a lot of time for a mortal to spend with someone voluntarily if they were going to turn on them.

For a while, I'd kept my eye on Gavin as well, keeping to the fringes of the afterlife so he couldn't see me. He was higher on my list. From the start, he'd made it clear he didn't think much of Kat, as though he blamed her for the magic that coursed through his veins. But all I saw from him was the same restless pacing as mine. He went from the beach to the house to the front yard. He walked along the perimeter and checked the mundane traps Barrett had set when Shogaur's mob had come for Kat. Once in a while, he summoned his magic and let the fire scurry over his bare arms, but his discomfort in doing so was written in the curl of his lip and the way he shook himself off and stomped away as though he could outrun his power.

In the afterlife, at least I had a reprieve from the worst of my fears and anxiety. They were present but muted, just as my grief had been after Adrian's death.

I escorted a few souls to the river that divided this liminal space from whatever came next—a mystery not even I was enti-tled to know—but none of them had any insight to offer. Ever since we'd dealt with Alodie, the gossip among the spirits had settled. I no longer heard murmurs about an immortal sorceress dragging death and destruction behind her. Of course I hadn't— that immortal sorceress was dead. Death itself had ensured no one would ever find her soul wandering the afterlife. At most, she was one of the wisps that floated on the non-existent breeze. There would be no *next* for her.

The longer I stayed on this plane, however, the more I noticed changes to the world around me. The murky monochrome I'd come to know had grown… brighter somehow. And less solid. To me, this place had always been as real as the mortal plane, just another layer of the world. But now it was like I could see through parts of it. The ground existed beneath my feet, but with a sense that it was only there because I wanted it to be there. The still river where the souls waited, where I'd shoved Mikhail to the ground, appeared less like water and more like a black line in the sand. To step into it would be to step into the void.

I didn't want to think about what had caused the change. After fifteen hundred years, I hadn't thought anything about this place *could* change. I feared what it meant.

I suspected the shift had something to do with my decision to draw more deeply on Death's power, deepening my connection to the afterlife, but I had no idea what the consequences would be. I hadn't noticed any new lost memories, and I didn't seem to have lost any more of myself… but I was different.

The realization chased me back to the mortal world, where I felt more like myself. More like the human I strove to remain.

I didn't regret what I'd done. I couldn't considering the answers Mikhail had provided. But I'd have to be on my guard. The fine knife-edge I walked was growing sharper, and I had to make sure we didn't save Kat only for me to fall.

21

Katerina

I WALKED OUT of the Listers' house without a word, crossed the fancy paved driveway, and climbed into the passenger seat of Barrett's SUV.

All without slamming any doors, or clenching my fists, or spitting on the perfect thousand-dollar flower arrangements.

But once Barrett pulled out of the driveway and drove down the street, I shoved my shaking hands through my hair and said, "That bitch needs to check her mouth before she gets herself into trouble. Who the fuck does she think she is? The goddess Hera reborn? Huh. I almost wish that were true. I've read all the stories about what Zeus put her through. He could come down here and deal with her for me, and I wouldn't shed any tears."

"Are you done?" Barrett asked.

I crossed my arms. "No, but I can continue in private later. Most of what I have to say about that witch isn't for your sensitive ears."

He chuckled—barely more than a low huff—then returned to his usual stoic self. "Do you believe her?"

I dropped my arms into my lap and glared out the window. "Unfortunately, I do. I don't think she would have told me the truth if she had done it, but she didn't seem surprised I was alive, and she didn't ask about my magic. The lack of either suggests she didn't know about the tea. Poppy was right. Hera's way more invested in her new ventures. Arnold might have done it, but I get the impression he doesn't breathe without Hera's approval."

Barrett nodded. "I got the same read. Wasted trip, then?"

"Not exactly. We ruled out one of my oldest enemies, so that's got to count for something. And now we have Hera working for us."

He shot me a sidelong glance. "How do you figure?"

"If one of her own is acting against me, she'll want to know so she can toss them out of her coven before I find out. As far as she knows, I'm at full strength and pissed off over a murder attempt. She won't want me sniffing around her meetings looking for the person who did it. With her power and connections, her network will be broad. She'll do everything she can to make sure this attack doesn't come back to bite her."

"That's something, then," Barrett said. "Think she'll tell you if she finds out?"

"If it means me owing her a favour? Our odds are pretty good. She's a politician to her core."

"Where to next?"

I rubbed my hands over my face and pulled out my phone. I'd missed a few texts from Poppy, but none that contained anything optimistic, and some from Rhys asking how I was doing, if he could do anything to help, and updating me on Maera's activities.

Rhys: Mum's paying house visits to people she knows bought the tea. So far she hasn't learned anything.

Of course she hadn't. Whoever had sold the tea had gone out of their way to cover their tracks.

I shared the news with Barrett, then said, "I think it's time we go about this the opposite way. The people who sold the tea might have closed up shop, but they exist somewhere. I say we track them down."

"So we head home?"

I hesitated before shaking my head. "Not yet. Not until we have a better idea where we're going."

Barrett frowned. "You don't think they're still on the island? Maera said the herbs in the tea were grown locally."

"It was chocolate mint and lavender, not exactly rare. I'm going to call Rhys and see if I can put him to work. Let's head to Toronto and we'll wait there until we have some direction. I need food. And sleep. This whole mortal body thing is more inconvenient than I remember."

There was that faint smile again, and I didn't know how I felt about it. Barrett wasn't supposed to smile. It scared me.

"Make the call," he said, and pulled onto the highway.

Three hours later, Barrett and I sat in the kitchen of Adrian's Kensington Market house, with two bowls of instant ramen on the table and Rhys between the two of us on speaker phone.

"There's good news and bad news," he said. "What do you want first?"

I tucked a mushroom between my chopsticks. "Bad news first. Always bad news first."

"I wasn't able to trigger much of a vision." His frustration rumbled through every syllable. "Two and a half hours, and all I got was that you were probably right to stay in Toronto. I swear, the CN Tower spends more time in my brain than it does on most tourist maps."

"Rhys, that's huge news. Why is that bad?"

"Because it's all I got," he grumbled. "I have no idea who you're looking for or where in Toronto they might be. Just that they *might* be there."

All right, I'd concede that wasn't ideal, but I wasn't about to tell him so. "What's the good news?"

"There is none, I just didn't want to be all doom and gloom. There is more bad news if you want it."

Barrett snorted, and I shoved a mouthful of noodles into my face. "Fine. Lay it on me."

"The packaging for the tea is all fake. Ow, Cuddles, get off. Don't look at me like that." He cleared his throat. "Anyway. The company name, the logo—none of it is registered to any known business. Someone put a lot of work into bringing you down."

"I'm flattered."

"According to the manager of the supermarket, the stall wasn't too busy while it was up, but a few people grabbed their sample boxes. There still haven't been any loud warnings on the news about mass hospital surges, so at least we can assume the tea didn't have a negative effect on anyone else."

"See? You did have good news."

"It gets stranger, though. While we were there, I asked Mum to tell me everything she remembered about the stall or the person who sold her the tea. I thought maybe if I had more information, I could use it to direct my visions."

"Sounds like a good strategy to me."

I didn't know much about how second sight worked. My grandmother had been Palonia's Seer, but she hadn't shared much about her experience. As far as she knew, she was a tool for the gods, passing along whatever wisdom they thought would best protect their people. I'd known a few others over the years, but most of them just went with it. The books weren't any more insightful, as we'd learned when Rhys was first learning to master his ability.

A few of Adrian's contacts had kept in touch with us to offer their assistance as they could, but for the most part, the overarching advice was, "Everyone is different. Keep having visions until you figure it out for yourself."

Incredibly helpful. No wonder Rhys was discouraged. That he hadn't given up was a testament to his perseverance. The gods had made a good choice when they'd chosen him for their gift.

"So?" I asked, drawing my attention back to the conversation. "What did your mum say?"

"I didn't remember anything," Maera spoke up. I didn't know if she'd been there the whole time or if she'd just popped in, but I imagined her leaning over Rhys's shoulder. "It's the strangest thing. I know where I was standing when I bought the tea, but the person's face, the colours of the stall—it's foggy. Like it happened in a dream."

I gathered more noodles with my chopsticks as I considered Maera's tale.

It sounded like a forgetfulness spell. An aerosolized potion, maybe? Something designed to kick in a few hours after inhalation. A few months ago, I would have thought no one would bother going through all that trouble, but we were dealing with a group that had found a way to create stones that contained spell circles. These people were out-of-the-box thinkers, and my inability to out-think them had landed me in this mess.

"We're looking at a group with money. Rich and clever are rarely a good combination." I tapped my chopsticks against my bottom lip. "What if we're not looking at an old group?"

Barrett frowned. "But Mikhail said—"

"I know what Mikhail said, but what if we're looking at a collection of people from old groups coming together to form a new group? We've suspected we were looking at an 'I Hate Kat Palon' fan club, so what if it's exactly that? A bunch of random people coming together over their hatred of me."

"Does that narrow things down at all?"

The rush of adrenaline that had crept up on me as I'd followed my line of thought crashed and burned, and I slumped over the table as I grabbed a carrot out of the broth. "No. Not at all. But I do think chasing covens is a waste of our resources."

"Wait, wait, wait," Poppy's voice came down the line as the sound shifted. There was a clunking noise of someone moving the phone. "Why are we not going after the covens? We're dealing with magic here, kitty Kat. I know you're going through some shit, but all this screams witchcraft to me."

"There's definitely some witchcraft involved—at the very

least a familiarity with it—but it would be a big risk for a single coven to make that kind of move against me. I like to think that for all the members of the 'I Hate Kat Palon' fan club there might be a few in the other camp who would be willing to fight alongside me. From what your mother told me—"

"Excuse me?"

The coldness in her voice sent a shiver down my spine, and I was surprised to discover frost hadn't coated my phone.

I looked up to see Barrett staring at me, an eyebrow raised with a mild "I told you so" arch. I stuck my tongue out at him and returned my focus to the phone, as though giving it my full attention would prevent Poppy from tearing my head off the next time I saw her.

"Evidence pointed us in her direction, so we took a bit of a drive. Your parents are doing well. Everything is polished and shiny and in full bloom."

Poppy snorted. "Of course it is. You think Hera Lister would allow scuff marks in her perfect life? I'm surprised she let you get close enough to see for yourself. She doesn't exactly have a high opinion of you. Or of me. Or of anyone who doesn't shape themselves to fit into her perfect world."

"She made that nice and clear. Your father, however, harbours a curiosity that refuses to be quelled by her nasty looks. He invited us in for coffee. Which we didn't drink because what the hell kind of coffee is that? It's a single sip. How much caffeine can you imbibe with a single sip?"

"It's a waste of space," Poppy agreed. "And so are they. As I told you when you asked if you should talk to them. I said no, remember? If dear old dad invited you in, he wanted to learn something. I hope you didn't tell them your magic is gone."

"Of course I didn't. I was my usual stoic self. They think everything is fine, I'm an immortal powerhouse, and I'm ready to tear the heads off whoever tried to kill me."

"Good. You'll be safer that way. If my mother realizes you lost your magic…" The way she trailed off made me imagine her shuddering in my kitchen. "Well, in case she figures it out, keep all the windows and doors locked, and maybe find yourself a protection amulet. I don't trust what she might try."

"No?" I narrowed my eyes. "Have you changed your mind about her being involved?"

There was a pause on the line. For a while I thought Poppy was working up the nerve to say yes, her parents could very well have stripped me of my everything, but at last she said, "No, I honestly don't think they had anything to do with it. She wouldn't want to draw that kind of attention from you or the rest of the magical community. Not when they're doing their best to change the stigma against witches in Toronto. Still… just be careful, all right?"

"I'm always careful." I stirred my noodles. The silence on the line drew out. The question on the tip of my tongue begged to tumble free, but my fears held it back. In the end, my desperation won. "I don't suppose you've had any more luck with the blood tests?"

"Not yet, Kat, but we haven't given up. We're going to get there."

"Right. Yeah. Of course."

I believed her. I just held little hope she would succeed before my time was up.

22

Katerina

After dinner, Barrett and I decided to head back downtown to drum up another lead.

The call with the others had lasted all the way through dinner, with everyone except Gavin pitching in to offer ideas on where we should start. With Muroppy's help, I had a list of ingredients they'd been able to identify from the tea—a mix of herbs that would have been impossible to track if not for the hint of magic binding everything together. Neither of them recognized the signature of the magic, but they guaranteed that if I sent samples back to them they could test for a match.

Rhys promised to keep working with his second sight, and Maera expressed her determination to wrestle her memories into shape and pull enough details for me to work with. Poppy had offered to come up with a potion to counter any possible memory spell, but Maera had insisted she do it magic-free.

"You two have enough on your plate," she said. "Work on that first. If I don't have results by the time you've cleared your list, we'll talk, but I can handle this."

I feared for Maera's memory. Nothing stood in that woman's way when she had a goal—not even her own psyche.

Before we left, Barrett and I came up with a list of shops we wanted to hit. Rune the Day was at the top—the occult store he and I had first checked out so many months ago. Most of the witches from the coven had died in the fight against Mikhail, but there were a few survivors I wanted to speak with. They had good reason to want me dead.

Or at least, they thought they had good reason to want me dead. But it was Mikhail who had killed their covenmates. All I'd done was warn them away. It was on them for not listening.

According to their website, Rune the Day had moved from their big location to a tucked-away strip mall on the other side of the city, closer to a suburban area and squeezed between a fast-food restaurant and a dry cleaner.

Was this really the home of the people who'd destroyed my life? Nine hundred years facing the worst magicals the world had to offer, and I'd been taken down by someone who worked out of a sit-com-worthy tourist trap?

Somewhere in the next life, Alodie was laughing at me.

The world over, witches and vampires were toasting my fall.

And here I was, sitting in a poorly lit parking lot staring up at the bright windows of this tacky occult shop with less power than the witch behind the counter.

Utterly useless.

Small.

My chest ached as my confidence circled the drain, and I hunched in my seat, unable to find the nerve to get out of the car.

"Stop it."

Emrick's voice pulled me out of my dark thoughts, and I jumped, not having realized he'd appeared in the back seat. I glanced at him as Barrett turned off the engine.

"Stop what?" I asked in a tone that said I didn't have the least idea what he was talking about.

"Your thoughts are written all over your face. Stop thinking you're not as capable now as you were a week ago."

Without saying a word, Barrett got out of the car and shut the door behind him, leaving the two of us alone. I watched the soldier through the windshield as he peered into the store window, pretending to be nothing more than a curious shopper.

I suspected he was thinking about how he'd love to call Public Health to have the place shut down for peddling quack cures.

While I brooded and stared and did my best not to give

Emrick the satisfaction of a response, Emrick summoned the mist around him and, a moment later, settled in the driver's seat.

"Kat," he said, as though my very name were the point he was trying to make.

"Emrick," I replied in kind.

"Please stop." His voice caught, weighed down with such sorrow my heart cracked—not only for the pain I'd unwittingly caused him but for myself as well.

For everything I'd thought I'd overcome and clearly hadn't.

For all the years I'd spent fighting only to wind up facing a battle I didn't know how to win. That uncertainty lay at the heart of the exhaustion that swept over me, as merciless as the tide.

"I grew up believing I could never be what my parents wanted me to be." I refused to look at Emrick but couldn't ignore the way his presence filled the enclosed space. "The only reason I ever became as strong as I did, as strong as I was meant to be, was because the bond between us gave me the chance to get there. *You* gave me the chance. Now the bond is useless, and I don't know what to do. I don't know how to be what I was. Not without my magic. One wrong move could kill me. With magic behind me, I can do anything, but as I am? I don't know what I'm doing."

Emrick rested his hands on the steering wheel, and in the

gesture, I understood his attempt to keep them off me. "Your magic doesn't define you, Kat. It never has. It wasn't your magic that earned you your reputation as the scourge of the wicked— it was *you*. Your drive, your unwillingness to ignore anything that damaged the balance you swore to protect. That hasn't changed. That won't change."

I wouldn't cry. Never mind the burn at the back of my throat and the sting in my eyes, I wouldn't do it.

"I could barely hold my own against Poppy's mom today." The confession burned. "If she'd wanted to, she could have crushed me under her Louboutin, and there would have been nothing I could have done about it."

"I don't believe that for a second." He spoke with such vehemence, I jerked my head towards him, and once I took him in, I couldn't look away. I devoured the sight of him, the stubble on his cheek, the muss of his hair, the same clothes he'd worn the last time I'd seen him. He was a servant of Death, a resident of the spiritual world who only became corporeal when he crossed onto this plane. His clothes were solid, but he hadn't purchased them. He imagined them, and they appeared.

For him not to have taken care of himself was evidence of his distraction.

Of his worry.

And if I'd missed it in his rumpled shirt, I couldn't have overlooked the fire blazing in his silver eyes, the bulge along his jaw, the stiffness in his shoulders. The man was a wreck.

"I'm sorry." I clasped my hands in my lap to prevent myself from reaching for him.

His eyebrows climbed towards his hairline. "For what?"

My grief stuck in my throat. An irrational guilt. A foolish sense of responsibility. "That you're caught up in my mess. Again. Every time someone comes after me, you always seem to get hit by it."

Everything came back to the bond between us, the tether that had been forged from a ritual neither of us had been a part of. Sometimes a blessing, sometimes a curse, it rested at the centre of every decision, every change—and right now, that centre was a whack-load of pain for both of us.

I wished I had a way to release him from it, no matter how much he'd fight me.

"Hey." He grabbed my hand, then let me go when we both flinched. The leather barrier of his gloves was worse than having him not touch me at all. He returned his hands to the steering wheel, and when he spoke, his voice was thick with restrained emotion. "There is nothing to apologize for, Katerina. I love you. More than anything. You're exhausted, you're hurting, and your mind is playing tricks on you if you think any of this is your fault."

His throat bobbed with a swallow, and I stared at the skin that rose above his dark sweater. Was he even paler now than he had been? He appeared less solid than I'd ever seen him, and a pang of worry cut through me.

"Where have you been? Not crossing more lines than you should, I hope."

His laugh was bitter. "No, I've been a good boy. Keeping to the afterlife for the most part. Where I belong."

Somehow that didn't put me at ease. There was something he was keeping from me, no doubt in an attempt not to add to my worries, but all that did was make me worry more.

"Otherwise, I've been with Muroppy, watching them carry out their tests. Whenever possible, I plan to stay there until they find answers."

I released a soft sigh. "You know you can't stay, Emrick. You have obligations to fulfill."

He scowled. "My obligations can wait. Nothing is as important to me as fixing our bond."

He pressed his hand to his chest, scratching at his shirt as though to alleviate some internal discomfort.

Anxiety rippled through me, tightening my stomach. "You know you can't. Your rules—your involvement—"

"I don't *care*." He struck the steering wheel, and the bleat of the horn drew Barrett's attention our way. As soon as he confirmed we hadn't wrecked his car, he returned to his browsing. Emrick sighed and sagged into his seat. "I don't care, Kat. Either we find a way to renew our bond so I can kiss you until you beg for air, or I fade into nothing. There is no third option. I won't live on this earth without you. I can't carry the memories of us knowing you're out of my reach forever. I won't do it. So I will push as hard as I have to."

My anxiety bubbled into frustration. "You can't."

"Like hell I can't," he growled. "You and me, Kat. It's the only way this world makes sense. Without you, I'm a shadow of myself anyway."

I didn't want to hear it. Didn't want to think of it. The idea of him fading into nothing, an empty, mindless wraith gathering souls without kindness or compassion—becoming a reaper of nightmare without colour or form or life—pained me more than anything my body was going through.

"I spent seventy-five years trying to save you," I said, hating the tears that rolled down my cheeks. "Don't make me regret letting you back in."

He shifted in his seat to face me, his expression tormented. "Kat—"

"I mean it, Emrick. Whatever happens to me happens. Whatever decisions you make after I'm gone, so be it. But while I'm still breathing, I need you to put yourself first. I can't risk having my last memories be of you not knowing who I am."

The silence that fell over the car left me unable to breathe. More tears fell, but I didn't bother to brush them away. I couldn't move my hands. Couldn't move my anything. I was too afraid that one shifting muscle would cause me to break down, so I remained statue-still until Emrick's shoulders slumped.

"All right." His voice was rough, his restraint slipping. "I'll trust Muroppy to work without oversight. But you better not give up. You better not lose faith in yourself or in the fact that fate bound us together. Some assholes might have torn us apart for now, but we will find our way back to each other."

I forced myself to nod, not for a second allowing myself to hope he was right. He reached his hand towards mine, then curled his fingers into a tight fist as he pulled back.

Then he vanished, and I bowed my head into my hands and sucked in three deep breaths to try to steady my heart.

Once I was sure I wasn't about to pass out, I allowed Emrick's orders to wrap around my thoughts, cushioning them against the fears that threatened to tear into me. No matter what, I would not give up. I would not falter.

With another deep breath, I opened the car door and stepped into the parking lot.

Barrett straightened from where he'd been leaning against the wall next to the door, and I nodded to reassure him I was all right. It was time to march inside and, store by store, own this city until someone gave me a lead or we stumbled across the people who'd attacked me and my family.

Halfway across the parking lot, my phone rang. As I reached for it, a shadow moved in my periphery. I turned towards it, extending my hands at my sides to summon my fire, panicked when nothing happened, and nearly missed the knife flying out of the darkness.

I dodged at the last moment, instinct taking over, but time stopped for me again as the blade lodged between my ribs.

A few inches over, it would have struck my heart... but I wasn't sure that it made much of a difference as the taste of blood filled my mouth. My breath came in stuttering gasps, and my vision closed in until only pinpricks of light remained.

I was vaguely aware of Barrett calling my name, vaguely aware of the shadow running down the street, but very aware when the temperature dropped and Emrick appeared beside me, begging me to hold on until the world around me disappeared.

23

Emrick

M Y HEART BEAT so quickly, I was amazed it hadn't yet flown out of my chest. Our frayed bond throbbed, pulled, a few more threads snapping as Kat's connection to the mortal world faded.

One second I was kneeling beside her, the next I was standing as her soul slipped from her blood-soaked body. She rose as a pillar of light, the same as the souls I spent so much time with, and the sight nearly wrecked me. Drawing on my power just enough, I focused on her form, until the Kat I knew—shimmering and translucent as she was—remained.

Her face was slack with shock, and as we stared down at her bleeding body, the knife still lodged between her ribs, I understood why. I couldn't process it myself.

Only a minute ago, we'd been sitting in the car talking. She'd been safe. Well, safe-ish. Now she lay on the brink of death, only a few breaths away from the tether between spirit and body snapping. Any moment now, someone would arrive to escort her to the afterlife.

Someone who wasn't me.

Without magic in her blood, she was no longer my responsibility. Instead, it would be some stranger—unless, like last time, Death came for her directly.

The thought made me cold. Numb. Torn with indecision. Because right now, what I wanted to do more than anything was to hunt down the son of a bitch who'd hurt her and tear their soul from their body. Human, magical, I didn't fucking care.

I wanted them dead.

The only thing holding me back was Kat. Not only had I just promised her—again—that I wouldn't involve myself, but I couldn't leave her here. Not in this moment of ultimate uncertainty. Not when it might be the last time I saw her until Death released me from my service.

A different sensation hummed beneath the pain of our fading bond. A different kind of pull. As though something far outside either was us was calling to me, urging me to go to it. I ignored it—nothing could be more important than staying right where I was—and in another moment, the feeling faded.

"Emrick?" Kat's voice wavered.

I stepped closer to her, reached out to touch her only to have my hand pass through her shoulder. My fingers grew chill. It was ironic that in this state she was once again safe from me, but only because I couldn't make contact.

Briefly I considered drawing on enough power to make her corporeal the way I'd done with Mikhail, but I brushed the thought aside. Mikhail was dead. Kat wasn't—not yet. I also didn't want to risk tying myself more securely to the afterlife while a single breath remained in her body.

"It's okay. It's going to be okay," I said, but I was in too much shock to sound as reassuring as I'd hoped.

"It's not, is it." She said it as a statement, knowing as well as I did she balanced on the precipice.

Side by side, close enough that I sensed the tingle of her energy against my skin, we watched Barrett leave her to tear towards the shop. He was inside less than a minute before he dragged someone out, his hands twisting the man's shirt.

"Help her," he growled.

The witch's gaze dropped to Kat, and in the dim light of the parking lot, his face paled to a sickly white. He wobbled on his feet, dragged his shaking fingers down his face, and swallowed twice before he stammered, "I-I—oh gods, I don't know if I can. This is—this is real bad, man. She needs a hospital. Let me call for an ambulance or something. I—"

"We don't have fucking time," Barrett snapped. "Your shop is filled with shit you claim will turn back time, so prove it. Get what you need and save her fucking life, or I swear to all the gods you pray to, I will punch a hole through your gut and rip out your spleen."

I didn't think it was possible for the witch to pale further, but he proved me wrong. A split-second deliberation passed through his head, then he nodded and darted back into the store.

I half-expected him to slam the door shut, lock it, and turn out the lights. I was ready to follow him and terrify him into compliance. To my amazement, I spotted him through the window gathering ingredients.

Barrett dropped down beside Kat and brushed her hair out of her face, his touch gentle. I waited for jealousy to strike, but it never came. This wasn't the touch of a lover. If I had to describe it, I would have said it was the fear of a brother.

A guardian.

"Goddammit, Kat, you stay with me, do you hear me?" He looked up and around. "Emrick, you son of a bitch, you better make sure not to take her too far. She needs to get back to work."

Beside me, Kat chuckled, but when I looked at her, her expression was contorted in pain. Not physical pain—this detached from her body, she wouldn't feel anything—but emotional agony.

"Emrick…"

She didn't have to speak another word for me to know everything she was about to say. She was tired. Leaving would be easier. It would be kinder.

"No." I cut her off.

"Emrick."

"*No.*"

A soft smile curled her perfect mouth but didn't reach her sorrowful eyes. "What if we're delaying the inevitable?"

"Then we delay. And we keep delaying. Saying goodbye now is not an option. I won't accept it. Not like this."

She closed her eyes, and her spirit rippled. On the ground, her body arched as though suffering the final pangs of life. I turned my back on her body to focus on her soul.

"You have to fight for me, Katerina. You have to fight with everything you have." Her eyes opened, and I stared her down, refusing to let her slip away from me. "Somewhere out there is a group who wants you dead. What do you think they'll do once they achieve their goal? Call it a day? They want you gone for a reason. It's their fault Alodie came back. Their fault Mikhail gained so much power and Shogaur was able to step foot on this earth a second time. Are you going to let them get away with that because it's *easier*? When have you ever chosen the easier path?"

The door to the shop flew open again, and the witch returned with his arms full of magical kit. He quailed under Barrett's dark glower, but to his credit, he didn't shy away from dumping everything on the ground and getting to work.

"She's losing a lot of blood, so we have to act quickly. When I tell you, pull out the knife so I can get these salves into the wound. They should stop the bleeding at the very least. Encourage the tissue to heal a bit faster."

Barrett scowled. "You sound like a quack. Tell me you believe in western medicine as well."

The witch shot him a glare that would have curled a lesser person's toes. "Hey, asshole, I'm the one who wanted to call for an ambulance. You want me to help? This is what I can do, so either shut up and help me or let the woman die in my parking lot."

I wanted to step out of the mist to slam both their heads together for wasting time, but because I appreciated Barrett making sure this guy wasn't about to stuff Kat full of poison, and because I suspected my sudden appearance might push the witch into an early heart attack, I stayed put and returned my attention to Kat.

She watched the events playing out around her body, fear mixed with uncertainty written all over her face. "I don't know," she said, replying to the question I'd left hanging between us. "Does it matter? Even if this person pulls me back, even if I survive this, what can I do against a group without my magic? They'll just come after me again. Next time they might succeed. How can I stop them?"

"You don't stop them alone. However you've felt about Barrett in the past, he's clearly on your side. You've got Poppy and Murisa working non-stop at home"—I swallowed my suspicions about Poppy, knowing this wasn't the time—"and Rhys's visions are on their way back. You also have Gavin. He might not want to get his hands dirty, but you know he'll step in if he has to. You've got a team, Kat. People who love you. People who are ready to help you." Except for whoever had betrayed her, but we could figure that out once she opened her eyes. "You can track these bastards down and give them the justice they deserve."

"Shit—shit!" the witch yelled, and I turned around to watch blood gushing from Kat's chest, seeping out from between her lips. "Apply pressure while I ready the next potion."

Her body slipped into convulsions as she lost more blood, and the spirit beside me stepped closer, her eyes widening. I wedged myself between her and the view behind me. "Look at me, Kat. Look only at me. Let them do what they have to, but you need to decide."

And it would need to be soon. I felt a stir in the air as another presence approached. Death was close on her heels.

She blinked, her long, thick lashes brushing against the

tops of her cheeks. I wanted to kiss her. If I'd been willing to risk melding myself more with the afterlife, I would have drawn on as much power as it took to feel her soft skin against the palm of my hand.

Instead, all I could do was hold my breath and wait for her to make up her mind. Would she embrace the rest she so richly deserved, or would she fight to stay with me?

Her gaze never left mine, her posture never shifted, but in her eyes I caught the exact moment she chose to stay. My heart resumed its steady beat, and the breath of relief I drew in was the sweetest I'd ever consumed.

Neither of us said anything, but her smile was determined, lined with steel and no small amount of righteous fury, as her spirit slipped away from me. Her form faded once more into a beautiful pillar of light and sank back into her body.

In another heartbeat, her bleeding frame sucked in a breath, and her eyes flew open.

24

Katerina

I WOKE UP in a bedroom that wasn't my own, and it took me a minute to recognize Adrian's Toronto house.

It took me another minute to remember how I got from the occult shop to my bed, but second by second, the fog in my head cleared and flashes returned to me of a knife flying out of the darkness, raised voices, Barrett carrying me to the car.

There was something else—a cool brush of air against my cheek—but when I reached for the memory, it vanished. A chill of unease scurried down my back with the suspicion that the memory wasn't for me to remember.

I huddled deeper under my blankets, wincing as pain shot through my chest, my back, and down my arm.

Afraid to see the damage for myself but unable to look

away, I peeled off my blankets and tugged down the neckline of my shirt.

A shirt I hadn't put on, I noted, and I tried to imagine Barrett wrangling me into it while keeping his eyes averted and avoiding any unnecessary touching.

The thought made me laugh, and I regretted it as the torn flesh beneath the clean bandages pulled.

I cursed and sagged against the pillows. I wasn't used to waking up in pain. Going to bed aching and bleeding, sure, but to wake up in the same state was strange and unusual, and I hated it.

On some level, however, I understood exactly how lucky I was. The way that knife had lodged in my chest, that missing memory I had of a reassuring voice and cool touch, was hint enough that I'd come terrifyingly close to the end. Maybe it would have been easier to let it happen, but fuck if I was going to let the bastards who'd killed Adrian and stripped me of my bond with Emrick get away with what they'd done.

I had no magic, I was weaker and slower than I'd ever been, but I would make them suffer for it.

Knifey Dude was just one more unknown to add to my list.

The fact someone had tried to kill me—again—told me one thing, though: we'd stumbled onto the right track somewhere along the way. Whoever had tried to off me with the tea knew I was alive, and the number of people who fell into that camp was small. Had they known from the start and bided their time until they got me out in the open, or had it been a recent discovery?

I set to work putting the list together until a knock at the door jarred me out of my thoughts. I almost shouted at them to go away so I could finish what I was doing but remembered in time that the knocker must be Barrett. Although the details were fuzzy, I knew I owed him a thank you for saving my life.

Gratitude. To Barrett. Weird.

"Come on in."

When the door opened, however, it wasn't Barrett who bustled into my room.

Maera, all white-and-red hair and blue shirt and soft jeans, started on seeing me. "You're awake!" Her green eyes lit up, and I caught the immediate well of tears before she blinked them away. "Thank God you're all right, Kat. You had us so worried. James called as soon as he put you in the car, and we were on the road within the hour. We had no idea what to expect. He said you'd pulled through, but a knife to the chest? In your current condition?"

She sat on the side of my bed, fussed over my pillow, and straightened my sheets. My heart warmed at her worry, but I was also distracted by a little detail she'd mentioned.

"We?"

"We're all here, of course," she said, as though it were a

given that an entire household would pack up on a whim to drive so many hours in the middle of the night to come see little old me.

Maera wasn't the only one fighting back a sudden sting of tears.

She took my hand and squeezed it tightly. "Are you all right?"

"No." I winced as my wound pulled again. "But thanks to Barrett, I'm alive, so that counts for a lot."

"Not just Barrett. That witch stuffed you full of potions that seem to have helped, and after Gavin arrived, he took over. Cleaned you up, bandaged you nice and tight. He didn't say anything, but I think he was impressed with the strength of those potions. All his fears for your life melted right out of him when he got a closer look."

Witch? Gavin helping me? I must have been out of it because none of that rang a bell. Unless I was still dreaming.

"That shop owner deserves a medal," Maera continued, "but Barrett deserves a smack upside the head for not getting you to a hospital. You could have died, Kat."

I grimaced. "I'm not sure *could have* is the proper choice of words."

Maera paled. "You mean…"

I considered the memory that wasn't a memory. "I don't know. It's possible. Just a gut feeling."

"Was Emrick with you?"

"I don't know." Which in itself was strange because he should have been. Unless Death had kept him away again. "I'd like to think so, but it's all a bit of a blur."

"Maybe that's for the best." Maera shifted on the bed. "I don't know if I'd like to see that man of yours in his official capacity." She shivered as though he'd shown up in my room with a cloak and scythe. She adored Emrick, but she struggled to balance who he was against *what* he was.

I didn't blame her. For most of my relationship with him, his duties to Death were theoretical. I never thought I'd have the opportunity to experience it firsthand.

"I do wish Rhys had been able to call you a few seconds earlier," she said as she brushed my hair out of my face. "You might have stayed safe in the car, and all this might have been avoided."

I frowned. "Rhys called?"

A memory came back to me of my phone ringing seconds before the attack.

"He had a vision of you on the ground covered in blood. The first clear vision he's had in weeks." A pained smile crossed her lips. "He's torn between pride and horror, I think."

I rested my hand on hers. "Tell him to stick with pride."

Maera tucked the blankets around me, unable to stop fussing. Then she bent over and kissed my forehead, and my breath caught in my chest. She'd never shown that level of affection towards me. Not since she was a child and I stood in the place of an older sister.

It both warmed me and terrified me.

"Get some sleep," she said. "Next time you wake up, I'll have your favourite foods ready for you, and we can talk about what to do next."

She left, and although I was certain sleep wasn't likely to come for me again, within minutes, I drifted off.

And woke up what felt like seconds later in a cold sweat.

My chest screamed at my sudden movements, but I was too busy trying to catch my breath to suffer much beyond the initial pang.

I'd dreamt that someone was watching me, about to kill me. I couldn't breathe, the weight on my chest was so heavy.

My eyes flew open, and I found myself staring deep into the yellow eyes of Poppy's undead cat.

"Gack! Cuddles, get off."

"*Mrow.*" His monotonous voice oozed contempt. He stood up, paws digging into my boob, and I swore he pressed his weight right into my healing wound.

I yelped in pain as he jumped onto the floor and stalked out of the room, then screamed when my gaze landed on a shadowy figure sitting in the armchair between the bed and the window.

"That little show was worth waiting for you to wake up."

Gavin's deep voice was laced with amusement.

I pressed my hand to my diaphragm to remind it how to function. "Are you trying to give me a heart attack?"

Considering Rhys's vision, I couldn't rule out the possibility, but if the sorcerer was my betrayer, I doubted he would be so open about it.

Then again, what couldn't he get away with? He was a nurse who had taken responsibility for my recovery. How difficult would it be for him to slip something into my wound and claim there had been complications?

My pulse lurched at the idea, racing faster as he pushed himself out of the chair and loomed over me, but I forced myself to breathe and calm down. I didn't have my magic, but I wasn't helpless. I had fists, and Poppy had already demonstrated the efficacy of a table lamp as an improvised weapon.

"You're bleeding through your bandages," he said with a huff. "Let's clean you up."

As he came into the light, I took in the hollows of his cheeks and the circles under his eyes.

"Trouble sleeping?" I asked, although I doubted he would be plagued by guilt-induced insomnia.

He snorted. "How is anyone supposed to get a full night in when you keep winding up in scrapes like this?"

I watched him closely as he set to work removing my bandages. Watched his eyebrows climb as he took in whatever state the wound was in, and felt relieved when I detected no trace of intense emotions. Fear might have meant I wasn't doing well; anger would have suggested disappointment that I was. Instead, there was only an intense focus as he grabbed his kit from the bedside table to clean my wound and apply new bandages.

"Whatever that witch gave you, it's working miracles," he said. "The wound looks days old instead of hours. It won't be a quick heal, but you'll be back on your feet faster than most of us would be."

That was a small comfort, at least. There were people out there who needed my foot up their ass.

I expected Gavin to leave now that his nursing skills had been applied, but he lingered at the side of my bed. His jaw bulged as he gritted his teeth, and he shoved his hands into his pockets. "What's it like?"

"Being stabbed in the chest? I can't say I recommend it."

His gaze dropped. "Being without your magic. Being normal."

I snapped my mouth closed and looked away from him. I shouldn't have been surprised by the question. If anything, I might have expected him to have asked it ages ago. For the past few months, he'd wanted nothing more than to be in the position I was now in. Of course he wanted to know.

It took me a moment to bury the pain of my situation and

even longer to find my answer. "I wish I could tell you it's the best thing I've ever experienced. That my body feels lighter, my mind clearer. But it feels like I've been impaled on a spike that's jostling me left to right and won't let me settle. It feels like someone's punched a hole through my chest, torn out my heart, and left the wound gaping and bleeding. Normal—whatever the hell that is—feels like shit."

His shoulders slumped, and he ran his hand through his hair. "I thought you'd say something like that."

I looked at him and caught the depth of despair in his dark brown eyes. "I know you wish Maera had saved you some of that tea. That you believe if you lost your power, your life would be easier or better, but denying who you are wouldn't make you happier. You could go back to your life, but you'd always know part of you was missing. Something you couldn't get back. You'd be miserable—all the more so because you'd have made this decision to be happy and it failed. We can't hide from who we are, Gavin. No matter how badly we might want to."

He pursed his lips, his eyes glazing over as his thoughts wandered far from this room. But as he started to speak, the door opened and Maera bustled in.

"Oh, Gavin, I'm sorry. I didn't realize you were in here. Should I come back?"

He cleared his throat. "No, it's fine. I was just leaving."

I wanted to shoo Maera away and drag whatever he'd been

about to say out of him, but on a gut level, I understood the moment had passed. Whatever was going through his head, he needed to work it out on his own first.

He left, and I sank back against my pillows.

"Is he all right?" I asked Maera. If anyone knew the goings-on of every person here, it was my housekeeper.

"He's stressed about your condition. We all are."

"I don't think anyone is as envious as he is, though."

Maera's eyebrows climbed towards her hairline. "Is that what you think? That he's jealous you've lost your power?"

"He hates magic. Even more than Barrett does." I frowned. "You did get rid of the rest of that tea, didn't you?"

"What I didn't throw out, Muroppy have used in their experiments. But I think you're missing the point, Kat."

"Oh?"

"He's been in the middle of a huge identity crisis since you saved him from that demon. Thanks to Barrett, Poppy, you, everything you've been through, he's had his eyes opened to this world. Now you, the only person who understands what he's going through on a magical level—the only person who could teach him anything about his abilities—is no longer in a position to help him. He's lost, Kat. Without some direction and support and kindness, I fear he'll never find his way."

And I'd been so distracted by his glares and his growling I'd missed all that.

If Maera was right, then somewhere along the way, his opinion of his situation had changed, and I hadn't noticed. If I had, maybe I could have helped him while I'd had the chance. I groaned and bowed my head, weighed down by the guilt that threatened to break my heart.

Now he'd come to me, and instead of assuring him that I would still be willing to help where I could, I'd loaded him up with platitudes.

Then again, if Maera was wrong—rare as it was, it happened—then I had to wonder if his reason for being here hadn't been with some ulterior motive in mind. After all, how quickly did one move from self-loathing to full acceptance? Goodness knows I still struggled after nine hundred years.

Regardless, I couldn't help but worry that my response might have sent him spiralling down darker, more dangerous paths.

25

Katerina

BY THE NEXT afternoon, I was able to leave my bedroom and head downstairs to the living room. The trip to my favourite armchair exhausted me, but it was better than being cooped up in bed for another day.

Poppy and Murisa had created some kind of goopy mess that they'd smeared over my wound, and most of the pain was gone—another debt to add to their tab once I was able to pay it. Unfortunately, my brush with death meant they'd had to put off their experiments on my blood, so I didn't have any updates to look forward to with the rising sun.

Maera had made my favourite breakfast of crepes with hash browns and fresh fruit, but somehow the indulgence struck me as a convict's last meal, and I hadn't been able to enjoy it.

I was hungry, grumpy, bored, and impatient on top of all the other negative emotions that had grabbed hold of me. A lovely picture for Emrick to walk in on.

Everyone else was busy with their own tasks. Muroppy were upstairs in their room across from mine, back at work now that they'd set up their equipment. Rhys was in the room he and Gavin were sharing on the third floor across from the master suite. He was determined to trigger more visions, wanting to know what was about to happen *before* I walked into it. Maera was in the backyard gardening, wanting to give me some space, while Barrett and Gavin were in the gym downstairs.

Which meant Emrick and I were alone as he dropped onto the couch across from me. My heart fluttered at the sight of him, followed by a sharp pang that, alone or not, I couldn't touch him.

He leaned forward and propped his elbows on his knees. "How are you feeling?"

I clutched my glass of water between my hands, propped my feet up on the coffee table, and met his stare. "Did I die again?" The question was out before I considered whether or not I wanted to know.

The corner of his mouth curled upwards, but his smile didn't quite reach his eyes. "Not exactly." His expression shuttered. "But it was close. Too close. You made the decision to come back, but if Barrett hadn't screamed that witch into submission, a few more minutes and the choice wouldn't have been yours to make."

I raised my eyebrows. "Barrett screamed at a witch for me?"

Emrick smirked. "Threatened to tear out his spleen."

I pressed my hand to my chest—the uninjured side. "That is so sweet. I never knew he cared so much."

"If you had any doubts, they should be gone now."

"Nah, he probably just couldn't imagine a world where he couldn't look down on me for something. And I get it. Not having him to rag on would create a void in my soul."

But I spoke without believing what I said. My heart was too full of warmth to give my griping any heat. Barrett had fought for me? What kind of world had we stepped into?

Emrick chuckled, and I forced a smile. It was nice to pretend for a moment that everything was as it should be.

"At the very least, I think we can rule him out as the person who betrayed you."

"I agree. No one threatens spleen-rippage as a cover-up." Being able to cross him off as a suspect brought a shocking amount of relief. A few months ago, James Barrett would have been at the top of my list of people who longed for my downfall, but after everything we'd been through together, that betrayal might have destroyed me.

"Are you going to answer my question?" Emrick asked, and I returned my attention to him.

"Which one?" At his arched eyebrow, I shrugged, then winced. "I'm still in pain. Not a fan of that. How do mortals deal with this constant discomfort? When I got out of bed this morning, my hips popped. Do you know how strange that is? It's like my body's forgotten how to move within itself, and I've only been mortal for a few days. What will it be like when I'm fifty? Sixty? As old as Alodie, with thinning hair and skin so wrinkled I can barely see past my eyelid folds?"

I was exaggerating, but not by much. After so many centuries of being young, the concept of aging terrified me.

"You'd still look as beautiful to me as you do right now," Emrick said. "As long as you kept that sharp tongue."

"From what I've seen of the fierce older women in my life, that's not a concern. If anything, it'll just get sharper."

"Then you have nothing to worry about."

We fell silent, and I watched Emrick as his thoughts drifted. If I had to guess, they hadn't travelled in a pleasant direction. His brow furrowed, and his hands clenched and unclenched in his lap. Although I tried to read him, I found myself having trouble interpreting the expressions I'd come to know as well as my own.

"Where did you go?" I asked.

He tore his gaze back to mine, and on a sigh, his shoulders slumped. "I can't stop thinking about Rhys's vision. That someone close to you might have turned on you."

His gaze flicked to the kitchen across the open-concept floor and towards the staircases that led up and down. We were still alone, but the knowledge didn't appear to put him at ease.

"I hate leaving you alone here, especially injured, when someone could sneak up on you and finish what that person in the parking lot started."

I chased away a shiver with a sip of room temperature water. "I won't lie and say the thought hasn't been keeping me awake as well. These suspicions aren't fun, but history's taught me I can't afford to overlook the threats that hide in familiarity."

"I've been keeping an eye on Poppy and Murisa as best I can, but there's only so much I can do."

I frowned. "Why do you suspect them most?"

Poppy had been nothing but helpful since I'd dragged her out of her cozy little life of minor necromancy and peddling tarot cards and fake curse kits. Since I'd used her to help me bring down Mikhail and caused her shop to be set on fire and—

"Never mind, I get it."

If Poppy was involved, it might also mean Hera's coven was on the table, regardless of what the woman said.

Exhaustion tugged me down, and I set my glass on the coffee table so I could sink deeper into my chair. My head swam and my body hurt. I wanted to go home instead of being stuck in a house that reminded me of the friend I'd so recently lost. This week was up there as the worst in recent memory. "Every time I think I cross off a name, more pop up."

Cuddles padded into the room, veered straight for Emrick, and at the last second recoiled, hissed, and jumped onto the back of the chair. He curled his paws under his partially decomposed body and glared at me as though I'd stolen his seat. Or he was waiting for me to fall asleep so he could reclaim his perch on my chest. Classic asshole.

Emrick kept his eye on Cuddles as he said, "I'm sorry, Kat. None of this has to be easy for you. I'll go upstairs and check in on what Muroppy's doing, but you need to keep your guard up."

A cruel truth, and one that left me feeling icky—as though I were the one betraying my friends by doubting them—but there we were.

He stood up and stared at me, his silver eyes gleaming with impossibilities. I pressed my lips together in an understanding smile, which he returned as he stepped through the mist and disappeared.

26

Katerina

Lᴛʜᴏᴜɢʜ I'ᴅ ʙᴇᴇɴ aware of Rhys's warning and what it would mean if someone in this house had turned on me, after Emrick's visit, I couldn't think of anything else.

My suspicions gnawed so deeply, they poisoned my view of every person sharing my roof. These people I'd spent months working with. Some of whom I'd known for years. With the exception of Rhys, I saw reasons that any of them might want me dead.

I'd returned to my room as soon as Emrick had left, feeling vulnerable out in the open. I'd tried to take a nap and failed when every noise throughout the house became someone creeping into my room. I'd debated barring the door with the dresser but couldn't move it. So now I sat in the armchair Gavin had occupied, having pulled it up to the French doors that peered out over a tiny balcony facing the backyard.

I missed the view from my balcony in Spring Bay. Sitting out there, I could look across the lake and see no one except the occasional boater. Here, I stared at the back of another house. But at least the neighbours' hideous curtains gave me more to focus on than the wall across from my bed.

As I pulled my legs up under me, my healing wound screamed. I embraced the pain. Discomfort aside, there was a certain reassurance in its steady pulsing, a comforting contrast to the cloud of doubts floating around me.

I'd spent my immortality trying to help people. Yes, I'd made many enemies along the way, but only those who strove to harm others or reveal the secrets of the magical world to the mundanes not ready to learn them. In order for our world to maintain the peace it had held for so many centuries, certain rules had to be followed. These days, it might be the witch or vampire hunters who doled out the consequences for breaking them, but for almost a thousand years, Adrian and I had been the magical bogeymen. At this point, I was a household name in most magical circles.

Show off your magic at your own risk.

But to know that at some point I'd also left myself open to being targeted by the people I cared about—I didn't know if my anger should be directed at them or at myself. Alodie, Mae, and

Blythe had taught me long ago that community meant nothing in the face of some people's ambitions.

Clearly someone close to me had gone the way of those sorceresses. They saw something they wanted—a world without me, or some greater end I couldn't yet see—and were willing to destroy anything as long as they got it.

In the face of a desire that deep, it became all too easy to believe every action was justified.

Five years ago, I'd dragged Poppy kicking and screaming out of her necromancer coven. I'd seen her potential for change, believed her motivations hadn't been as destructive as those of her coven leader, so I'd made a deal for information in exchange for her life. Since then, she'd shown no sign of wanting to return to her old ways, but that didn't mean the wish wasn't there.

That might have been enough for her to turn against me, but I'd twisted the knife by using our deal to get information about Mikhail. She'd been afraid to help me, and I'd forced her into it. Her fear of being ousted from the community had pushed her to hide in a graveyard and summon a zombie body-guard for protection.

I'd tracked her down again, and what had happened? Alodie had burned down her store.

So no, I couldn't discount the possibility that she wanted to kill me and return to her corpse-controlling ways.

As for Murisa, who was she, really? She'd come into our lives out of the blue to help with the Shogaur situation. Although I'd dug a bit into her past, I hadn't found much. She was a self-taught witch, had never belonged to a coven, and had to keep her witchcraft secret so her magical-hating parents didn't disown her. But she was a skilled tech witch, so how much information could she have hidden from me? Even if her own motivations were clean, that didn't mean she wasn't working with Poppy. The two of them had become a formidable team, and I didn't know how far Murisa might go to give Poppy what she wanted.

While Emrick and I had ruled Barrett out, there was still room for doubt. He'd made his dislike for me clear enough, and this recent show of camaraderie could hide a more malicious turn of that dislike. Adrian was no longer in the picture to stand between us, so there was nothing stopping the ex-soldier from killing me and staking his claim among the witch hunters.

What about Gavin? Mr. I-Would-Rather-Die-Than-Be-A-Sorcerer. Maera said he was lost, but that didn't mean he was confused. It was possible his sad puppy-dog expression the past few days had nothing to do with not knowing how to use his newfound power and everything to do with disappointment over his failed attempt to get rid of me. What if he did hold a grudge that his grandmother was dead because of me? Or that I hadn't left him to die in Shogaur's custody rather than dragging him into this new life?

Maybe it was Maera, looking to prevent me from pulling her son deeper into my world. No more Kat putting Rhys in danger. No more cleaning up after me or dealing with my problems. After fifty-five years, I could understand her being tired of it.

The more I considered every option, the more depressed I became. Was it possible my decision to embrace some kind of connection in this world had hidden the truth from me? Left me vulnerable where I thought I was safe?

I wished Adrian were here to talk me through it. I would have appreciated his insight. Or his reassurance that I was jumping at shadows. Or, at the very least, to have someone at my back ready to tear out the throat of whoever it might be, even if it was his beloved thrall.

I was so deep in my brooding I didn't hear the door to my room open. When Gavin walked into view and leaned against the wall by the window, my heart nearly leapt out of my chest. It took me a good second or ten to settle my pulse so I didn't jump out of my seat and throttle him.

He offered me time to calm down—or time to gear himself up for whatever he wanted to say—and stared into the middle distance, his expression thoughtful.

I held myself back from pushing my chair away to put more space between us. He was larger than I was and had his fire magic. If he wanted me dead, there was little I could do in this enclosed space to prevent it. I didn't even have my knife on me, and I heard Adrian's voice in my head calling me a fool for believing I was safe in my own room.

Gavin shifted his weight to his other foot, and his jaw flexed with every clench of his teeth. I could practically hear his thoughts whirring in his skull as he carried out some internal debate, but I didn't rush him, not sure I wanted to know which side of his psyche would win out.

Finally, after an age had passed, he said, "When Maera called and told us what happened with that tea, I admit, I was happy about it. I thought I'd finally found my escape from this hell ride." He glowered at the floor. "I also thought you had it coming."

I bit my tongue to prevent any sarcastic quips from bursting out.

"You saved me from being tortured by that demon," he continued, "but ever since, you've been pushing me to learn my magic when all I've wanted is to turn my back on it. When Barrett told me you lost your power, my first response was to laugh. The irony of you demanding I accept what I am only for you to lose everything you are." He lifted his chin and met my eye squarely. "I'm not laughing anymore."

My damn tears returned, the strain of holding them back clawing at the back of my throat and making my nose weep. I looked away from him and focused on the leaves of the tree blowing in the breeze over the backyard. Anything to stop the tears from falling.

Gavin crossed his arms and shifted his weight again. "As soon as the reality sank in, I got angry. With you, in part, for proving yourself wrong. For showing me that, even if I did accept what I was, there was always the chance I would end up losing it, and then where would I be? As bereft as you?"

He scratched his head, adjusted his shirt, dug his toed sock into a dip between the floorboards. "It's taken me a few days to realize who I'm actually angry at, Kat, and it's not you. I'm angry at myself for being a hypocrite. For swearing all this time I didn't want to learn my magic only to have the option be stripped away. I've been left wondering what my life might have looked like if I'd taken your offer and your time seriously." With a rough sigh, he shoved his hands in his pockets, and his restless energy seemed to settle. "What does that make me if not the worst kind of asshole? Being angry I can't have something now that the door is closed to me."

I listened to him with an ache in my heart, appreciating how correct and incorrect Maera had been.

A tiny voice in the back of my head shouted that his feelings weren't my problem. I was going through my own shit right now, and his "wah, now I can't learn magic" tale of woe should have been nothing but a whimper in the face of my internal roar. But it wasn't. He hadn't removed himself from my list of suspects—he could be regretting spiking my tea—but I did feel bad for him. I knew what it was like to have doors slammed in my face, cutting me off from possibilities. Whether he was the cause of my lost magic or not, he was suffering because of it.

"Hey," I said, drawing his gaze to mine. "It doesn't make you a hypocrite, Gavin. It makes you human. No one likes change, and to wake up one day to find out you're a walking incinerator, that's a bigger change than most people face. I'm sorry I pushed so hard. I should have understood that accepting you're a believed-to-be extinct species of magic user might take more time than a single day in the middle of a world-threatening crisis. Or the next world-threatening crisis. Or the one after that. It's been a busy few months."

"You wanted to help me. Hell, you wanted to save my life."

"I did, but strong-arming someone to face reality is not usually the best way to go about it." I paused for a moment to let my apology sink in. "If you're ready to learn, we still have options. It might take longer, and it might not be traditional training, but we can find you a teacher. Or I could help you. Maybe."

The offer burned my tongue. The thought of helping him master his power when I could no longer access my own would be no small amount of torture. But I couldn't abandon him.

He curled his hands at his sides, and his dark eyes kindled with a fire I couldn't interpret. Frustration? Pride? Anger?

In the end, he bowed his head. "With you teaching me, maybe it would have been different, but as it is… Seeing what I might stand to lose… I can't do it."

Without another word, he left, closing the door softly behind him. As I sat in the silence of my room, I couldn't help but wonder how many lives my change in circumstances might affect.

27

Emrick

ALTHOUGH I WATCHED Muroppy work and saw nothing that proved my suspicions, I also couldn't shake them. Too often, the two exchanged dark looks that didn't seem to have anything to do with their findings. More like they were sharing unspoken thoughts related to a conversation they'd had out of earshot.

For the most part, I remained in the afterlife, hovering on the edge of the mist so they didn't know I was there. I hoped they would talk and reveal their secrets if they believed themselves to be alone—and felt no sense of guilt about doing so with Kat's safety at stake—but there was nothing.

They worked in silence, took turns sleeping, and allowed Maera to bring them plates of food so they didn't need to stop to eat.

Cuddles sauntered in and out of their room, rubbing his long grey hair over the furniture, losing tiny bits of himself as he went. Poppy had created a stasis enchantment that prevented him from decomposing, but it didn't hold all his pieces together. Both witches regularly gave him pets "for luck," but if he was their good luck charm, he wasn't pulling his weight. All they found was failure after failure after failure, until finally, a little before dawn the next morning, Murisa threw up her arms and released a crow of victory.

Poppy was at her side in a second, rubbing the sleep from her eyes. "What is it? What did you find?"

"I may have isolated one of the proteins in the potion. If I'm right, it's possible that not only can we backtrack it to the ingredient that was used to strip her magic, but maybe we can… I don't even know. Do something with it. Synthesize it? Create a vaccine?"

Poppy frowned. "She's not sick, Ris."

Murisa buried her head in her hands and let out a growl of frustration. "I know, I *know*, but her magic can't have just *disappeared*. It's part of who she is. It's in her genetic makeup. There's a lot we can manipulate in the genes, but we can't change them completely. If that were possible, we'd have people lined up to drink teas that changed their eye colour or their metabolism." She sat up straight, her expression wide. "Oh, wouldn't that be cool?"

"Focus, sweetie. What are you saying? You think she still has her magic? It's just, what? Dormant? Locked in?"

"Yes!" Murisa sat forward. "That's exactly it. If we can figure out the makeup of the potion she ingested, maybe we can pinpoint precisely what's affecting her magic. Find a way to break it apart, and *bam*, she'll be all fire-fingers again."

Poppy grunted a laugh. "Fire-fingers. I don't want to imagine what role they'd play in her and Emrick's love life."

I rolled my eyes at her predictably immature thought process but couldn't deny the hope that had woken at their theory. If they were correct, it would mean Kat wouldn't be defenseless. Her life span might be reduced to a normal number of decades, but she would be herself again. If that was all we could be sure of, I would be satisfied.

Murisa's shoulders drooped, and the excitement on her face turned wistful. "I hope I'm right."

"Me too." Poppy slid her hand over Murisa's and intertwined their fingers.

With her free hand, Murisa rubbed her tired eyes. "I don't know what will happen if we don't figure this out. I've just found all of you. I don't want to lose this family."

"Hey." Poppy sank into the chair next to Murisa's and slid her arm around the other woman's shoulders. "Whatever happens, you won't lose me, all right?" Cuddles hopped onto

Murisa's lap and purred deeply. Poppy nodded. "Either of us."

Murisa wrapped her arms around her. "To feel like I finally have a family—one that accepts me, is *proud* of me. I can't give it up."

Poppy's expression hardened over Murisa's shoulder, and I watched with interest. "I'll make sure you have whatever you need. I promise. It's you and me against the world, okay? But that won't matter because we won't fail."

I prayed they were right—and that Poppy proved to be as loyal as she acted. My suspicions about Murisa had all but vanished, but the necromancer remained a question mark. She didn't appear disappointed that Murisa might have found a path forward, but my ability to read people had diminished over the years as I'd drifted further from humanity. I didn't know if I was missing something.

But these witches had given me something to hope for, so I would make damned sure no one stood in Murisa's way of making it happen.

28

Katerina

I stood in my room staring mindlessly out the balcony's French doors into the neighbour's empty dining room. I didn't know what to do with myself. Between the potions the witch from Rune the Day had given Barrett and Muroppy's healing salves, I was pretty much back on my feet—from death to walking in three days was pretty spectacular; I was never ragging on witchcraft again—but had nowhere to go.

We had no leads.

So far, Hera hadn't contacted me, which told me she hadn't sniffed out any of the rogue witches behind the attack. Tony was supposed to get in touch if he found anything else, but it was silence from the hunters as well.

We could rule the vampires out because magic was involved

and they hated using magic. They would have been far more likely to send someone to tear my head off, especially now that Adrian's protection no longer covered my vampire-hating ass.

Rhys had spent half of yesterday walking around Toronto, trying to identify anything from his most recent vision without success, and the other half at home trying to trigger more visions. The only thing he'd Seen was me standing on a crowded bus, which—if a psychic hadn't told me—would have sounded more unlikely than me losing my magic.

Poppy and Murisa were still cooped up in their room doing who knew what with my blood, and Emrick continued to avoid me.

He wouldn't call it avoiding, of course. He would say he was giving me space to process and adjust to my new state of being. But I called bullshit. When I'd first discovered our bond and my immortality, he hadn't left my side for fifty years.

No, in truth, he couldn't cope with what had happened to me, and I didn't blame him. Every day, I became a little less grounded. It felt like the early days after I'd sent him away seventy-five years ago. The constant ache for his touch had become a physical strain, and I'd nearly floundered beneath it. Back then, I'd had Adrian to lean on. Now…

Grief simmered under my skin, and I paced the length of my bedroom. I needed to get out of here. I needed to get some fresh air or punch someone.

Maybe Barrett was free.

As though my thoughts summoned him, I heard his familiar baritone drifting up from the backyard below. I pulled one half of the French doors open to better hear him, peering down over the railing from where I stood on the threshold of the balcony to find him and Gavin standing close to each other. By their expressions, their conversation was far from light and fluffy.

My stomach tightened, and my fingers curled around the edge of the door frame.

Gavin squeezed his fists at his sides, and fire wrapped around his bare arms, swirling in a riot of oranges and reds as it crept towards the hems of his shirt. With a growl, he spread out his arms and dispelled the magic. His chest heaved, and his entire body trembled. Barrett rested his hand on the other man's shoulder, said something, and Gavin appeared to calm down.

The two of them stood like that for a while until finally Gavin nodded. Barrett patted him on the back, and the two stayed where they were, staring at the small but beautiful garden bed Adrian had created and Maera had spent the morning tending.

I wondered what they were talking about. My paranoid brain worried they were coming up with new ways to kill me now that their other options had failed. The rational part of me, shrinking though it was, guessed that Barrett was trying to help Gavin work through his issues.

After a moment, the men returned inside, leaving the backyard empty and my thoughts ping-ponging between suspicion and reassurance.

The temperature in the room dropped, and a moment later, Emrick stepped out of the afterlife onto the balcony. His silver eyes swam with longing and sorrow, and my cracked heart splintered.

I sucked in a breath at the sharp pain, and my knees trembled.

It was too much. Everywhere I looked, I was surrounded by everything I'd lost. Emrick, Adrian, my magic, my trust in my people. All these facets of my identity that had been smashed or stolen or drained, and if I kept going as I was, I would wither into an empty husk with no chance of coming back.

"I can't stay here," I said.

Concern flickered across Emrick's face. "What do you mean?"

"I just watched Barrett and Gavin talking, and my brain interpreted every gesture as an attack against me. Are they the ones behind it, or were they talking about the cost of property taxes and how Gavin trying to buy a place in Hamilton on a nurse's salary is as likely as Maera buying non-brand-name laundry detergent? I feel uncomfortable every time I leave my room, but I have nowhere else to go. The longer I stay cooped up in this house, the more certain I am that they're all out to get me."

The creases around Emrick's eyes tightened, and he squeezed his hands at his sides. Then he dropped his gaze and rested his palm against the glass.

"I'm sorry, Kat. You don't need doubts on top of everything else."

I bowed my head against the window pane and set my palm against his. It was cold, impersonal, impossible to imagine he was truly touching me, but it was as close as we could get so I forced myself to accept it.

"I miss you."

As soon as I said it, I regretted it. It didn't do to dwell on things we couldn't change.

"We'll get through this, Kat. Just like we've gotten through everything else."

"You're the only person left I can trust, and you can't even—" A bitter laugh escaped me. "I need to get out of here."

"And go where?"

"I don't know. Home? Leave everyone here to continue their research and go back to Spring Bay where I can finally breathe."

The corner of his mouth kicked upwards. "Hide?"

I scowled. "No, not *hide*, Mr. Smart Ass. I don't hide. I

fight. But it helps to know who the hell I'm supposed to be fighting. Right now, I'm stuck looking over my shoulder, not sure if someone in this house is going to stab me in the back—maybe literally—and I'm tired. Exhausted. At least at home, I'll have space to think."

"And be on your own without reinforcements if someone comes for you."

The picture he painted was grim. No matter where I looked, danger loomed. Was this what it was to be mortal, constantly expecting Death around every corner? How did the average life expectancy keep getting longer if that were the case? The stress was already about to knock me over.

I sagged against the window, and Emrick stroked his gloved thumb over my palm through the glass. He opened his mouth, closed it, then settled against me. By all appearances, we were holding each other up, and I appreciated how true that was on a deep, visceral level.

"I've been thinking," he said softly, hesitantly, as though he weren't sure whether he should continue. Finally, he shrugged. "What if the traitor isn't someone here?"

I frowned. "What do you mean? I thought Rhys told you—"

"I know what he said, but you know better than I do there's room for interpretation. According to his vision, it's someone you know and trust, but that doesn't mean it's one of these six."

"These six are pretty much the extent of my list that fit the criteria."

"What if that's not true? I don't know—I've been watching Murisa and Poppy, and I'm not seeing it. Same with all of them. They're grieving with you, Kat. They're busting their asses to find answers. It wouldn't make sense."

I hoped he was right. I hated that, until we discovered the truth, we couldn't be sure.

As the weight of the past few days swept over me, I closed my eyes and drew in a deep breath, inhaling the soft scents of campfire and loam as they wafted off Emrick.

The smell of him was followed closely by the cool touch of mist as it stroked my bare arms and wrapped around my waist. I sank into the sensation, greedy for more. I imagined his hands sliding around my waist so his front pressed against my back, his fingers sliding up to caress my neck, my cheek. Yearning cut through me with its bittersweet kiss.

I was wrong earlier. Being apart from him now was more painful than it had been during the seventy-five years he'd stayed away from me. At least then, the separation had been my choice. This forced divide was more torturous than feeling the tick of every passing second or being without my magic.

If whoever had created that tea had wanted to cause me soul-destroying pain, they had done their job well.

The door to my room flew open, and I jumped at the

sudden chaos. The mists evaporated, the feeling of Emrick's closeness faded, and I stood alone in my room, with him on the other side of the glass.

"Maera, what the hell?" I asked as my housekeeper rushed towards me.

Her green eyes were wild, and she was out of breath. Instinct had me reaching for my hip, but of course my knife wasn't there. Again, Adrian's voice was in my head, chiding me for not taking the proper precautions.

I was somewhat reassured by the sight of Rhys coming in behind her, but even his eyes were shining, and he exuded a sense of excitement that buzzed across my skin from the other side of the room.

Instead of attacking me, Maera grabbed my hands and squeezed them tightly. "I saw her, Katerina. The woman who sold me the tea."

My thoughts fizzled into silence, and my face went slack as I struggled to process the words spilling from her mouth.

"Here? You saw the person from home here?"

"Yes, Kat." She jerked my hands for emphasis. "The person who poisoned you is in Toronto."

29

Katerina

I WAS STILL reeling with the news by the time Maera had gathered everyone in the living room for an urgent meeting.

Ever the efficient woman, she'd rounded up the entire household within three minutes, all without raising her voice to shout down the stairs as I might have done.

Not once did she release my hand until she'd shoved me into my favourite chair, but as soon as she let go, her attention moved to everyone else. I watched them come in, their expressions ranging from curious to irritated at being interrupted to showing nothing whatsoever because Barrett's face was chiseled out of granite.

Emrick stood behind my chair. Of course he'd followed Maera and me downstairs, and I appreciated his steadying presence because I was about to vibrate out of my seat.

Finally, we had a lead on an actual human being behind the attack. Muroppy could do whatever they wanted to figure out the nature of the potion, but there was only so far a counterpotion could help me. Only by tracking down the source would I get to stare into their eyes and watch their life drain out of them.

Or maybe I wouldn't kill them. We'd have to see how I felt in the moment. Right now, I felt pretty fucking homicidal.

"I was at the pharmacy on the corner getting more bandages," Maera said as soon as the witches entered the room. She didn't bother with a preamble, understanding we had no time to lose if we didn't want this trail to go cold. "A woman, mid-thirties, blonde. Bright pink T-shirt, jeans."

"And you're sure it's her?" Emrick asked. When Maera shot him a look, he held up his hands. "You said before you couldn't remember what the person looked like. I don't want Kat to get her hopes up if you have any doubts."

Maera nodded. "I get that. I saw her out of the corner of my eye first, and for a moment—just a moment—I remembered her face. Then I looked at her and wasn't sure, but the moment she saw me, she reacted, and I knew. Everything came back like it had been there the whole time. She likes neon-bright colours, this one. It stands out."

Barrett cursed and grabbed his keys from the bowl on the

counter. "Why didn't you call us instead of coming back here? She's probably gone by now."

Maera huffed. "I tried. I tried calling everyone, but no one answered."

Barrett started towards the door, and I stood to follow him. Immediately, six angry people shouted at me to sit down, each of them explaining why their plan was better than anything I could come up with.

"You're still healing," Maera pleaded, at the same time Barrett stated, "I'm in a better position to defend myself if she attacks," even as Poppy said, "Oh hell no, I want to get my hands on the bitch giving us witches a bad name."

I looked at them as their voices floated over me, hearing nothing but the tick, tick, tick of time passing, giving this woman more of a window to get away. This was the first luck we'd had in days, and I wasn't about to squander it by trying to force the issue.

"Fine." I crossed my arms. "Barrett, Poppy, you two go. I'm going back to my room. Emrick, you go with them—just to play messenger."

Emrick's eyes narrowed, and I sensed his gaze between my shoulder blades as I left them to organize themselves. Without looking back, I went up the stairs and closed the door behind me.

The arguments in the living room changed to a few barked

orders from Barrett. Less than a minute later, the front door slammed shut as Barrett and Poppy left.

I gave it another thirty seconds. When I was sure neither Maera nor Rhys was about to come up to check on me, I went to the balcony, threw my leg over the glass railing, and shinnied down the drainpipe.

Metal and plastic creaked under my weight, but I only needed to brace myself for a few feet until I was close enough to the ground to jump the remaining distance. I landed in the low hedges and sent an apology to Adrian for ruining his greenery before rolling to my feet—checking through the window to ensure no one inside had noticed me and breathing through the stabbing pain that sliced through my chest—and cut across the backyard.

Barrett would have driven to the pharmacy, meaning the main street wasn't an option for me, but I'd lived in this neighbourhood the ten years I'd spent in Toronto. I'd walked every path, every alley, every route until I knew each one with my eyes closed. Down to the smells.

So I knew that if this woman wanted to get as far from the pharmacy as possible without anyone tracking her, she would avoid the main roads and stick to the alleys.

I followed the lane that backed the properties on either side, skirting the cars parked there. Graffiti covered the garage doors and fences, but none of my team was around to spot me or call me out for leaving the safety of home.

Only too late did I think of my knife sitting on my bedside table.

I paused, debated the wisdom of returning for it, but if I wanted to find this woman, I didn't have time to go back. Resigning myself to the danger, I kept my eyes peeled for something to arm myself with and settled for a sturdy piece of broken fencing about the length of my arm and a closed plastic water bottle filled with not-water. Littering was a disgusting habit—especially when it included bodily fluids—but given my circumstances, I gave the litterbug a pass. Neither item was likely to save me, but if they helped me escape a sticky situation, it would be worth having to wash my hands a thousand times once that water bottle spilled.

I followed the lane towards the pharmacy, wondering how long it would take the others to realize I was gone and figure out what I was doing. All I had to do was move faster than they did.

A few blocks before I reached the pharmacy, a flash of bright pink caught my eye, and I upped my pace to get a better view of the source before it hurried away. I had to pass a few more cars, but sure enough, there was a blonde in a pink shirt, and she walked with the speed of someone eager to make tracks. I half-expected her to look over her shoulder to ensure she wasn't being followed, but not once did she look behind her.

Smart woman. Looking back only increased your odds of

tripping and falling on your face. Better to focus on where you were going and stand a chance of getting there.

I took my own advice and broke into a slow jog, swallowing my curses with every step as the jarring motion tugged at my healing wound. But what was a little pain if it meant catching this woman and encouraging her to tell me everything she knew about the group who wanted me dead?

She rounded another corner, and I worried she was going to reach Bloor Street before I could stop her. If she made it that far, there would be too many witnesses for me to tackle her to the ground. Here, at least, the alleys were relatively unpopulated and anyone hanging around would be wise enough to look the other way.

Hopefully, anyway. I was willing to take the risk.

But just as I was about to launch myself at her, practicality bade me hold back. In my current state, what were the odds I would be able to wrangle her to the house? She would overpower me—possibly throw some spell at me—and either kill me or render me unable to follow her.

If I found out where she was going, maybe she would lead me right to this mystery group. Save me from having to question her. Save us from wasting any more time.

Not that I could do much about an entire group on my own, but I was so close to understanding what had happened to me I could taste it.

So, despite my better judgement screaming at me to hit her over the head with my piece of fence and drag her unconscious body inch by inch over the rough terrain to our backyard—or, smarter still, leave and let the others try to catch up with her—I tucked my piece of fence into my leggings at the small of my back and under my shirt and stayed on her tail.

As she struck onto Bloor, I was ready for her to hail a cab, but she hopped onto a streetcar, and I gave it a few seconds before I got on behind her. Another of Rhys's visions coming to pass.

She was easy to spot in her bright shirt. In the middle of summer there were a lot of vibrant colours bobbing around the crowd, but this shade of pink was eye-watering. It left the rest of her washed out, but I doubted many people were looking at her face.

The streetcar wound its way across town, and the longer I stood there, my body swaying with the movement, the more time I had to ask myself what the hell I was doing.

I pulled my phone out of my bra to update Barrett on our quarry only to find an unread text from the man in question waiting for me.

Where the fuck are you?

He had such a way with words. I tapped my thumb against the side of the phone and debated my response. A not small part of me was tempted to leave him on *Read* to mess with him.

Either now or later, I was in for a lecture, and I wasn't in the mood to get an earful on a crowded bus.

The rest of me, the parts clinging to reason, knew it would be smart to have backup available whenever I reached my destination. Wherever Blondie was leading me, I was in no place to deal with her myself.

Being the grown-up hunter I was, I replied with my current location, rough direction, and told him I'd update him as soon as I knew where I was going.

He was going to be so angry.

With my team having realized I was gone, I expected Emrick to show up and repeat Barrett's question with an even greater tone of frustration, but considering how crammed the streetcar was, I hoped he deemed it wiser to stay away.

Twenty minutes later, Blondie moved towards the door. She didn't look over her shoulder, which suggested she was either very innocent or very confident, but it also meant she didn't notice when I fell into step behind her. I waited until just before the doors closed to climb down and kept her in sight as she made her way down the street.

We were back in a residential area, the streets quieter and the houses only slightly less squished together. At a two-storey red-brick house, with an attic loft that stared down on the street, Blondie climbed the stone steps to the metal front gate, hurried up the walkway, and went inside. A wooden porch stretched the width of the house, the garden was well tended, the windows new, the brick clean.

Nothing stood out as unusual or evil, but goosebumps bubbled across my skin as I stood staring up at the place, far enough away that anyone looking through the windows wouldn't spot me but close enough to appreciate that if I wanted to know anything more about the house, I'd have no choice but to go up to the front door and knock.

Which I was not about to do. Did I enjoy making Barrett squirm? Yes. Was I stubborn enough to follow this lead on my own rather than risk losing it? Yes. Was I *that* stupid? Not anymore.

Not without a huge burst of power behind me and the ability to heal from any spell hurled at my head.

I pulled out my phone to put Barrett out of his misery. I texted him the address and a picture of the house, promised him I would wait around the corner until he got here, and offered a bright, "You're welcome!" although for a change I didn't feel smug about ignoring his orders.

I was buzzing too much to feel smug.

Inside this house could be the people who'd ruined my life. I was so close to finding out who they were and why they'd done it.

And if there was a way to reverse it.

My stomach twisted, my palms grew clammy, and I brushed

my hair behind my ear with a shaking hand. Exhaling sharply, I walked towards the corner, ready to uphold my promise to stay out of sight until Barrett arrived, when a young man with brown hair, glasses, and an army-green T-shirt covered in cheese powder stepped in front of me.

"Tony?" I asked. "What the hell are you doing here?"

30

Emrick

I GROUND MY teeth as I pulled myself towards the soul awaiting my attention.

I'd been on my way to the pharmacy when this witch's death had called to me, and I cursed my inability to ignore it. Especially when I didn't want to go to the pharmacy, either. There was nothing I could do to help Barrett and Poppy, and I wasn't needed for communication when the others had cell phones.

Kat had been trying to get rid of me—trying to get rid of everyone—and I'd let her, fully intending to give her a moment before returning to her side to find out what her real plans were.

I hadn't had time to do more than pop in and watch her slip through the back gate before this soul had summoned me, and now I was champing at the bit to return to her. First I'd rush this soul to the river, then I'd give my sorceress a piece of my mind.

The room where the witch had met his end was in an apartment outside Ottawa. The man lay in bed. He'd been older, almost skeletal. Potion vials lay scattered across the desk in the corner, herbs hung from the ceiling, and magical tomes, open and closed, rested on every available shelf. A certificate on the wall congratulated him on fifty years of service in the Hunter's Guild, which explained the heavy feel of grey magic in the air. Not oily enough to be dark, but certainly on the dodgy side.

The spirit hovered in the corner, a pillar of light waiting for me to shepherd it to safety.

It huffed as I stepped into the room, and I got the distinct impression it was judging me. Curious, I drew on a hint of my power to bring him into clearer focus, and I found myself staring at a younger man than the one lying in bed, but with the condescension in his expression that denoted every year of his advanced, magically elongated years.

"This is what all the fuss is about, is it?" he asked. "We spend our lives asking what happens when we shuffle off this mortal coil, and the answer is some romance-novel model come to whisk us away? I'm sure a fair few of your souls love that, don't they?"

He wasn't wrong.

"So tell me, what happens next? You show me the door, I go through it, and…"

"I don't know."

He huffed again. "This entire system needs an overhaul if you ask me." He looked around his room, and his gaze fell on the certificate. Sadness overshadowed his features, and his glowing shoulders slumped. "But what do I know? I spent fifty years herding people around, and what did it get me? A fancy watch and an escort to the door. No one heeded my warnings about what's coming, and now where are we?"

A chill ran down my spine. "What warnings?"

The man shot me a dark look. "What does it matter to you? Whatever's coming affects the living, not the dead. Though I suppose you'll find yourself a bit busier. Death will have to dispatch more of your kind to deal with the overflow."

"What. Warnings?"

It had been months since anyone had talked to me of danger on the horizon, but this man spoke as though he *knew* something. Not just the whispers and growing unease of the other witches I'd escorted, but something certain.

The witch's eyes narrowed, and he watched me closely. He was a quick one, even in death. Most spirits stumbled when they made their transition from living to not, but this man seemed to have crossed the boundary as gracefully as one might step off a curb.

"We had a Seer among the hunters," he said. "Not a very good one, I'll grant you, which was why no one paid her much attention. But I did, because the times she was right were worth it for all the times her visions were vague or inaccurate. And in this, she was too consistent to disregard her."

I clenched my teeth to stop from rushing him along.

"She spoke of war. A war between magicals and mundanes. Something earth-shaking. Millions—*billions*—dead, the magical world in tatters."

The ground trembled beneath my feet. "From what?"

"She didn't know. She told me there was darkness at the heart of it. A shadow that obscured the truth." He drew his shoulders back. "Beside that shadow, however, was a beacon of fire and lightning. The immortal sorceress."

My mouth went dry, my fingers numb. It wasn't possible.

"Alodie is dead," I argued.

His face crinkled in disgust. "Who is Alodie? I speak of Katerina Palon. The self-proclaimed guardian of the balance. All the chaos and destruction about to tear this world apart starts with her, and no one listened to me."

I staggered backwards until my back hit the wall. "It can't be. Kat's lost her magic. Someone is trying to kill her."

The witch's eyes widened, and his disgust morphed into something akin to hope. "Then someone did believe me. Perhaps there's still time to change the course of the universe. Perhaps someone will succeed in getting rid of her before she can destroy everything."

Red flashed in my vision, and before I knew I was moving, my hands wrapped around the witch's suddenly corporeal throat. Terror cut through his eyes, but I had no patience for it.

"You have no idea what you're talking about," I growled. "Kat is the only person who has dedicated her life to standing between peace and chaos. Your precious *guild*, the other hunters, they've done nothing compared to the sacrifices she's made. Be grateful you won't be around to see how the world crumbles if these people succeed in their mission."

With my fingers still tight around his neck, I jerked him through the mists into the afterlife. The second we crossed the barrier, I released my hold on the power I hadn't meant to draw, and the witch transformed once more into a faceless pillar of light. Wordlessly I led him to the river, tempted to leave him in the wasteland to make his own way—or not.

But my debt to Death bade me carry out my obligations, and the journey gave me time to think and accept that the witch wasn't at fault. He was afraid of whatever the Seer had shared with him, and by all accounts, Kat was at the heart of it.

Because again I'd been wrong.

After everything I'd heard, I'd been certain the spirits were speaking of Alodie, the immortal sorceress who wasn't above working with ambitious blood witches or summoning fear demons in her efforts to regain her youth. If anyone was capable of bringing destruction in her wake, it was the woman made of pure evil.

But it was Kat all along. My poor sorceress who'd lost so much and now, according to this witch, stood to lose so much more.

If she weren't the cause of so much worse.

31

Katerina

Tony STARED AT me, his expression as impassive as Barrett's usually was. Did everyone who hated magic suffer this chronic stoicism, or did the chronic stoicism push people to hate magic?

I'd have to ask Barrett which came first.

For now, I was alone with the guy who'd gone out of his way to try to make me feel uncomfortable since we'd met. This was the first time he'd come close to succeeding.

"Are you going to answer my question or keep staring at me like you're trying to unpuzzle my brain? Do I have something in my teeth?" I ran my tongue over them to make sure my breakfast hadn't lingered, but nothing I did earned me a flicker of a reaction.

"I could ask you the same question." His voice was filled with suspicion, and I noticed his hand reaching for something behind his back.

I refrained from doing the same, wanting to keep my fence piece to myself for the time being. The water bottle was a comforting weight in my hand, however. "I followed the blonde who went inside that house. Do you know who she is?"

"She's part of a pretty powerful group." His lip twisted with scorn. "This is one of their headquarters."

A witch, most likely. I looked to the house, wishing I knew how big the coven was. We'd have to plan for a fight, and here I was without my magic.

"Is that why you're here? A scouting mission?" Tony pressed his lips together, and I rolled my eyes. "Fine, keep your witch hunter secrets. I'll wait here and watch you deal with them."

He snorted. "What else would you do? It's not like you have your magic."

I pressed my hand to my chest, careful not to put pressure on my healing wound. "Ouch."

We glared at each other for a beat, then he said, "Fine. We're planning a raid. One that's been a long time coming."

I looked around the empty streets. "More of you are on the way, I hope? Barrett has a lot of faith in you, but unless Blondie's the only person inside, I think you're outmatched."

Tony scowled. "There'll be enough of us. We've worked too

hard on this not to go in fully prepared."

I looked again at the house. The windows were dark, with no sign of movement within. Were they expecting an attack tonight? Were they readying their defences?

"I have reason to believe that woman had something to do with my power being stripped away, so whatever you're planning, I want in."

"Again, I ask—to do what? They'll crush you before you cross the threshold."

I opened my mouth to argue, but dammit, he was right. I might have my trusty fencing and my water bottle of questionable fluid, but they would be useless against a house full of witches. If the hunters were on their way, they'd stand a better chance of success.

I shoved aside my frustration. "Fine, but I want to talk to your leader when they get here. Someone in that house has to know what was in the tea they gave me, and I need to talk to them."

"We'll see what we can do, but I wouldn't get your hopes up, sorceress. Our plan is to go in hot and heavy, and the goal is that, by the end of the night, only the hunters will be left standing."

That didn't bode well for getting me what I needed. I wished Barrett were here. Tony might not be willing to make a deal with me, but maybe he would have listened to someone he respected. I'd have to grab an opportunity for myself. Watch the doors, wait for the witches inside to scatter, and catch one alone while the hunters weren't looking.

"I know what you're thinking, but I wouldn't get too close to anyone in that house." Tony crossed his arms and stared at me from behind his thick lenses. "No one in there is a particular fan of yours."

I raised an eyebrow. "Oh? What do you know about them? Who are they?"

He shrugged. "They're a recent group. A decade or so ago, they broke away from their home groups to form something stronger, and they've been working in the dark ever since. Gaining power, gaining followers. They're over a hundred strong now, and more members are coming in from all over the world every week."

He spoke with a passionate hiss underlying his words, and I wondered how many times the witch hunters had attempted to shut this group down.

"Why didn't you mention them when we were at your house? You've obviously known about them for a while."

He dropped his gaze. "Known about them, sure, but we've never been able to pin them down long enough to get much information for the hunter files."

"They keep getting ahead of you, huh?" Was this the best time to poke the bear, when my defences were low and he was priming for a big attack? Probably not, but I couldn't resist. He was so pokable.

I shifted to stand beside him so we could both look up at the house. He stepped away to widen the distance between us, and I bit my tongue to stop myself from calling him on it.

"What's their aim?" I asked.

He cast me a sidelong glance. "The same as most of these groups. To stake their claim. Get rid of the competition. Deal with the problems riding their ass. The difference between them and other groups is they've proved they have what it takes to do it. And our intel says they're ready to make their move."

"So this is the hunters' last hurrah to get in their way?"

"Something like that."

A tingle of unease skittered down my spine, and I checked the street again. Still no sign of Barrett, and the other hunters had yet to arrive. How long would the two of us be stuck standing here shooting the shit while the people in the house prepared for an assault?

But while we were waiting, I could at least make use of the hunter by my side.

"What else do you know about these people? Who did they split off from?"

"A few different organizations," he said without looking at me. "They obviously have a real rage against you."

Another shiver ran through me, although I didn't know

why. He was right—of course they did. Why else would they have tried to kill me?

"Any thoughts on why that might be?"

"If I had to guess, you've taken down too many of their people. From what we've learned over the years, they've been trying to kill you for longer than you know. Magical creatures, poison—but you keep avoiding them."

I shifted to face him. "You seem to know an awful lot about this group the hunters have no file on."

He didn't break eye contact. "Do you know how frustrating it is to come up with plan after plan only to watch them fail because of one woman's refusal to get out of the fucking way?"

I blinked and stepped away as the significance of what he was saying sank in. "Yeah, I can see how that would be pretty infuriating."

Rhys had told me my betrayer would be someone I knew—someone I *trusted*. I didn't think I trusted Tony, but it turns out you learn something new every day, because this was a real slap in the face.

Tony turned, his hazel eyes bright behind his glasses. "So here we are. Ready to make one last attempt while the enemy is weak so we can finally be free of it. Free to run this show the way we see fit. Free to arrange the world the way it was meant to be without some out-of-date hag standing in the way of progress."

I bristled. *Hag?* Excuse me very much.

But the sting to my pride was overshadowed by the growing appreciation of my predicament. I was standing outside a headquarters filled with people who wanted me dead, my way out blocked by a man who had obviously joined them.

I scanned the street, once more looking for Barrett. "Do the witch hunters know you've turned on them?"

His smile was cold. "The hunters know everything. Who do you think is inside that house?"

The ground wobbled beneath me, and my vision went dark around the edges. He couldn't be serious.

If he was telling the truth, the witch hunters had betrayed everything they stood for. All to what? Come after me?

I looked around again, and this time Tony followed my gaze. "Who are you looking for?" He darted closer and closed his hand around my arm. "You did say you were alone, didn't you?"

The flicker of concern in his eyes gave me hope that I could bluff him into letting me go.

"I didn't say anything of the kind. Whatever you've told me tonight, it's about to get out. And whether I take you down or not, someone will."

I tugged on my arm to free it from his grip, but he didn't budge. The man carried more muscle on him than I would have guessed by his weighty build and penchant for empty calories.

I tightened my grip around the water bottle and wished I held the piece of fence instead.

His sharp gaze bored into mine. "I think you're bullshitting me. If anyone else was here, they would have stepped in long before now. With you as powerless as you are, they wouldn't take the chance I'd win."

He was right, which was more than a little embarrassing. There was no way I could take him by myself. The muscles in my chest screamed at me. Fatigue hugged my joints, making every move sluggish and jerky. I had to get away from him. Stall him if I could. Barrett would be here soon.

Tony leaned in closer. "Which is too bad for you, sorceress, because you just ran out of time."

I caught the glint of murder in his eyes seconds before he swung his knife at me. I twisted the arm caught in his grip to dodge the strike. The blade sliced through my T-shirt. Sacrificing the water bottle, I grabbed hold of my makeshift wooden sword and parried his follow-up attack. His knife came down again, this time aimed at my neck, and I jabbed the tip of the fence into his armpit. The wood sank in deep, and he cried out as his arm went limp. The knife clattered to the ground.

I jerked the fence free, wrestled my arm from his grip, and fell into a fighting stance. He glowered at me, pulled a second knife from his belt, and sprinted forward. I hopped to the side, light on my toes and feeling confident after my recent lessons with Barrett. I was out of practice, but my muscles remembered the moves. Duck, block, dodge, parry. Tony was no slouch with his blade, but he was no Barrett.

Unfortunately, he also wasn't recovering from a stab wound to the chest.

Too soon, my breaths grew heavy and my healing flesh screamed at me to slow down. I couldn't—to slow down would be to die—but I had no way of escaping this fight.

I swung my fence again, this time using it as a bat, and clobbered Tony over the head. He staggered on his feet, hand to his skull, and I threw myself at him to take him to the ground. Once I pinned him, I could hold him.

But when I slammed my body into his, a sharp pain shot through my side. His dazed expression faded into a feral grin as he hiked his knife up and twisted.

"Good night, sorceress."

32

Katerina

LIGHT DANCED IN my eyes as my gut wavered between numbness and burning agony. I stumbled backwards, my hands on the knife, too stunned to evade the backhanded blow Tony delivered across my cheek. I tripped over my feet and hit the ground hard, landing on the knife and driving it deeper into my flesh.

Gritting my teeth and sucking in breaths to ground myself in the pain, I swept out my leg as the hunter came closer. He jumped over my first swipe but missed the second as I shot out with my other leg. He landed on his back with the air bursting from his lungs.

At some point during my fall, I'd dropped my piece of fence, but my trusty water bottle was within reach. I twisted off the lid and gave the plastic a hearty squeeze. Yellow liquid squirted into Tony's face and dripped into his mouth. He rolled onto his side, gagging at the stench and what must have been a putrid flavour. While his back was turned towards me, I dragged myself to my wooden sword, wrapped my trembling fingers around it, and swung it into his shoulder. The jagged tip pierced his flesh, and the wood cracked towards my fingers. He cried out, and I jerked the slat free before he could roll away.

Tony didn't let his urine-obstructed vision or the bleeding holes in his shoulder and armpit slow him down. He hurled himself at me, and I rolled, this time unable to hold back my scream as the knife burrowed deeper into my side.

I had to stay conscious—had to keep moving. Barrett would be here any minute. All I needed to do was keep Tony occupied until he arrived, and then whatever happened happened. If I died too soon, Tony would slip away and no one would ever know the witch hunters were involved.

Latching on to the adrenaline pumping through my veins, I tightened my grip on the fence and swung it again at his head, hitting him so hard the wood burst into flying splinters. Blood ran down the side of his face as he flew off me.

"Why do the hunters want me dead?" I rasped as I propped myself up on my hand.

Tony rolled onto his knees with a groan. The blood from his head mixed with the red stain spreading across his shoulder, and his glasses sat at a broken angle across his nose. Hatred burned bright and unquenched in his eyes.

"You are an evil on this earth, sorceress." Spittle sprayed from between his lips, the title coming out as a curse. "For eight hundred and fifty years, you've spread your corruption and no one has been able to stop you. That kind of power shouldn't be held by anyone, let alone an arrogant, power-hungry bitch."

I couldn't help it. I laughed. Not even the shooting, throbbing, flaring ache in my side was enough to stifle my amusement in the face of Tony's blaring hypocrisy.

"Thanks to you, Alodie walked this earth for sixty years," I hooted, then gasped as another wave of agony swept through me. "That bitch trained Mikhail. She summoned a demon. She went after the people most likely to put her back in the ground. You think *you're* worthy of power?"

"It was for the greater good." He hauled himself to his feet and slammed his foot into my side.

I yelped and curled in on myself. I refused to cry. This bastard didn't deserve it. But fuck, I wanted to. The pain was taking over, consuming me, making my head swim and my fingers tingle.

"Nothing else could take you down. She was a lesser problem. If she'd succeeded in killing you, we would have ended her in a breath. But she failed like everyone else did. The only thing she got right was cooking the vamper who stuck so close to you.

The vampire hunters were thrilled to see him go."

For a flicker—the briefest moment of time—fire flashed through my veins, burning hot enough that if I'd been able to grab hold of it, I would have burned Tony to cinders where he stood.

He *dared*?

Fury choked me. It slid its molten fingers through my blood and fueled my determination to rip this slug limb from limb. Oh, I wasn't dying here tonight. Not until this son of a bitch lay on the ground bleeding in front of me.

But it wouldn't be now. Already, my strength was waning. If I went after him here, I would fail, but I clung to hope that if I kept him talking, Barrett would arrive to finish the job for me. He'd earned that right.

"The vampire hunters and witch hunters are working together?" Every word hurt, every breath was torture, but I pushed beyond it. "That's a pretty big crowd. It's good to know you were so weak on your own you had to pool your resources to come after me."

Tony scowled and drove his foot into my ribs again. The world went black. Digging my fingers into the cracked asphalt beneath me, I dragged myself towards consciousness.

Where the hell was the guy who lived in his basement with his junk food and questionable blanket? This witch hunter soldier bore no resemblance to that person. This guy could eat that guy for breakfast.

Even as the thought came to me, another one chased it. "All those times we went to you for help, you strung us along to get us into the worst possible position. That's why your people never showed up when we went after Mikhail. That field lock-down—all lies. Every step of the way, you set us up to die."

Tony knelt beside me and grabbed me by the hair, tugging so tightly my roots shrieked.

"You've got that right, sorceress. Believe me, we were all rooting for the bad guy if it meant bringing down the worst guy."

I clenched my teeth as the pain in my side melded with the pain in my chest and absorbed the pain on my head. Every inch of me cried for mercy, but all I could do was keep breathing. "Is that really the tagline you're running with?"

I knew I should bite my tongue and not goad this asshole, but he was pushing my buttons.

What I was most grateful for was that Emrick wasn't here. I didn't think I'd have it in me to stop him from grabbing hold of Tony and turning him to compost, consequences be damned. For Adrian's sake, for Gavin's, for the poor woman in the park who'd wanted to read her tarot cards on her lunch break—for all the people who'd been harmed over the past few months when they shouldn't have been involved at all.

"Don't worry," Tony hissed in my ear, "you won't be around to hear many more of my taglines. Your time is at an end, and it's long overdue."

He curled his fingers around the hilt of his knife and twisted, drawing a scream from me. Then he tugged the blade free and set it against my throat.

I met his eye, refusing to be cowed in my final moments. If he wanted to kill me, I would force him to watch it happen. He deserved to know I'd use my last breaths to promise that my death would not be his victory.

The blade had only nicked my skin before a car door slammed nearby.

Tony's hand hitched, and the blade cut a little deeper, but a moment later, he was gone and the back of my head smacked the pavement.

Stars burst in my vision and the world exploded in a flash of light that didn't fade in a hurry, blending instead with a deeper darkness around the corners.

I tried to press my hands against the wound in my gut, but my arms were numb, the muscles too weak to move with any kind of faithfulness. Soon enough, they fell still at my sides.

I sucked in breath after breath and stared up at the sky.

"*Fuck.* Again, Katerina?" Barrett demanded. "What the fuck are you trying to do to me? Emrick's going to fucking kill me."

"Is she okay? Oh goddess, fucking hell. Kitty Kat?"

"You have your kit?"

"Yeah, but fuck me if I have a cure for being gutted in here,

Barrett—what the fuck."

I did my best to focus on Barrett's stoic face as he knelt at my side and pulled my head onto his lap.

"Shit." He gently turned my head. "We have a head wound, too."

"She's conscious at least. You know, aside from the gaping wound in her organs. We'll deal with that first, shall we?"

A porch door slammed somewhere out of sight, and Barrett cursed again. "We'll have to do this on the road."

"If we don't do this now, she won't make it to the car."

The mist around me was growing deeper, and I wondered if Emrick would be waiting for me.

Again.

Then Poppy shoved something in my side that sent lava racing through my veins. I hissed through my teeth. My back arched, causing the heat to spread through my muscles so every shift was torture. Beyond the haze of creeping unconsciousness I heard her apologize.

"That's the best we can do, or none of us are making it out of here." Barrett scooped me into his arms. "Come on, Kat. Stay with us for a few more minutes."

I did my best to keep my eyes open, anchoring myself to the pain that speared me with every step, but before the car door opened, I was out.

33

Emrick

I PACED KAT'S room in the Toronto house as Murisa and Gavin fussed over her.

Maera stood at the end of the bed with clean towels piled in her arms, and I wondered what she intended to do with them. Kat's bedding was ruined, and the mattress likely was, too. We'd have to burn most of her furniture to avoid the police showing up to investigate if we hauled it out to the curb.

For the fifth time, I extended my pacing into the afterlife to see if Kat had somehow crossed the barrier without me noticing, but she was nowhere to be found.

Which should have reassured me she wasn't as close to death this time, but it didn't.

She looked as though she was already gone. Her bloodless

face, the lack of response, the seeming stillness of her chest.

But every once in a while, I caught a flutter of a pulse in her throat and the shallow intake of breath. She was here, hanging on by a thread.

I should have left that witch to wait for me and gone after Kat. If I'd been with her, I could have…

Even as I imagined squeezing her attacker's throat until they were nothing but dust in my fist, I knew I couldn't have done it. Not without risking the last pieces of my soul and leaving Kat alive but alone.

Now she was slipping away from me, but there was hope we could bring her back. Just like last time.

Damn, my sorceress knew how to keep me riding the edge of terror.

I stalked the length of the room again, then stopped to see how Gavin and Murisa were progressing. Gavin's attention was focused on Kat's side as he dabbed the blood away, and Murisa was steadily pouring a potion into the gaping wound.

Once the vial was empty, she set it on the bedside table, reached into her satchel, and pulled another vial free.

"How is she?" The question left me before I could stop it. So far, I'd held my tongue, needing them to concentrate on what they were doing, but now that Murisa had pulled away— now that Gavin's gaze had dropped, as though he couldn't bring himself to look up—I had to know.

"The bleeding's slowed," he said.

I waited for him to say more, but he dabbed again at the wound, his lips pressed tightly together.

"And?"

Murisa drew her arm over her brow. At first I thought she was wiping the sweat away, but when she spoke again, her voice was choked with unshed tears. "It's not enough, Emrick. I don't know what to do. The blade nicked something. We can call someone, try to get her to a hospital, figure out a story to tell them—but I don't know if we have enough time."

Barrett came in off the balcony. "No. The hospital's not an option. Not when we don't know who did this to her. These people have come after her at every turn—the hospital wouldn't be safe. Keep working."

Murisa raised her hands, her bloody gloves dripping. "There's nothing else I can do. I'm not a surgeon. Gavin, do you—"

He shook his head and threw a towel into the corner with the other soiled linens. "This would need an OR and a team. I'm amazed she's lasted this long."

Kat groaned and rolled her head towards me. Her eyelids fluttered open, and I swore her mouth curled into a small smile at the sight of me. I stepped closer, dropped to my knees beside the bed, and, saying to hell with the risk, took her hand in my gloved ones.

"You've lasted this long because you're a fighter, Kat," I told her. "You always have been. Keep fighting a little longer."

The bond burning in my chest grew taut.

Murisa whimpered at Kat's shallow breaths, and she bowed her head onto her arm. Behind me came the sound of drywall smashing as Barrett drove his fist through the wall, and Maera choked on a sob.

I squeezed Kat's hand and waited. Waited for the last threads between us to snap. Waited for the sense that her body had emptied of the light that kept it going. Waited for the sensation of Death coming into the room to take her away from me.

Every moment was torture, a stone fist squeezing my heart and rending it into a fine paste. Beneath the pain came a rage so sharp, so hot, I half-expected steam to rise from my pores.

Gavin stood, looking at Kat with his shoulders hunched and his fists clenched so tightly his knuckles bled white. "I'm going to fucking burn that street to the ground to find who did this." We all looked at him, expressions ranging from agreement to shock. When he met my eye, he said, "I let her down. She wanted me to learn my power so I could stand by her and help. If I had, someone would have been with her today."

Barrett rested his fist on the wall. "She shouldn't have gone alone."

Kat always gave the man hell for not having any emotions, but no one looking at him right now would believe that for a moment. Only at Adrian's death had I seen him so broken.

"Did that blonde do this to her?" Maera asked. Guilt was written in every line on her face, and it cut through me like a cold wind.

Barrett stared at Kat, his expression closing in on itself. "Someone was kneeling over her when we arrived. They ran off when we got out of the car, so I didn't see who it was—but it wasn't the blonde."

Maera released the faintest of sighs, but her regret remained. I understood her guilt—almost agreed with it. She should have known what Kat would do once she learned the woman who'd poisoned her was nearby.

But what else could Maera have done? Kept it from Kat? That would have gone over as well as pouring kerosene on an open fire.

"Do we know what house they came from?" Gavin asked. "Poppy said people tried to chase you before you left."

Barrett nodded. "I know what house."

Gavin's face flushed red. "Then what the fuck are we doing here? Let's go tear them apart."

Barrett hesitated, and in that brief pause, my heart stopped. Did he know the house from tonight—or was it possible he knew because he was involved?

Before I had a chance to accuse him, before Barrett had a chance to speak for himself, Rhys stepped into view. His face was slack, his eyes white.

"A house full of colours. Full of buzzing. Full of screams. You'll get some answers but more questions. Satisfaction. Fear. Revenge."

He stumbled into the door frame as his eyes cleared.

Everyone held their breath, waiting for him to explain, but just as he opened his mouth, Poppy shoved him out of the way and ran into the room. "We did it!"

The silence grew tenser as everyone turned to her.

"It worked, Murisa! We figured it out! We found a way to counter the spell—we can get Kat her magic back."

34

Katerina

I AWOKE TO the taste of rancid meat slipping down the back of my throat.

My gag reflex tried to kick in, but hands pressed my shoulders down, and more of that foul liquid dripped into my mouth.

I refused to drink it. I knew what that stuff did. It would make me itch, leave me vulnerable to Alodie's ritual to drain my blood from my veins and consume my immortality. I squeezed my lips together. I might be weak, but I wouldn't give in.

"Come on, Kat, you have to drink. Stop fighting us on this."

Barrett's voice—serious, hard, coming through gritted teeth.

Memories flashed behind my eyelids. Tony standing outside a red-brick house, telling me the hunters had been coming after me for years. His shoe driving into my ribs. Barrett introducing me to Tony as an old friend. Him admitting the hunters had wanted to recruit him.

Adrian's friend, his thrall, his lover, and now he was trying to kill me. With Alodie's potion no less.

I thrashed against his hold, heard the gasps of other people in the room. Who else had turned on me? Had Poppy sided with Barrett? Gavin? Were they all trying to take me down while I was weak to clear the way for their own ambitions?

Pain cut through me with every movement, but I didn't care. If I was going to die, I would go down fighting. I opened my eyes but couldn't see. Panic and agony left everything too hazy to make out.

Suddenly all hands were off me, and I stilled, struggling to catch my breath.

The bed shifted as a weight settled beside me, and someone caught my fingers. Their touch was rough on my skin. Not a soft, bare hand—leather.

"Kat, please." Emrick. The only voice that could have calmed me. Filled with desperation, as though, like me, he was on the verge of madness. "Let them help you."

I didn't trust the others, but I did trust him. My only constant in this world. The one person I believed had my interests at heart.

Although I was terrified of the unknown, I was exhausted.

So I put my faith in him and sagged against my pillows.

The vial returned to my mouth, and this time I didn't fight as the disgusting drink touched my tongue. It oozed down my throat, and I realized it wasn't the concoction that had killed my family. Vile, but not the same. Alodie was dead, her ritual gone with her.

Thinking only of Emrick, I downed this unknown potion like an obedient child until the last drops were gone.

"It's working," Murisa said. "Her blood is responding better to the healing potion I used earlier. It's not immortality-level, but the bleeding has stopped."

"You hear that, kitty Kat? You're not dying on us today."

The relief in Poppy's voice was so palpable that the first stirring of uncertainty knocked on my distrust.

Emrick squeezed my hand, and slowly, too slowly, my vision cleared, and his face came into focus.

His silver eyes appeared first. They swam with tears, creating a vision of moonlight reflecting off a still lake. I wanted to lose myself in them until this pain went away.

But I didn't have that option because Poppy was on my other side, taking my free hand in hers. Murisa sat beside her, tears streaming down her cheeks, smiling so widely I was concerned her facial muscles might lock.

At the foot of the bed stood Rhys. His arm was around Maera's shoulders, her arms hooked around her son's waist.

Both of them were crying.

Gavin stood in the doorway with his arms crossed, his jaw flexing as he attempted to maintain his composure, but even his eyes were red.

And beside Emrick stood Barrett. No tears on his face, of course, but his eyes burned with relief, and when I met his stare, he nodded his chin in the equivalent of a giant bear hug.

My throat closed as my own tears threatened.

How had I ever doubted these people?

Guilt hit me like a punch to the gut, and it took me a second to realize it wasn't my emotions but my internals healing. Not nearly as quickly as they would have if my bond with Emrick were intact, but faster than my poor, magicless body would have been capable of.

I frowned and held up my hand as a familiar warmth buzzed around my heart. Faint, like the effects of a few drinks on a hot day, but hope sparked deep within me.

"What did you do?" The question came out rough, barely more than a whisper, but Poppy and Murisa exchanged a smile of such pride and excitement that I couldn't prevent my hope from growing brighter.

"It was all Murisa," Poppy said. "She broke down the protein from the magical traces we found and created a counterpotion."

Murisa wiped her face. "I don't know if you'll get all your

magic back, but you should start feeling some."

I reached for it, and although it was sluggish to respond, it was *there*. After so many days of having nothing, the sensation of power running through my veins was sweeter than any pie Maera could make.

"Thank you." I looked between the two witches. "Seriously, you two, thank you. I owe you forever."

Poppy squeezed my hand so tightly I flinched, and her expression was steel. "You owe us nothing, kitty Kat. Nothing. Do you know what you've put us through the past couple of days? Do you know—" She choked on a sob and turned away. Murisa slid her arm around Poppy's waist and pulled her into her lap.

"We've been so worried," Murisa finished for her. "You're..." She trailed off, swallowed hard, and shrugged. "You're the heart of this family, Kat. Without you, I don't know where any of us would be."

I couldn't speak. The expressions on their faces confirmed what Murisa had said, and my guilt over suspecting them twisted my already tangled insides.

When I caught Emrick's eye, he smiled as though he heard every thought, every emotion running through me, and he raised his gloved hand, reaching out to brush my hair behind my ear. Before he made contact, he stopped, pulled his other hand out of mine, and rose from the bed to cross the room.

My heart and soul screamed for him to come back, but I swallowed my cries, understanding why he had to leave. He wanted to comfort me as much as I wanted him to stay, but that lay way certain death for me.

My magic might be returning, but our bond was still *off*. Not broken, but… suppressed. An uncomfortable, clogged feeling in my chest.

The hunters might have failed to kill me—again—but they had succeeded in separating us. A crime I didn't intend to leave unpunished.

At the thought of the hunters, I forced myself to laugh, a short, sharp sound. My confession caught in my throat, but I had to get it out. I wanted my team to know the worst. If they were going to fight by my side, they deserved my honesty.

"I admit, I thought all of you might have had a hand in it." I looked to Rhys. "Your vision did a number on me. Made me think all of you might have decided I'd be better off dead."

He smiled through his tears. "Sorry. I wish I could have been more specific." He frowned. "You don't suspect us now?"

I shook my head. "How can I when we know who's behind this? Behind everything. Your vision was right, though. I never would have suspected the hunters. Despite all my bad opinions of them, it turns out I did trust them to have my back." I looked at Barrett. "You sure know how to pick your friends."

He frowned. "The hunters? What do you mean?"

My brow furrowed to match his. "You were there. You didn't see Tony trying to impale me on the toe of his custom Converse?"

He stilled, and his nostrils flared. "Tony? Are you sure?"

"I got a pretty good look at his face while he filled me in on the wheres and whys of their plans."

Maera cleared her throat. "Why don't you fill *us* in? There's a lot I don't understand."

"I followed Blondie and was waiting for Barrett to join me when Tony showed up. He told me the hunters were on their way and that they were planning a big raid. I thought he meant they were going to attack the house. I thought it was a coven base or something."

I shook my head as it kicked in how badly last night would have gone if Barrett and the others hadn't shown up when they did. "The house is a hunter base. The raid he talked about must have been to finish me off. Maybe it's a good thing I went out there. I can't bear to think how it might have gone down if they'd taken us by surprise here."

The house was hardly defensible, snug as it was in its row of townhouses. These hunters had allowed Alodie to summon Shogaur. They wouldn't have cared about Maera being collateral damage.

By the time I shared the rest of what Tony had said, fatigue was slurring my words and sending my thoughts adrift. There was so much to take in, so much to work through. I needed to stay awake, but all I wanted was to sleep. I pressed my hand to my side where a deep itch had set in as the tissue pulled itself back together. I didn't look forward to seeing what damage had been caused or the kind of scar it would leave.

It would be strange to see new scars marring my skin after nine hundred years waking up to the same ones every day.

But what was life without scars? Maybe it was a good thing mine would start to show again.

"Son of a bitch," Barrett shouted as he drove a fist into my wall. Based on the hole on the other side of the room, it wasn't his first. "That fucker. The *hunters* summoned the demon bound to that sorceress? They're the reason Adrian—"

His throat worked, but he couldn't get the rest of his sentence out. Not that I needed to hear it when I carried the same rage. Everything Tony had said… I'd do Adrian's house the favour of not sharing that part of my night with Barrett. None of the walls would be left standing.

And after this, neither would Tony.

Again, I reached for my magic, and this time I grinned when my fingers warmed. Still not enough juice for any actual flame, but it was coming. When it did, I would invite Tony to a private barbecue.

"We'll get him, Barrett," I said. "For what he did to Adrian, we'll make him pay until he's begging us to end his life."

"Not alone this time." Gavin stepped away from the wall, held up his hand, and summoned a fireball into his palm with remarkable control. I waited for it to flare or shoot sparks, but he held it steady, and the flame reflected the burn in his dark eyes.

A chuckle rumbled in my throat. "Look at that. I'm impressed, Gavin."

"I've been working on it. Our conversation—my conversation later with Barrett—" His gaze jumped to the other man with an expression I recognized. My curiosity awoke, but I quashed it down. This wasn't the time. "It made me realize I was tired of running. You say I'm a natural-born sorcerer? The first one to be seen in centuries? I never would have been born with power if Alodie's demon hadn't been summoned. I think it's about time I thank the hunters for making it possible."

I winced as I tried to shift position. "At least one of us will be able to show them there are consequences for their short-sightedness."

He squeezed his hand shut to extinguish the flame and took another step closer. His intense gaze bored into mine. "No, dammit, it won't just be me. That's bullshit. I've only been in this world a few months, and even I see the good you do here. Someone's taken you out of the game because it makes life easy for them. It's not right, and it doesn't help anyone other than the people who stand to gain from it. Tell me you're not going to sit back and let them win."

A thrill ran through me at his anger, and for a moment, I was Katerina Palon, sorceress and sword, guardian of the magical balance.

I latched on to the feeling, the first time I'd experienced it since waking up powerless. "I'm not. I'm going to keep moving and keep fighting until whoever's leading this cause understands what a mistake they've made."

Barrett grunted his approval. "Then I think it's time we make our plan."

35

Katerina

WHILE I ADMIRED Barrett's get-to-itness and wanted nothing more than to join him and Gavin in their bubble of asskickery, my body had other opinions on the subject.

Within ten minutes of my emotional outburst over everyone swearing loyalty to our family, my eyelids sagged, and it took all my effort to remain coherent and not drift into that in-between stage of consciousness where everything I said was gibberish.

Maera ordered everyone out and shooed Barrett through the doorway after Gavin. Rhys patted my leg and looked so reluctant to leave me that I managed to contort my exhausted face into a wink to reassure him I would be all right. Poppy and Murisa gave my healing wound another quick check before they also disappeared, leaving me alone with Emrick.

He stepped away from the wall, which made me happy enough, but only came as far as the chair in the corner of the room, not even pulling it closer to the side of the bed.

"I can't believe they did it." I was barely able to string my words together, but it needed to be said. Celebrated. We were one step closer to everything going back to normal.

Emrick swept his hand through his hair, and his smile was dazzling. Though maybe my fatigue exaggerated the sparkle of his perfect teeth. His grin faded all too soon into an expression of remorse. "I'm sorry I wasn't with you. I should have been."

"It's a good thing you weren't. You wouldn't have been able to stop yourself from destroying him. Not in the moment."

His silver eyes blazed so brightly everything else in the room faded. "And he would have deserved it. You would have been in the right to stand by and let me deal with him."

"Never," I swore. "I won't lie that in the moment I might have wished it, but I'll never accept you fading away for my sake, Emrick."

It was the last thing I remembered before sleep took me.

The next time I woke up, I was amazed by how good I felt.

Far from top shape, but better than I'd expected to feel given my state when I'd fallen asleep.

I knew I should get out of bed and check myself over, but greater than my curiosity over how badly Tony had beaten the shit out of me was my need to confirm that the results of Muroppy's hard work hadn't been a sweet, taunting dream.

For a full minute, I sat bound, unable to bring myself to draw on my magic, terrified I would discover it hadn't come back.

A low *mrow* from the corner of the room drew my attention to Cuddles. He was reclined on the armchair, his grey fur spread out like a monarch's mantle. Everything about him was regal and confident in spite of the kinked tail, the chunk missing from his ear, the strange angle of his jaw, and the patchiness of his long hair.

Even broken, he knew he owned the room.

I chuckled and shook off my fear. If the undead cat could be so certain of himself, the least I could do was test my new limits.

With a deep breath and a firm finger-wag at my hopes not to get too high, I held my hand out in front of me. "Here goes nothing."

I closed my eyes and searched deep within me for the spark of power I'd taken for granted for so many centuries. At first, I felt nothing, and despite my finger-wag, tears welled in my eyes. Whatever power had been there yesterday, it was gone now. The potion must have offered a temporary reprieve. Still room for hope, maybe, but not the grand return I'd wanted to show the hunters.

My shoulders slumped, and as the muscles in my back sagged, my knife wound yelled at me to stop moving so much. The flash of pain served to pull me out of my sorrow and focus on my wins instead of my losses.

Despite all logic, I was feeling better than I should have for nearly dying—again. I hadn't imagined the sensation of power running through me, and I refused to believe it had been a fluke.

I met Cuddles's eye across the room. "Soon enough, you won't be the only resurrected life in this house, I promise you that."

I summoned my courage and once more sank into my breath.

Seconds passed, minutes. At last, I sucked in a gasp as a zap of magic shot from my chest down my arms and ended in a tiny flame in the centre of my palm.

A cheer slipped through my lips that morphed into a laugh, even as tears spilled down my cheeks. I gently reversed my heat and allowed joy to swim through me as the flame was replaced by a lace of frost that crept over my bare hand and up my forearm towards my elbow.

The effort drained me, and the emptiness of my power sat like a void behind my heart, but I didn't care. It was back. *I* was back.

Riding the high as my sense of worthlessness slid away, I threw back my covers and eased out of bed.

"What do you think you're doing?" Poppy asked as she stepped into my bedroom. After a night of shadows and murky vision, she was a rainbow of vibrancy. The tips of her brown curls were now a deep fuchsia, and her nails were a swirled blend of orange and blue. The combination both clashed and complimented her bright green T-shirt. The only darkness about her came from her washed-out black jeans. Only now, seeing her at her brightest, did I realize that over the past couple of days, she'd worn nothing but neutrals.

At the sight of me attempting to stand, she broke into a run and reached the side of my bed in three steps. She set down the tray of food she'd brought in with her, and I noticed another vial of the putrid potion she'd forced me to drink yesterday.

"You shouldn't be out of bed. You're not nearly strong enough to—huh." She stood back and eyed my naked body. "Well, I didn't expect that."

Another woman might have blushed under her appraising stare, but I didn't get the impression that she was checking out my assets.

Following her gaze down the length of me, I took in the

yellowed bruises on my chest and along my ribs. My thighs were covered in similar yellow-green patches, and even more bruises stretched out from around the bandages.

"Can I take a look?" Poppy asked.

I nodded, and she set to work unwrapping me. When she stepped away, her eyes flew wide, and I angled myself to get a better look at the wound, which didn't look nearly as bad as it should have.

In fact, there was hardly any wound left to notice.

"Son of a bitch," Poppy breathed. "How are you feeling?"

"Sore. Like I got the crap kicked out of me… a few days ago."

The witch shook her head. "People would kill to have your healing ability. Even if it's slower than it used to be, you're still a few weeks ahead of where any of us would be. Come on, let's get you cleaned up. I came in to see if you wanted help taking a shower. Gavin says you shouldn't get your wounds wet, but I don't know if that's a problem anymore."

I considered sending her away to shower by myself, but Poppy seemed eager to help, and I had to admit the strain of getting out of bed after channelling that tiny flame had taken a lot out of me.

"That'd be great."

"I'll start the water and come back to get you. Do not move." She looked to Cuddles. "Make sure she does not move."

"*Mrow.*"

But she didn't need Cuddles to order me around. For a change, I did as she said. It felt strange to follow someone else's lead, but I reminded myself how I'd felt sitting on the porch thinking about all the reasons these people had to turn on me. Poppy could very well have reached out to her old coven to find ways to destroy me. Her reasons would have been solid, if twisted.

But she hadn't. More than that, she'd busted her ass to return a piece of myself I'd believed lost. That deserved enough respect to stay put.

When she came back, she slid her arm around my waist, and together we walked across the bedroom to the en suite. The shower was running, and, by the time I'd relieved myself, steam filled the bathroom. It stroked my skin, teased the hair on my arms, and danced around my fingers as I grabbed hold of the wall and stepped into the tub.

Poppy grabbed the sprayer from its place on the wall. "We'll start with your hair and work our way down. Maera gave you a sponge bath to get most of the blood off when Barrett and I brought you back, but you stink of… pee? I won't ask why."

I let out a harsh chuckle. "Thank the laziness of nighttime revelers for that one." Bitterness coated the back of my throat, and I raised a shaking hand to the healing bump on my forehead. "Fucking Tony. Months of pretending to help us and saying he couldn't, and all this time he was feeding the sons of bitches coming after us. He deserves more than the little magic I've gotten back. The bastard deserves to burn, Poppy. They all do."

Poppy replied with a firm nod. "And he will. Based on the war plans going on downstairs, Barrett's not fucking around."

"What about defences around the house in case they come here?"

"We're on it. Wards, traps, cameras. They won't be able to sneak up on us."

She sprayed down my hair with gentle hands—her orange-blue talons never once scratching me—and although I tried to help her with the shampoo, I quickly realized raising my hands above my head was not a smart move, so I left her to it.

She worked in silence for a while, and I closed my eyes under the warm water, luxuriating in the sweetness of knowing I wasn't dead yet. Twice this week I'd come closer than I had in eight hundred years, but twice my team—my family—had shown our enemies we wouldn't be bossed around.

"You had us really worried, you know," Poppy said after a while, and at the strained emotion in her voice, I made the decision to keep my eyes closed and allow her some privacy. "Murisa said it yesterday, and she's right. Without you, none of us would have a place in this world."

My throat threatened to close, but I pushed through.

"That's not true, Pop. You're all amazing at what you do. You'd have found your way."

"Not like we have." She combed her fingers through my hair as she rinsed out the shampoo. "Do you honestly think I'd be working on potions to help people? Creating defensive knick-knacks and spells that will keep Rhys safe in a fight? Enchanting Barrett's weapons? No, I'd still be summoning corpses, trying to gain more power to show off to my coven. Trying to prove to Mom in all the wrong ways that I'm not her. Or worse, giving in. You met them—you can imagine what I would have become. Thanks to you, I'm not there anymore."

"You also don't have a shop. Or your apartment."

"Spaces, kitty Kat. Just spaces. Besides, what we've been doing for you—the potential of what we *can* do for you—is so much more incredible than selling fake baubles to witches out for their own. I want to make a difference, Kat. I want to help magicals come into their power in ways that will make our slice of the world a bit more positive. Like you do. And Murisa— where would she have been if you hadn't ordered her to come to you? Still cooped up in a crappy little apartment, lying to her parents about how she was using her six-year degree. Her family might be worse than mine. They don't want a witch for a daughter. They don't think it's practical or stable enough employment." She chuckled. "I mean, they're right, but that's not the point. No one could have done what Murisa did with your blood samples. The woman's a genius."

"I won't argue with you," I murmured. My heart was full with what Poppy was saying, but my body was too relaxed to put much effort into speaking.

She turned the sprayer onto my back and slowly made her way across my skin with the sponge, staying conscious of my bruises and being careful to avoid the stab wounds.

"As for Gavin," she continued. "That man would have killed himself. Either by accident or on purpose once he realized he couldn't get rid of his fire magic. I don't know much about what he and Barrett talked about the other day, but I can tell you Gavin left your room looking like a man drowning in uncertainty and despair, went outside with Barrett, and came back in as driven as Indy when he catches wind of some ancient relic."

She turned off the water and hung the sprayer on the wall. I was torn between disappointment that my moment of peace was over and relief that it meant I could crawl back into bed and take a nap.

Poppy handed me a towel, and I set about patting myself dry, careful with all my bangs and scrapes.

When I wrapped the towel around me, Poppy held my hand to help me out of the tub. She caught my eye, and her expression was one of abject seriousness, with not even a hint of her usual sparkle.

"Never do anything like that again, all right? You're mortal,

Kat, and you're vulnerable. You might not want to accept it, but I'm telling you it's not up for discussion. You have a lead? You take someone with you. You're going into a fight? You bring backup. No more going out there on your own."

"No more," I agreed. "It's going to be a tough habit to break, but I promise. You lot will be my first port of call."

I meant it, too. My family had earned whatever trust I had to give.

A knock sounded at the open bathroom door, and we turned to find Barrett standing in the doorway.

He looked me over, and if he was surprised to find me on my feet, he didn't show it. "We're about to put that promise to the test. Are you ready to help me take down Adrian's killers?"

36

Emrick

KAT'S MAGIC WAS back.

While I'd hoped for some miracle, I'd never expected Murisa and Poppy to actually find one, let alone create one. But they'd done it.

Kat's smile when she'd sensed her power had lit up my soul like the first touch of bright sun on a cold winter's morning, and never had I resented this forced divide between us more.

I rubbed my sternum and walked along the black river. The burn was still there. I wouldn't let myself admit that some small part of me had hoped our bond would repair itself along with Kat's power, but the disappointment was a heavy weight in my heart.

Half the world was set to rights, but while the tether

between us remained frayed, life would always be off-kilter.

All because of the hunters.

Anger sparked deep within me, and I stopped along the water to glower into its dark depths. How had I missed it? How was it possible such a large organization had turned its intentions to such evil, and I hadn't noticed?

They'd played their hand well, hiding behind Alodie, Mikhail, Shogaur. Aside from summoning Alodie's demon, they hadn't needed to lift a finger. And they hadn't, as Kat had explained. They'd refused to step in when she'd asked for help and failed to appear when they'd promised they would. The hunters were supposed to protect mundanes *and* magicals. Over the years, they'd put the latter into question, enforcing strict rules that often oppressed law-abiding magicals instead of allowing them to flourish. But not for a moment had I suspected their intentions ran darker than that.

How far had this change spread?

According to Kat, this group of hunters had split off from the rest, but was that true? I prayed it was. If not, Kat's team would be standing against three international organizations looking to crush her. There was no way they'd succeed.

The spark of anger flared into something brighter, creeping through my limbs, tempting me to step out of the afterlife and storm that house. I could reduce every hunter within its walls to piles of dust and ensure their souls never reached the afterlife. I could keep Kat safe—keep the whole damn magical world safe.

Life and death. Magical and mundane. Me and Kat.

Everything was about balance, and these hunters threatened to tip the scales. We couldn't allow it to happen.

I squeezed my hands at my sides, indulging in the mixed heat of my rage and the burn of our fractured bond. They had stolen Kat from me. They deserved whatever I brought to them.

As though a curtain had dropped on the world, the river in front of me dissolved into darkness. The wasteland behind me vanished, and the blips of souls wandering the shore popped out of view. I was surrounded by an impenetrable fog, and my heart stuttered at the sensation of being closed in. Smothered.

Visions of me appearing in the hunters' headquarters and tearing out their souls as I longed to do filled my head. Of me rending their spirits and leaving them bereft of an afterlife. Of me fading... fading... becoming part of the fog that now squeezed around me tight, until I couldn't move—could barely breathe.

In another heartbeat, the pressure on my chest cleared along with the fog, and I was back on the shore with the souls and the still water.

I dropped to my knees, gasping to remove the discomfort that had gripped me, trying to reassure myself I was here and myself. Death's warning had been harsh, but I couldn't begrudge it. I had to release my desire for vengeance. It wasn't my place to punish the living.

But once Kat was finished with them? I would make their souls scream before the mundane herder escorted them to safety.

37

Katerina

IT TOOK ME longer to get dressed than my patience would allow, every wriggle into my black leggings and long, fitted blue T-shirt sending pain through every corner of my body. But by the time I made it down to the kitchen, I wasn't as exhausted as I thought I'd be. My legs felt looser, my back not as stiff. It was amazing what a hot shower and a bit of magic could do.

The water's restorative effects were bolstered by the expression on Barrett's face when I sat down across from him. War was written in every line of his mouth and around his eyes, and the sight stirred my blood.

Gavin sat beside him, arms crossed and legs stretched out under the table so he slouched in his chair. Rhys sat at the head of the table swirling the ice in his glass of cola.

Murisa sat at the other end, and she reached for Poppy's hand as the necromancer pulled out the chair beside mine.

Emrick stood against the wall as far as possible from everyone else. His hands were stuffed in his pockets, and a lock of blond hair had fallen over his silver eyes, which were fixed on me. His expression gave me pause. He looked as though he were confused by something, but when he caught me staring, the furrow on his brow smoothed out and he flashed me a wink.

My heart fluttered at that wink, desire and longing tightening my insides and making me wish we were alone. And properly bonded.

I forced my attention back to Barrett. "What's the plan?"

"We storm the house," he said without hesitation.

Maera frowned as she bustled about the kitchen. The kettle was boiling, the coffee was percolating, and something delicious-smelling bubbled on the stove. Every sign pointed to my housekeeper being stressed out of her mind, but she didn't say anything.

Nope, not a single word passed through her lips.

She simply threw a spoon into the dishwasher and slammed the door closed, dumped a pan into the sink, and sprayed the water with such ferocity a few droplets backfired and reached us at the table. Cuddles hissed at the attack and darted under the table with a low grumble of discontent.

I smiled at her back. "Care to share?"

She grumbled a few words under her breath, and I looked to Barrett, who said, "Maera has some issues with my plan. She doesn't think we should take the fight to them."

My housekeeper broke her silence. "That's not what I said. I said I hate that there has to be more violence when so many lives have already been lost. I hate that everything about the magical world—even between mundanes within this world— has to turn to bloodshed."

My smile faded. "If I had a choice, I would walk away and let them chase their tails until they ran out of steam. But their actions hurt my family. Stole people from me. Threatened the lives of millions. Forget resetting the balance for a moment—if someone doesn't stop them, they won't stop. And right now, the only someones ready and willing to act are us."

Maera finally turned around. "They'll stop if you're dead."

The room fell silent. Emrick pushed away from the wall, and although his hands stayed in his pockets, his shoulders hunched as he readied himself to step between us.

I blinked at Maera, and she blinked back. Her mouth fell open, and as though she heard the words that had come out of her mouth, she rushed to say, "I'm talking about faking your death."

The tension in the room seeped out on multiple inaudible sighs, and Maera crossed her arms. "Tony probably thinks your last encounter did you in. He's not wrong. That was way too close. Why not let them believe they succeeded? Why not disappear for a few years? Or retire? Even with your magic, you're in no position to go up against the monsters you have in the past. Let the hunters believe they've won. They'll go back to hunting the real threats, and no one here gets more blood on their hands."

I couldn't deny her suggestion tempted me.

I was exhausted.

Even with my magic trickling back, these past few days had proved that, although my body didn't show it, I was getting old. Getting stabbed had never been the best time, but I'd endured it because I knew within a few hours I'd be as good as new. With my healing ability slowed, even if I was back on my feet faster with power in my blood, the idea of hunting down threats and standing between them and a world that neither knew nor appreciated my mediation sounded like a world of pain.

Did I want to suffer through it for the rest of my now-normal lifespan, or did I want to follow in Adrian's footsteps and spend my final days enjoying my life? Disappearing, as Maera suggested. No longer being *Kat Palon*, but simply Kat. A twenty-four-year-old woman with enough money to travel and experience the simple joys, helping my friends, staying under the radar, and letting the world carry on without me.

My ego fought against the idea, but since when had it been a good idea to let pride take the reins? That was how I'd wound up facing giants by myself and getting pulverized by flying boulders when I'd refused to wait for Adrian to accompany me.

On the other hand.

I looked around the room at the people staring at me, waiting for me to speak. Where would they be if I left? Would they pack up and come with me? We'd be our own little band of miscreants travelling the world doing a whole lot of not much.

What had Adrian always called it? Spending time by spending time. It had been his worst nightmare, even though, by all appearances, he'd embraced the change.

If he hadn't died in that fight against Alodie, how long could he have remained in that sort of stasis before being pushed by boredom to reenter the world?

With most of us in this room being in our twenties, we had at least another sixty to eighty years ahead of us. I didn't see any one of my team being satisfied spending those years hiding.

If we did, we'd have to ignore every magical threat. We'd have to turn the other way as the balance between magical and mundane shifted and no one else stepped in to right it.

Because the hunters wouldn't do it. Without me standing in the way, the transformation of the organization from protector to oppressor would continue—unless this group of Tony's grew large enough to replace the original and they kicked off a full-on war.

In this room was enough power, smarts, and muscle that

we'd be doing the world a disservice by staying out of the fight. Even if the others wanted to step aside, my conscience wouldn't let me sit on the bench while others did the work for me. Not until I was no longer capable of doing it myself.

When I met Barrett's eye and saw the fire burning deep in his dark gaze, I knew I wasn't the only one at the table with the same answer in my heart.

"No." I looked up in time to watch Maera's shoulders sag. "I'm sorry to disappoint you, but I can't do that. Because of these people, Adrian is dead. Because of them, Rhys was possessed by a demon who nearly turned the entire province against innocent people. I can't let those crimes go unanswered. They claim to stand for justice and balance, but their idea of both is to bring magicals to heel."

Maera held my gaze for a moment, and her eyes softened. "I'm not disappointed, Kat. I may not be happy, but I knew what your answer would be. I hoped it would be different, but I didn't expect it. You are who you are, magic and immortality or no. Knowing that, I brought these from home before we left." She crossed the room to the cupboard above the stove. When she returned, she carried a familiar wooden box, long and narrow. My throat tightened as she opened it to reveal my gloves. "I just hope you know what you're in for. These hunters are not meek. They won't go down without a fight."

"They won't," Barrett agreed. "They'll see us coming, and

they'll be ready."

I looked around the table. "Then we'll have to find a way to surprise them. They have their fancy kit, but we have something they won't expect."

Murisa arched an eyebrow. "And what's that?"

I looked at Rhys, and his eyes widened. "I told you once you would be our secret weapon, and I hold to that."

He shifted uncomfortably in his seat and ran his fingers through his hair. "You know I'm not back yet. I don't want to—"

"You had a vision," Gavin interrupted. "Before we brought Kat back, you Saw something about the house."

Rhys flushed bright red under everyone's stares, but I couldn't protect him. Not when we needed to use every resource we had.

He cleared his throat. "It wasn't too clear. Starts and stops, mostly. But there's definitely a fight in the house. It's an enclosed space, so you struggled. You were all there. I saw potions flying. Not much else."

"What about the hunters? What did you See of them?" I asked.

Rhys closed his eyes, and his brow furrowed. "That's the weird thing. I can't See much of anything. In what I remember, it's like the house is empty except for you. I'd almost say it wasn't worth going, except I See you talking to someone, Kat.

You'll get answers if you do, but they won't be the answers you want."

I rested my hand on his shoulder and squeezed. "See? This is why we need you." I turned to Muroppy. "How were the enchantments going before my life crisis so rudely interrupted you?"

The witches exchanged a glance, and Murisa's eyes twinkled. "Well enough. We have a few things to share."

Barrett frowned. "If this group is as strong in numbers as Tony said, they won't run. Not while they think you're weak. So if Rhys says the house will be empty, we need to prepare for traps."

"We need to prepare for everything," I agreed. "We'll load up on potions and enchantments."

"Will that be enough?" Gavin asked.

Rhys looked around. "What else do we have?"

Even as he asked the question, a familiar tingle coiled around my heart and ran down my arms. Faint but growing more intense. A trickle that became a deluge until the tidal wave settled into its steady ebb and flow.

I grinned and held up my hand. With a surge of power, flames wound around my fingers and formed a fireball as large as my head. "A very pissed-off sorceress who just got her magic back."

38

Katerina

THE REST OF the planning was short and sweet. Every now and again, I had Rhys try for another vision, and although he succeeded twice, he Saw nothing except a dark house. I tried not to let the lack of details worry me.

A few hours later, under a dusky sky not yet fully populated by stars, we stood on the street outside the hunters' base. I was back in my hunting uniform of black T-shirt, leather pants, runed gloves and felt more like myself than I had all week.

Poppy and Murisa stood on my left, armed to the teeth with spells and potions that would keep them safe and, hopefully, put us on strong footing as we entered the house.

Barrett and Gavin were on my right. Gavin's hands were clenched at his sides, and I caught the faint glow pouring through his fingers. The sight made me look around at the other houses, taking note of the windows, searching for any nosy neighbours peering through. Although a few houses were bright with life—the flicker of televisions, shadows moving beyond curtains closed for the night—nothing stood out. We'd need to limit our magic to inside the house, but so be it. I'd fought under worse conditions.

Barrett rested one hand on the enchanted semi-automatic at his hip, modified to eliminate noise and never miss its mark. On his other hip, he carried a four-inch blade in a sheath Murisa had lined with an enchanted compound. The compound would coat the blade when he unsheathed it, letting every stab cauterize on strike. Perfect if we wanted to inflict pain but keep someone alive. For questioning.

And maybe a bit for fun.

While Rhys had wanted to join us in case he had another vision, the rest of the team had vetoed his request.

"If the house is empty, what does it matter?" had been his argument, but Barrett had managed to talk him out of it. While the house might be empty, we didn't know what awaited us.

Emrick had also made himself scarce, which was both a relief and a surprise. After my last two forays out of the house this week, I'd expected him to want to stay close by my side to ensure the third attack wasn't the charm, but at least I wouldn't have to fight to keep him off the people who'd come between us.

I turned my attention to the house. Like last night, the windows were dark. No cars were parked out front, no one peered out from behind the curtains.

I didn't trust the silence.

Readying myself, I patted the satchel at my side, which was filled with potion vials in case my magic gave out on me, and the knife at my hip. My blade was the opposite of Barrett's. The coating that lined the sheath had been compounded with a magical anti-coagulant. A small nick would be enough to bleed someone out if they didn't get it treated quickly enough.

Aside from the enchanted weapons, Murisa had also armed us with a collection of enchanted mechanicals. Some were like the beetles we'd used against Alodie, containing potions Murisa could pour onto the unsuspecting from above. Others would be our spies, checking rooms so we didn't have to. If anyone lurked in the shadows, we'd know it before they attacked.

I drew in a deep breath and let it out slowly. "You ready?"

"More than," Barrett said.

Poppy and Murisa nodded, and I allowed Barrett to take the lead. I was supposed to be recovering from a beating, after all. We didn't want to give away my surprise return too early.

In fact, I barely felt my injuries. I'd taken another nap after our session at the war table and devoured a plate of Maera's roast beef, and I felt ready to kick down the door and unleash hell. Only the occasional twinge in my side and tenderness of my bruises reminded me that a day ago I'd straddled the afterlife.

Oh yeah, Tony and Blondie were about to regret many of their life decisions.

Barrett opened the gate into the front yard, and Poppy and Murisa followed. Murisa's wheelchair hovered up the two steps to the small courtyard thanks to her enchantments, and I wondered if she'd added any other secrets to the chair's mechanics. Knowing her, fireworks would burst out from the wheels. Though, considering Murisa's surprisingly darker side, flamethrowers weren't out of the question.

Gavin and I brought up the rear. I watched the windows and did my best to anticipate what we might find inside. If Rhys's vision was correct, I wouldn't find out anything definitive tonight, but I wasn't about to let my guard down.

Having learned from Poppy's shop, Barrett checked the door handle for any potions or caustic powders before he opened it, and then, gun at the ready, he stepped into the house. Gavin stayed close behind him, shifting to put his back to Barrett's as they moved out of the doorway. The moment Gavin was beyond the neighbours' view, he summoned his fire, and the flames licked over his hands and up his arms until he looked more demon than human. We needed to figure out how to make the poor man some gloves like mine.

The house remained quiet, and Poppy and Murisa went in

next.

With every moment that passed, my adrenaline surged. I was braced for our plan to blow up in our faces—possibly literally. I clung to Rhys's vision, believing he would have Seen something as massive as an explosion, but I couldn't shake the feeling that the trap was about to snap shut.

My instincts were sound. The moment the witches were far enough inside, a shout cut through the night. I ran in just in time to see Murisa reach into her satchel and pull out what looked curiously like a small toaster. It spread a pair of fine mesh wings and launched itself into the air, disappearing into the shadows before I could figure out what it did.

Three hunters stood on the stairs above us, guns in hand. I threw myself to the side before a bullet lodged in the door frame where I'd been standing. The sounds of gunfire had been dampened, but I thought of all those houses outside, all those neighbours. How much would it take for them to call the cops on us?

Then again, what would the cops do? No doubt the ones who responded would all be hunters, and they'd focus more on securing the neighbourhood than putting down the fight.

But our enemies' guns were soon useless as Gavin threw a fireball in their direction, catching one of the three directly in the chest. The other two dropped their now scalding-hot weapons and barrelled down the stairs away from the blast. I expected them to throw potions, but instead they drew knives, no magic to be found among them.

Poppy charged forward, brandishing a few vials of her own, but halfway across the room, she triggered something in the floor, and a silver net closed around her, binding her in fine wire.

She screamed as the mesh tore into her skin, and red flickered in my vision. I reached into my satchel, pulled out a vial and threw it at the two hunters moving towards Murisa. The glass smashed at their feet, and a green-tinged potion splashed over their pants, eating through the fabric and burning into their skin.

Their hisses turned to shrieks of pain, and one of them dropped to their knees. As they did, Murisa wheeled towards them. A bright flash blinded me to the room, and when it cleared, I found her as trapped as Poppy, the wheels of her chair caught in something slick that had spilled across the floor.

They were caging us, and I could guess why. Once we were all caught, it would be easy for them to mow us down or set the house on fire. They could get rid of us without any extra effort. They believed it would be that easy.

Murisa dumped the rest of her gadgets out of her satchel, and they rose in a swarm. Half of them darted into the hunters' faces, and the screams that filled the house would haunt my nightmares for years to come. The rest of the mechanicals burrowed into the floorboards and the cracks in the walls. As soon as the hunters' corpses collapsed, their faces red and swollen from dozens of tiny potion-filled stings, the other half of the swarm joined the first. Within two minutes, the mechanicals were out of sight.

The fire on the stairs spread upwards, and more hunters sped down, leaping over the flames so they wouldn't be trapped on the second storey once their only escape was blocked. Barrett was ready with his gun, firing off shots as two, then five hunters came into view. Gavin followed up his attack with another.

They pursued the hunters out of the foyer and into the dining room.

I made to join them when a floorboard creaked behind me. I turned and found Blondie standing in the doorway of the kitchen with a gun aimed at my head. Her sneak attack had failed, giving me the second I needed to leap out of the way before a bullet tore a hole the size of my fist in the drywall.

I followed up with a tiny fireball—a baby compared to what I usually worked with, but I didn't want to drain my uncertain reserves before we'd even started. The flame struck her in the chest, and she threw herself into the kitchen as the fire spread across her yellow T-shirt.

Barrett came out of the dining room, blood smeared across his bare arms but otherwise unhurt.

"Everyone's dealt with?" I asked, keeping my hands raised

and my magic at the ready. That had been a small force, barely a nuisance, and I refused to believe we were finished.

"Could someone get me out of here?" Poppy called. Blood dripped through the mesh where the wire had sliced into her skin. Barrett pulled another knife from a sheath at his hip. He flipped the back open to reveal a pair of wire cutters, then set to work cutting through the bottom of the net.

Gavin returned to the foyer, his eyes narrowed, his fire quenched. "I don't like this. I know we expected the trap, but I expected a *trap*, you know? That was…"

I agreed with him. That had been a prelude. But for what?

I approached the kitchen where Blondie had disappeared. The room was empty, and the back door was open. The coward hadn't bothered to fight beyond her initial volley.

While Gavin set to work carefully heating the sludge around Murisa's chair so she could get her wheels free, she flipped through an app on her phone. Her brow contorted in confusion. "According to my spies, the house is clear. There's no one else here."

Rhys had said there would be answers, but if that was true, we wouldn't find them standing in the living room. And now the upper storeys were out of the equation. Oops.

What upset me most was that Blondie had seen me use my magic, so we'd lost that element of surprise as well.

I heaved a sigh. "Let's get out of here before we're burned

out. We might have missed our shot, but we can regroup." I looked to Barrett. "Think Tony's at home? We could always pay him a personal visit."

He scowled. "He's probably expecting us to do exactly that, and probably with nastier traps."

I knew he was right, but I hated that I'd have to wait to watch that asshole breathe his last.

Frustrated and unsatisfied, I led the way down the hall and jerked open the front door. I wanted to hit something. Set something on fire. These bastards had stolen so much from me, and they deserved my wrath.

"You just won't stay down, will you?"

The voice that greeted me as I stepped outside ignited the fury that had bloomed the moment I'd discovered the hunters' treachery.

Tony stood on the street, with a pissed-off-looking Blondie on his right and another guy I didn't know on his left. Four more hunters were positioned behind them. The three in front stood with their guns raised, all trained on me.

"That stops tonight, sorceress," Tony said.

I had no time to speak or move before the three fired and pain exploded in my chest, my gut, my knee. I crumpled to the ground.

Screams sounded beside me, followed by a soft popping noise as Barrett fired off a shot of his own. It hit the unknown guy in the middle of his forehead, and he dropped without a sound.

Blondie shrieked and fell at the guy's side, her wails piercing the night.

Tony didn't bat an eyelash as he stepped forward. Barrett made to intercept him, but the four other hunters raised their weapons, holding my friends firmly in place.

I sucked in air through what I suspected was a hole in my goddamn lung and pressed my hands against the bleeding wound in my gut. Blood trickled down the corner of my mouth, and I blinked through the haziness that once again clouded my vision.

Beyond the four hunters, I spotted the swirl of mist as Emrick arrived, but he remained in the shadows. Waiting to see what became of me? To see if the hunters had finally won?

"We expected your team to show up looking for revenge, but you... You're a surprise." Tony tilted his head and stared down at me with a smugness I wanted to punch off his face. "I could have sworn I'd beaten you into submission."

A laugh burst out of me, sounding oddly like a metallic clink against stone.

"You're like a child wearing his dad's clothes, aren't you?" I wheezed. "But you can't even take care of his clothes—you get junk food all over them. You're standing here thinking you've won, but you haven't come close. We're only getting started."

I might have been out of the game, but the others weren't. And Maera and Rhys knew where we were and who the enemy was. Regardless of what happened tonight, this fight wouldn't end here.

My stomach itched, and I rubbed at the wound, hissing through my teeth at the burn. Across the street, Emrick stepped forward, his silver gaze fixed on me with an intensity I couldn't interpret, his hand pressed to his heart. Did he feel the pull on the remains of our tether as my life dripped out of me?

"Shut the fuck up." Tony raised his weapon again. "One more word, and I'll put a bullet right through your brain."

I met his eye. "Do it, then. What's holding you back? Afraid the second you do, that half-spirit over there will dash across the street and turn you to dust before you can take your next breath?"

Tony's hand trembled, and although I watched him try not to look behind him, his curiosity won over his show of confidence. In the glow of the streetlight, I watched his face pale.

"Do it, Tony," Blondie screeched. "Shoot her in the fucking head like they shot Mark. What the fuck are you waiting for?"

I laughed again. "If you're waiting for me to submit, we'll be here for a long time. I don't bow to anyone."

To prove my point, I dragged my shaking leg beneath me and fought to rise to my feet.

The gun in Tony's hand trembled. "Stop it. Stay down."

"What are you afraid of?" Poppy's voice shook with rage. "You've already put three bullets in her. You don't think that was enough?"

I found it funny she'd said that, because at this very moment, I felt more than ready to throw myself at Tony and smash his head into the ground. I felt strong enough to summon my magic and lob a fireball at the four bastards standing ready with their guns.

Out on a public street, I wouldn't do it even if I had the strength—I refused to become the very threat I guarded this world against by exposing magic to the mundane—but the desire was strong.

I waited for my injured leg to give out under my weight as I rose to my full height, but although the gaping hole below my kneecap pinched and pulled, it held steady.

And now that the initial shock of the bullet wounds had passed, my breathing wasn't nearly as laboured.

It was almost like...

Another sound of metal hitting asphalt caught my attention, followed by a third. I looked down to find the remains of three bullets lying in the street.

"What the fuck..." one of the four murmured.

I followed the hunter's gaze to my chest in time to watch my wound close, leaving only a thick, red scar in its place that soon paled.

My breath caught in my throat, and I looked up to meet Emrick's eye again. He stood frozen in the streetlight, and now the hand on his chest made perfect sense.

My hand rose to mirror his, and I swallowed hard to work some moisture into my suddenly dry mouth.

The hollowness in my chest that had started the moment I'd lost my magic was gone, and in its place was a gentle pulsing, soothing and familiar.

My shock transformed into a wild giddiness as I turned my attention back to the six witch hunters in front of me.

"You should have taken your shot while you had the chance," I said to Tony.

His eyes widened. "Oh shit."

39

Katerina

I RAN AT Tony. More gunshots rang out from the other hunters, but I ignored them as I grabbed Tony's T-shirt and threw him to the ground.

Over my head, a blue potion bottle flew and struck one of the four hunters in the chest. The reek of smoke and burning fabric filled my nose, and the guy dropped to the ground, screaming as though his insides were being torn through his outsides.

A second man dropped as Barrett squeezed off another shot.

In another moment, the street descended into chaos. Between Murisa's mechanicals and Poppy's potions, the air was filled with projectiles. Barrett stood with his weapon raised, holding off on taking everyone down until we got the information we needed, while Gavin stayed close by his side, ready with his knife if anyone got too close.

I left them to deal with the other hunters, rolled Tony onto his stomach, and pressed my knee into the middle of his back. "What do you think, Tony? Do you want to go the way Adrian did? The way Shogaur's victims did? The way Alodie did? I'll tell you now, that route involves a lot of fire, but it's up to you."

"You wouldn't," he spat, showing remarkable bravery for someone trapped under a sorceress with both the desire and the power to roast him one limb at a time. "You have your *balance* to uphold. Fucking hypocrite. If you don't see how you throw off that balance, you're clueless."

I curled my fingers through his thick hair and yanked his head back so I could whisper in his ear. "If you think I haven't weighed every angle of my immortality, you're the clueless one. You've had, what? Twenty-eight years on this earth to decide you have all the answers?"

"And because you have more than that, you think you know everything?"

"Because I have more than that, I accept I know nothing. We're all winging it, hunter. The only difference between you and me is that I consider the long-lasting effects of my decisions, not how they'll affect my ego or my reputation."

He barked a laugh. "That's a joke, sorceress. Your ego is so big, you can't see past it. You think everything is about you."

He didn't have time to explain before Muroppy shouted a warning. I looked up to see Blondie swinging a fallen branch at my head.

Stars burst in my vision as I flew off Tony, and Blondie swung the branch down again. "Stop talking!" she screeched. "I don't want to hear your stupid voice anymore. Mark is dead, you bitch!"

I rolled out of the way of the second blow, and the branch struck Tony on the back of the head as he tried to climb to his feet. He sprawled forward on his face, and I jumped up to grab the branch out of Blondie's hands.

She jerked it away from me, hauling me with her, and by chance, I missed a bullet that came from one of the remaining hunters, who now had no idea what to do with themselves.

"Get rid of her!" Tony shouted.

At his battle cry, the hurricane of chaos closed in around us. Murisa unleashed more of her enchanted mechanicals, and they swarmed the two hunters. They tried shooting but soon ran out of bullets, leaving them to run around swatting at the air, screaming as the bites grew more intense.

"Keep them alive!" I ordered. One of these bastards had the answers we needed about whoever had made the tea. I wasn't about to let our chance to wipe out this hunter problem die with them.

Poppy held a vial at the ready but hesitated to throw it at

Blondie, not wanting to catch me in the crossfire.

Tony gained his feet, staggering for balance after the clock to the head. Barrett strode towards him, and Tony pulled his gun. "You chose the wrong side, Barrett."

Barrett ignored the weapon and threw himself at him. Tony fired, but the shot went wide as the two crashed to the ground.

In my distraction, Blondie almost succeeded in snagging the branch away from me, but Gavin rushed to my side to claim it first. Tears streamed down her cheeks, taking her thick eyeliner with it. The poor creature looked so pathetic I almost wanted to let her go to grieve over her dead friend.

Until the bitch pulled a knife out of her pocket and drove it into my forearm.

I snatched my arm away, taking the knife with it. Gavin shoved her to the ground, and her eyes widened at the flames licking over the backs of his fingers.

She scrambled backwards to her buddy's corpse and pulled Mark's gun out of his holster. With trembling hands, she aimed it at Gavin, and even as Gavin raised his hands, ready to defend himself, I jerked the blade out of my arm and threw it.

Blondie froze, then looked down to find the hilt embedded in her chest. A gurgle escaped her before she collapsed over Mark's body.

Eat it, Romeo and Juliet.

Gavin heaved out a breath. "Thanks."

I winked at him. "No problem. Can't have you showing off to the neighbourhood, now can we?" It'd be enough of a problem explaining all the screams and pops to the police who were undoubtedly on their way.

He squeezed his fists tight to extinguish the fire.

A cry cut through the night as Barrett landed another punch in Tony's gut. Unfortunately, Tony was too slippery. He managed to escape Barrett's hold and scrambled to get away, but Barrett tackled his legs and brought him back down.

I sucked in a breath to get my bearings, and as I scanned the street to assess our situation, I found Gavin staring at me.

"How is this possible? I saw you get shot. You should be dead."

My smile widened. I felt lighter than I had in weeks. Maybe even in years. "You know the saying about gift horses, Gavin? Well, I'm not looking this one in the mouth."

At Murisa's cry, I whipped around to find one of the hunters had escaped the mechanical swarm. He'd grabbed two and hurled them at her, and their stingers had sliced across her brow. Poppy reached for her satchel, murder in her eyes, and I stepped in before she could throw a vial.

Seeking the stillness in the air, I grabbed hold of the static and channelled it into my fingers. Sparks jumped across my curled palm, and I rested my hand on the hunter's chest.

"I strongly suggest you hold still, my friend."

He craned his neck towards me, bared his teeth, and spat in my face. "Eat shit, sorceress."

Original.

He reached for something at his hip, but I didn't give him a chance to piss me off further. I released my magic, and his body jerked once before he collapsed to the ground, his heart still.

I looked up to find Emrick standing on the outskirts, watching everything but never stepping in. Gratitude filled me. Soon enough, I was sure, he'd start clearing the bodies before the massacre could be discovered, but for now he kept his distance.

I turned my attention to the final hunter. Murisa recalled her mechanicals, and they returned to her waiting satchel, leaving the man wobbling on his feet, dazed and more than a little confused. His gaze landed on where Tony and Barrett wrestled on the ground.

He started towards them, but I stepped into his path and wrapped my fingers around his throat, summoning just enough fire for him to know it was there.

"I think we should leave them to their dance. You and I can chat instead."

The hunter froze under my touch, his hand halfway to his knife, and I clucked my tongue at him until he relaxed his arm.

"Who created the tea?" I asked.

He glared at me and pressed his lips together.

I increased the heat in my fingertips by a few degrees. "The tea."

A hiss escaped him, along with his stubbornness. "Her name is Sarah."

"What was in it?"

"I don't know." I increased the temperature again, and panic dripped into his eyes. "I swear I don't know. She's a scientist. She was doing experiments on some kind of compound. The general ordered her to do it. That's all I know."

The general? A witch hunter general? This little group of theirs had climbed higher than Tony had let on.

Impatience held me bound. This guy had to know more than he was saying, but if I unleashed any more of my fire, he wouldn't be around to tell me anything.

Cold air wrapped around me, cooling my blood with the comfort of Emrick's proximity. The hunter squirmed in my grip as he took in the man who would have seemed to appear out of nowhere. Emrick wouldn't touch him, but he didn't know that.

"Tell me about this compound," I said calmly.

"She—she got the recipe from that woman. That sorceress. Abigail. She said it would protect us. That it was the only thing that might. Please let me go. I swear, that's all I know."

The stink of urine tickled my nose, and I curled my lip in disgust. This man had come out here to put me and my team in our graves, and now he was afraid to die?

"That's what's wrong with you hunters." I drew my fire back

in but tightened my fingers around his neck. "You're all talk, but when it comes to laying your life down for what you believe in, you don't have it in you."

His eyes hardened, and I smiled at him. I had to give him credit—he knew how to hide his terror.

Emrick vanished from my side, leaving me to finish up, and I debated my options. I couldn't let this guy go running back to his general or the scientist with her anti-Kat compound, but I wasn't about to torture him any more than I had. I released my magic and grabbed my knife. Before he noticed it, I drove it into his heart. He gaped at me but was dead by the time he hit the ground.

Leaving only Tony.

Barrett had him pressed against the asphalt, his hand wrapped in Tony's collar as he whaled on him with his bare fist. Tony's face was pulp, blood soaking his shirt, the street, Barrett's clothes.

I rested my hand on Barrett's shoulder to pull him back from the dark corners of his mind. Was he even aware of the tears streaming down his cheeks?

He drew in a sharp, shuddering breath and released the hunter, who sagged against the ground with a groan.

"You bastard." Barrett made a futile attempt to wipe the blood off his face as he stood up and staggered backwards. "Because of you, the man I loved is dead. People have suffered.

Innocent people. You have no idea the trouble you've caused."

Tony rolled onto his side and spat a glob of blood onto the road. "You more than anyone should understand what we're trying to do, Barrett. This is what you wanted. To put magic down before it has a chance to ruin everything. How can you side with these people against us now that we're so close to making that future happen?"

Barrett gritted his teeth and bowed his head. When he looked up, shame was written in every crease of his brow. "I can admit when I've made a mistake. Can you say the same?"

Tony's gaze was filled with disappointed rage as he hobbled to his feet. "Don't be such an idiot. You know what this woman is capable of. What every creature like her is capable of. No one is safe. The *future* isn't safe until every last one of them is dead or leashed."

"No."

There was no inflection in Barrett's voice, no room for argument. He'd reverted from emotional wreck to stoic automaton in the blink of an eye, and I didn't know if I was reassured by the familiar lack of expression or afraid of what the emptiness meant. After seeing for myself the passion and intensity Adrian must have known existed all these years, I didn't know how healthy it was for the ex-soldier to bottle it up again.

But this was hardly the time for a therapy session. Even if I'd wanted to pry, Barrett gave me no opportunity.

He raised his gun and aimed it at Tony's face.

"Barrett, man, come on," Tony pleaded.

"Adrian didn't have time to beg for his life. Be grateful you did."

He squeezed the trigger, and Tony fell to the ground.

Barrett shuddered, and when he spoke, his voice was low and husky. "Come on. Let's get out of here."

40

Emrick

I STAYED OUT of view until Kat and the others climbed into Barrett's SUV and drove off.

I needed a minute to figure out what it meant that my sorceress was still standing. Shot three times, and those bullet holes had closed up just as they always had. Just as they were supposed to.

For the first time in a week, the burn in my chest was gone. The bond was whole. Complete. I'd noticed the change after Poppy had dosed Kat with that potion, but it was only an hour ago that I'd realized the fullness of the shift.

I didn't trust it.

So instead of going to her to celebrate her victory, I'd stayed on the edge of the afterlife as she'd looked around the silent street, searching for but not finding me. I'd caught the hurt in her eyes that I hadn't come to see her. But I couldn't. Not yet.

Once they were gone, I made my rounds with the corpses. Starting with Tony. The other hunters may have wanted to hurt Kat, but this was the son of a bitch who'd played her for a fool. Barrett had gotten his revenge, and now it was my turn.

I sensed the mundane herder approaching so wasted no time in drawing Tony's soul to me. In a flash, his spirit was within my reach. I didn't bother making him corporeal. Barrett had already done an impressive job pulverizing his weak flesh. Instead, I punched my fist into the centre of the pillar of light and released a shot of Death's power. The light flickered and burst apart, drifting in thousands of directions as it tried to put itself back together. I wished it luck. In another century, maybe, enough pieces would have reunited to let him cross over into what came next, but until then, he'd be lost in the after-life, a tortured spirit who had no choice but to consider all the mistakes he'd made in life.

The mundane herder arrived—an empty-eyed shadow that didn't acknowledge me as it gathered the souls of the fallen hunters. It offered no conversation, no personal touch as it opened the barrier between this life and the next and ushered them through.

The same future that awaited me if I wasn't careful.

Fortunately, my revenge on Tony had been in the clear.

And my next move would be as well. While the hunters were mundane, their work among the magical meant their corpses followed the same rules as the witches and shifters and creatures. Allowing their bodies to be found by the mundane neighbours would raise questions and direct attention to areas that were best kept secret. So, corpse by corpse, I knelt down and turned them to dust. Within a few minutes, nothing remained of the battle that had happened here except for a few spatterings of blood and some dirt for the street cleaners to take care of. And the burning house, but sirens in the distance assured me help would be here soon.

If only the rest of the outcome could be so easily dealt with.

What did it mean that Kat was once again immortal?

What did it mean that her immortality had been blocked?

Rhys's vision had indeed come to pass, and we were left with far more questions than answers.

The tug of the bond in my chest urged me to follow Kat, but still I held off. Until I understood what had happened, I wouldn't risk her life. She would be angry with me for it, but I could live with that—as long as it meant she did, too.

41

Katerina

OUR DRIVE BACK to the Toronto house was silent, and when we walked through the front doors, Rhys was ready with the first aid kit, and Maera had already prepared a spread of tea and cookies at the kitchen table.

"More visions?" I asked Rhys as I dropped into a chair.

His skin was ashen under the bright kitchen lights, and his throat bobbed as he struggled to find his words. "They came hard and fast for a while. Glimpses of tonight, a few flickers of what's coming."

Maera pressed her lips together, her expression grim. "From what he told me, we should take advantage of whatever peace we have tonight. I don't know how long it's going to last."

On that joyous note, everyone else grabbed a seat and tore

into the fresh-baked cookies. I, however, avoided the tea, still not ready to take that risk.

No one said anything until the cookies were gone and more than one teacup had been drained. Only after Maera had cleared away the dishes did she sit down at the foot of the table across from me and take in the state of us.

"About what happened tonight," she said. "Who's going to start?"

As one, everyone turned to me.

I looked at each of their curious faces, trying to frame my answer. Maera and Rhys wanted to know who we'd fought and how the fight had ended. The rest would want to know how I was sitting here after being shot three times.

They probably suspected—especially when Emrick appeared in the kitchen, taking his place against the wall next to the counter—but they needed it confirmed.

They also needed to know what, or what little, I'd learned from the hunters. If we were about to go to war, they deserved to know the details.

"I think…" I began, then trailed off and considered everything I'd heard tonight, not only what the hunters had said but what they hadn't. What had slipped from panicked mouths and what those mouths had bitten back. "I think we've been wrong about a lot of things. Not just about my magic but before that. All the way back to Mikhail. All the way back to the summoning of Alodie's demon. All this time, I thought someone was out to get me. Now I have reason to believe this is bigger than me."

Rhys frowned. "What do you mean?"

I felt Emrick's stare on my profile like a tangible force, but I couldn't look at him yet. The desire to leave everyone in suspense and run into his arms was too great after so many days apart, and I had to get this out. Everyone in this room needed to know what I did so we could figure out what to do next. We didn't know how much time we had before the hunters struck again.

I rubbed my thumb over one of the runes etched into the wrist of my glove. Blood had spattered across the leather, and it was going to take me hours to clean it.

"Something Tony said. And Blondie. And the other guy. Getting rid of me wasn't the endgame. And if that's the case… what is?"

Everyone around the table exchanged glances while I picked at the blood on my gloves.

My stomach twisted as my attention homed in on the red stains. My life had become nothing but blood over these past few months. I was tired of it. Sick to death of it.

Not wanting it pressed into my skin anymore, I stripped the leather off my arms and slammed my gloves onto the table. As I did, the etching compound used to create the runes caught the overhead lights, glinting silver, and I stiffened.

Alodie had said it was ironic I'd kept them with me all these years. She hadn't explained why, but the answer was coming to me.

"Kat?" Emrick asked, his voice filled with concern.

I drew the gloves closer and used my thumb to clear the blood out of one of the runes. The etching shimmered faintly with the slight movement.

Just as my blood sample had done in the microscope.

Bile crept up the back of my throat, and I set my gloves down.

"Alodie was behind the tea." I swallowed my disgust. "She gave the hunters the recipe for the compound my community used to make these runes."

I handed one glove to Murisa, who held it up to the light and squinted to get a better look.

"The recipe was a secret among my people. We used it to create… wards of a sort. Between the compound and the runes, this leather is indestructible, but it also restrains my magic. Like a leash." I turned my attention to Emrick, who'd pushed away from the counter.

His silver eyes blazed, awareness and anger vying for dominance in their depths.

Poppy's eyes widened. "If the witch hunters have this recipe…"

I grimaced at the bitter flavour of what I had to say. "They could find a way to nullify my magic again. All our magic."

Poppy blanched, and even Gavin looked a bit ill. Barrett gripped the sorcerer's shoulder to steady him, and Gavin rested his hand on Barrett's in thanks.

Murisa sucked in a sharp breath. "That explains it! I knew the potion I gave you would work because I saw how it reacted to the proteins in the tea, but I was wrong about *why* it worked. I suspected your magic was blocked, not gone, but had no idea how it was possible. This compound must have bound it, hidden it." She looked between me and Emrick. "In doing so, it did the same to your bond."

I rubbed my chest where the tether between Emrick and me had awakened, a warm pulsing that connected me to the here and now better than any kind of mindfulness practice. When I looked up, Emrick's hand mirrored mine. I wondered what he felt now that everything seemed to be back to normal. Did he feel the burn in his chest, or had the pain eased as mine had?

Murisa squinted at the runes. "Somehow, the hunters turned the etching compound into an edible substance. I'd be impressed if it weren't so damned terrifying. But at least now we have a counterpotion in case they try it again."

I met Emrick's eye but directed my question to Murisa. "Is the counterpotion a permanent solution, do you think?"

Emrick dropped his gaze, and in that small gesture, I understood his fears. I shared them to a point, but I suspected the strain between us was far from over, restored bond or no.

"We can check your blood again later to make sure," Murisa replied, "but I think so. I suspect even without my potion, the blocking agent would have worn off eventually unless they forced a steady supply on you. The protein in the sample I had was already degrading. Slowly, but it was. It would have taken a few more weeks." She frowned. "Maybe long enough for them to get what they needed."

I shuddered. "Let's make sure they don't get another chance, all right?"

"Yeah, Maera," said Poppy. "No more random teas."

Maera flushed red and blinked back tears. "Nothing but standard black tea from now on."

I forced myself to look away from Emrick to take in my housekeeper's shame. At her inability to lift her gaze from her untouched cup, I pushed back my chair, rounded the table, and threw my arms around her neck. "I don't blame you, Maera. I promise I don't. These people were determined to get that compound into my system, and they took advantage of you. They'll pay for that as much as everything else."

She patted my hand and cleared her throat. "Thank you. Still, lesson learned. An important one, if you're right. This time was tea, but who knows what else they'll try."

"For whatever their next plan is," Gavin said.

Barrett flexed his jaw. "Whatever it is, I think we need to

assume it's already underway."

I nodded. "And they're going to be prepared." I bowed my head into my bare palms. "I wish we had some way of getting ahead of them." A dark chuckle escaped me. "Maybe we should have kept Tony alive. I bet he would have been eager enough to share the details with a bit of pressure."

"Death."

Silence fell on the room as Rhys's empty voice spilled across the table.

I raised my head, and my breath hitched on seeing my friend with his eyes as white as the tiles on the backsplash.

Maera stiffened and gently took her son's hand. "What do you See?"

She caught my eye, and I recognized the concern lurking in her expression. Rhys had said he'd had multiple visions while we'd been gone, and now here was another one. Whatever blocks he'd suffered had clearly passed, and I wondered what it meant for him that his second sight was once more gaining power.

"An empty room," he intoned. "A world of grey. Thousands of empty eyes. Fire extinguished. Ice melted. Words silenced." His eyes widened as he sucked in a breath, and panic filled his final words as he added, "Death is coming for Death."

With a final gasp, he collapsed into his mother's waiting arms.

42

Katerina

IT TOOK TEN minutes for Rhys to revive. We moved him to the couch, and Maera prepared a cup of hot chocolate for him when he woke up—something comforting for the soul and sweet for the system.

After confirming he had no other details to add, I left him with the others, needing some time to myself to process everything that had happened over the past few days. What I'd learned. Where I now stood in the world. How the hell I was going to stand in the way of three international organizations.

I climbed the stairs on tired legs, closed my bedroom door, and sank onto the edge of the bed.

I longed to be at home, somewhere safe and familiar and *mine*. I wanted to sit in my Muskoka chair on the balcony and listen to the gentle lap of Lake Huron against the beach.

Instead, I was stuck in the middle of this big city, being serenaded by the traffic a few blocks over and suffocated by the reek of car fumes and cigarette smoke drifting through the window.

I struggled to ground myself in the sensory maelstrom, longing to find my centre while my thoughts tumbled through a few separate hurricanes.

The storms came screeching to a halt when Emrick stepped out of the afterlife into my room.

The coolness of the mist swept over my skin, tickling the back of my neck, soothing the uncomfortable heat in the small of my back.

I released a slow breath and rose from the bed to face him, but he kept his distance against the wall, half in shadow, not fully corporeal. As though he were ready to step back into the afterlife at any moment.

Exactly as I'd feared he would.

I stepped towards him. "Are you really doing this?"

"Stop there."

I obeyed. Not because I wanted to, but because I knew if I got any closer, he would leave. Right now, more than anything, I needed him to stay.

I wanted to press him on what worried him, wanted to address the tension buzzing between us, my returned immortality, my magic, but my courage failed. Instead, I focused on the other giant, looming problem.

"You didn't have much to say downstairs. About the hunters having some greater plan than taking me out of the picture."

He canted his head. "I didn't have anything to offer. Not yet."

"You agree with me, though?"

"I do. There's been—" He cleared his throat and shifted on his feet. "The rumours floating around the afterlife are back. Nothing specific, just whispers. Worries. I've been back and forth on what they mean, but an impressively lucid soul filled in the blanks for me. Whatever's about to happen, you're at the heart of it. You're going to light a lot of fires and get a lot of people dead." The corner of his mouth kicked upwards. "I guess that's nothing new."

I batted my hand at him. "Oh, stop it, you flatterer."

The banter didn't hold its usual comfort. It was too strained. Too fake.

I dropped my arm and sank back onto the bed. "What do you think we should do?"

He crossed his arms. "I wonder if what Maera suggested before has merit. Maybe disappearing for a while is the best option. You have your magic back—possibly your immortality. You could step away from the world for a few decades, let the hunters believe you're gone, and make your plans to come after them when they no longer suspect it."

So much was packed into his suggestion it took me a while to rifle through it.

He thought I should run. After everything we'd learned tonight, he believed my best option was to turn tail and flee until it was safe for me to come out.

As though I'd ever been the sort of person to run away from anything.

I'd made that mistake once in my life, and it had cost me my son, my husband, my parents. I'd lived with that decision for eight hundred and fifty years. Spent my entire existence since striving to wipe that failure from my past.

And he thought I would be willing to do it again now? Leave Barrett and Poppy and Gavin to pick up my slack?

He had to have lost his mind.

I knew he hadn't, though.

At the heart of his fears was that one word: *possibly*.

He worried Murisa's potion would wear off and the bond between us would fade again.

As long as he believed that, I would be stuck this far apart from him and he would never support any plans to take the fight to the hunters.

"Emrick…" I stood again and took another step closer, but he narrowed his eyes at me, and once more, I stopped. "Our bond is solid. You know it is. You have to feel it."

He rubbed his chest and closed his eyes. "I do. After a week of suffering nothing but that burn in my chest, to feel you in here is a dream I never thought I'd experience again." When he opened his eyes, his expression was one of silver fire. "But what if Murisa's wrong? What if whatever they gave you is strong enough to overpower her counterpotion? What if in another breath, you're mortal again? I won't take that chance."

"We've been through this before." Eight hundred years ago. "My stance hasn't changed."

Back then, I'd told him I would rather burn than live an eternity without passion. I'd been given good reason to test that opinion over the past seventy-five years as I worked to keep him away from me, hoping to save what remained of his soul. I'd never wavered.

His throat strained with a hard swallow. "Mine has."

My heartbeat stuttered, and I clenched my fist to my chest as though that would keep the shaken pieces of it inside my ribcage.

Emrick squeezed his eyes shut. "I'm sorry, Kat, but it has. I love you too much—*too fucking much*—to risk your life. To know you were mortal and lost to me was bad enough, but to have this hope renewed… to risk believing you're mine again only to lose you. It would break me into more pieces than I would ever be able to recover from."

"So… what?" I had to clear my throat to prevent my words

from coming out thick and choked. "It's your turn to walk away? You're going to leave me, put our relationship behind you *just in case*?"

"No!" His eyes flew open, and he stepped forward, then stopped himself and retreated. His chest expanded with a slow, deep breath, and, more calmly, he said, "I say we wait. We make sure Murisa is right."

"How long?" I forced myself to sound calm when what I wanted to do was rage. I had walked through hell, stepped onto the shores of the afterlife *twice*, and the one person I'd fought to come back to was pushing me away.

"I don't know. Until after we deal with the witch hunters? Until after we find out exactly what the full effects of that compound are?"

"Emrick, I—"

"Please, Kat. Do this for me. Do this so I don't make an awful, horrible, irreversible mistake."

We stared at each other, and I read the torment in his eyes that matched mine. Neither of us wanted this, but there would be no talking him down.

"Fine," I said stiffly. "We'll do it your way. After all, if I'm right, we have the rest of eternity ahead of us. What's a little bit of time?"

He exhaled sharply with a nod. "Thank you." He hesitated, then stared at me until I met his gaze. "I love you."

My throat tightened. This wasn't how our reunion was supposed to go. Before he'd left that morning so many days ago, he'd promised to pick up where he'd left off. I'd thought if some miracle restored our bond, we'd lose ourselves in each other while we figured out how to proceed against whoever had blocked it. We'd plan our revenge between peaks of pleasure.

Instead of heat, all I had to offer was a restrained, "I love you, too."

He clenched his hands at his sides, and his jaw ticked. By the tension radiating from his coiled muscles, I suspected his thoughts had travelled in the same direction as mine. But the man was nothing if not stubborn.

With one last look, he disappeared, leaving me alone with my thoughts and my fears and a raging impatience for the hunters to strike. Once they did, we would fight, and we would put them down once and for all.

Maybe after that, maybe after the last battle was won, my life would finally make sense again.

Thank You for Reading

Thank you so much for taking a chance on an independent author. We're living in a wonderful age where it's easy to upload a book to the internet, but that doesn't reflect the blood, sweat, and tears that go into making a book the best version it can be. It takes time, patience, perseverance, and to have the final result end up in a new reader's hands is the best reward. You are the reason we keep writing, so thank you.

If you enjoyed the read, please help support the author by leaving a review at the retailer where you purchased the book. Reviews make a world of difference for an author, helping us reach new audiences and bringing more people into the worlds you've spent time in.

For exclusive character content, announcements, promotions, and special offers, sign up for Krista's mailing list at https://www.kristawalshauthor.com/pages/about-the-author

Acknowledgements

As we gear up towards the finale, I'm on tenterhooks to hear what you think of Kat and her crew so far. I've been having the time of my life getting these books ready for publication, and so many people have helped make it memorable.

As always, my deepest thank you to Kate Sparkes, the FAKAs and the Blood & Pulp gang, and Christopher Barnes for helping me shape this book into what it is.

I want to say a special THANK YOU to the folks on my Street Team (we still need to come up with an awesome name). This group has hyped up every title in this series, helped me with my social media coverage, flagged last-minute typos, filled my inbox with reactions as they read, and brought so much life to their reading that it never fails to motivate me to make the next book even better than the previous. You guys are awesome, and I'm so grateful for you!

I also want to thank my Patrons for your ongoing support. It always gives me a thrill to share the early chapters with you.

Chris Reddie, my partner in crime, your support is a never-ending joy. I love getting random texts from you when you're reading my latest, cursing my characters and throwing your fave lines my way. I never feel more proud than when I get a reaction out of you. And my darling daughter, you have no idea how warm and fuzzy I feel every time to point to a book and say, "Is this your book?" even when it's not.

And thanks to you, my wonderful readers, for continuing

on this journey with me. You make it easy to face the drudgiest parts of this job with a smile on my face.

See you at the next one!

About the Author

Known for witty, vivid characters, Krista Walsh never has more fun than getting them into trouble and taking her time getting them out.

When not writing, she can be found reading, gaming, or watching a film – anything to get lost in a good story.

She currently lives in Ottawa, Ontario with her husband, toddler, and epileptic blue heeler.

You can find her at www.kristawalshauthor.com or at the local Second Cup coffee shop... but only if you come bearing a Vanilla Bean Latte, half-sweet.

Other Works by Krista Walsh

Epic Fantasy

The Meratis Trilogy
The Cadis Trilogy
The Nayis Trilogy

Urban Fantasy

The Dark Descendants
The Ghostmaker Trilogy
The Immortal Sorceress Series

www.ingramcontent.com/pod-product-compliance
Lightning Source LLC
Chambersburg PA
CBHW020242010826
48973CB00006B/1621